BEASTHEART

Special thanks to Andy Prentice

ORCHARD BOOKS

First published in Great Britain in 2022 by The Watts Publishing Group

1 3 5 7 9 10 8 6 4 2

Series created by Beast Quest Limited, London

A CIP catalogue record for this book is available from the British Library.

ISBN 978 1 40836 370 6

Printed in Great Britain

The paper and board used in this book are made from wood from responsible sources

Orchard Books
An imprint of Hachette Children's Group
Part of The Watts Publishing Group Limited
Carmelite House, 50 Victoria Embankment, London EC4Y 0DZ

An Hachette UK Company
www.hachette.co.uk
www.hachettechildrens.co.uk

BEASTHEART

SLAYER

A.H. BLADE

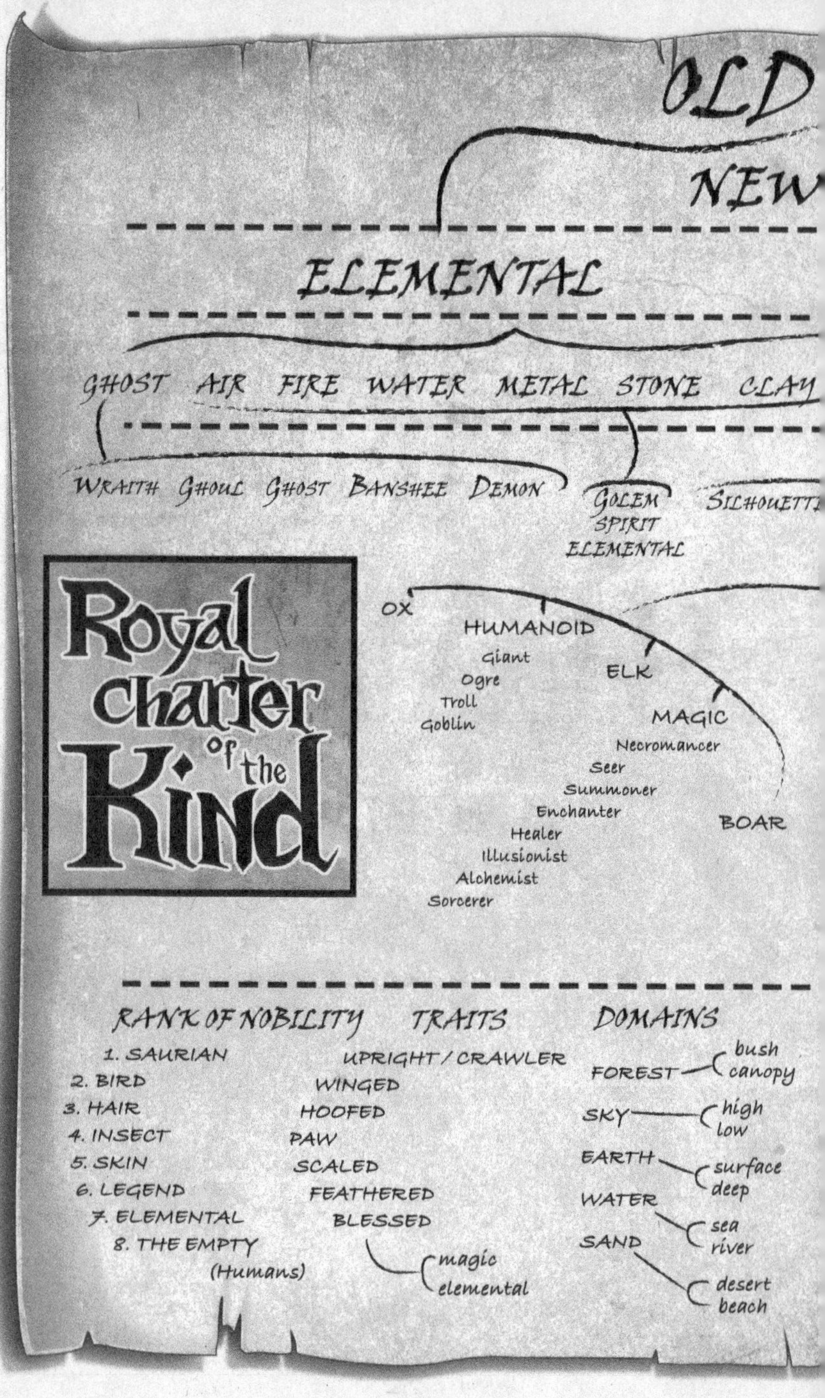

OLD

NEW

ELEMENTAL

GHOST AIR FIRE WATER METAL STONE CLAY

WRAITH GHOUL GHOST BANSHEE DEMON

GOLEM
SPIRIT
ELEMENTAL

SILHOUETTE

Royal charter of the Kind

OX

HUMANOID
Giant
Ogre
Troll
Goblin

ELK

MAGIC
Necromancer
Seer
Summoner
Enchanter
Healer
Illusionist
Alchemist
Sorcerer

BOAR

RANK OF NOBILITY	TRAITS
1. SAURIAN	UPRIGHT / CRAWLER
2. BIRD	WINGED
3. HAIR	HOOFED
4. INSECT	PAW
5. SKIN	SCALED
6. LEGEND	FEATHERED
7. ELEMENTAL	BLESSED (magic, elemental)
8. THE EMPTY (Humans)	

DOMAINS

- FOREST — bush, canopy
- SKY — high, low
- EARTH — surface, deep
- WATER — sea, river
- SAND — desert, beach

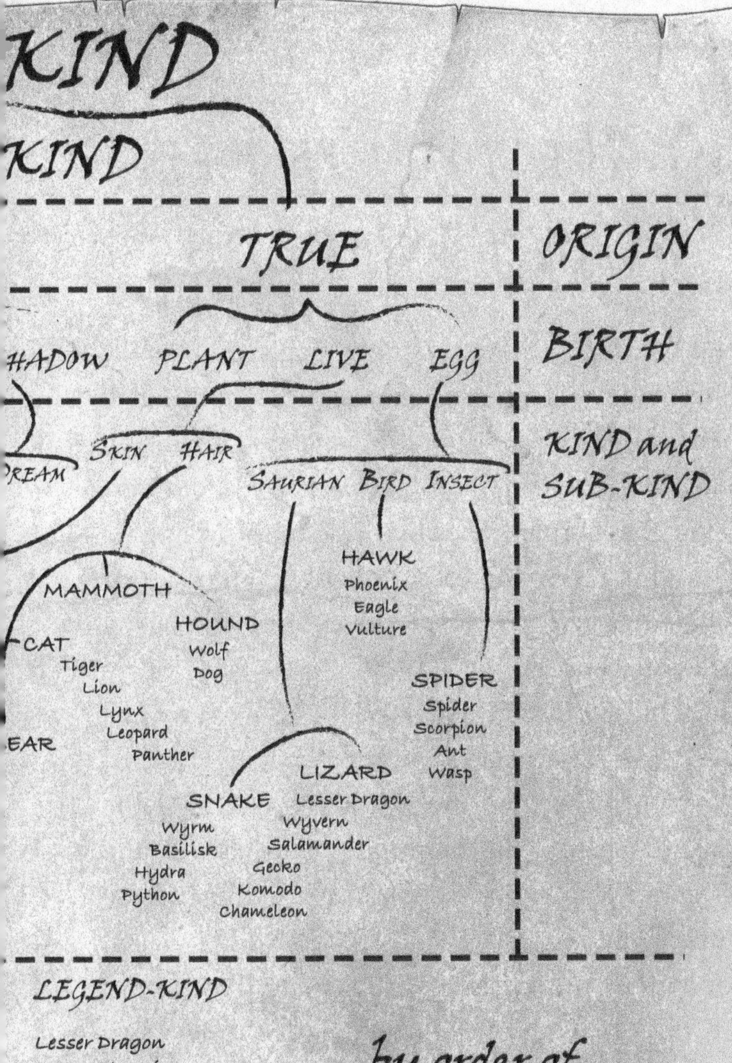

LEGEND-KIND

Lesser Dragon
Lesser Phoenix
Lesser Hydra
Lesser Centaurs
Lesser Griffins
Lesser Minotaurs,
Ogres, Giants, Trolls

by order of

Malachai

First of the Learned Kind
Year 503 after Spawning

A History of the Many Worlds

In the beginning there was only magic.

This magic was raw, unstable and full of potential. It existed entirely within the timeless dimension of the Netherplane – a nightmarish sea of ever-shifting chaos, ruled over by the God of Magic.

Until this god – who we now know as the Creator – decided to use raw magic to conjure the Many Worlds into existence.

First, he stabilised this material into what we call shadow, the base element of pure magic. He used shadow to forge the other elements, to build the land and the sea, the mountains and valleys, the forests and plains, the realms of the living and the realms of the ghosts.

Among all the creatures, the greatest were the old-Kind – colossal beasts who guarded the natural places of the worlds. The old-Kind carried elemental magic in their veins. They worked in alliance with chosen human warriors called the Masters of the Kind. Together the old-Kind and the Masters preserved peace and balance. Harmony reigned.

Until the humans' desire for dominion saw them spread in increasing numbers.

The humans drove the old-Kind from their homes, imprisoned these mighty demigods, even slew them.

When it looked like the old-Kind were all but destroyed, the Creator intervened. Using the dying life force of the old-Kind, he spawned a new race. The new-Kind.

The new-Kind were smaller and less magical than the old-Kind, but far greater in number. They rose up and defeated the humans. Now it was the humans who were forced from their lands and threatened with extinction.

The balance once kept by the old-Kind and the human Masters was all but gone. Conflict reigned. The vision of the Creator was no more.

And if imbalance is not cleansed from the Many Worlds, then their very existence remains under threat.

Gael,

Gateway Keeper, Custodian of the Many Worlds

1

The Death-Song

Jonas spotted a broken twig, almost hidden among the reed stalks to the side of the path.

He crouched low for a closer look.

Fresh sap gleamed on the break, snapped by some-Kind in a tearing hurry. His quarry was getting careless. But which way had they gone? This mist-choked bog held many hiding places.

Jonas heard his mother's voice telling him to look *harder.* She had taken him hunting before he could walk. She had patiently taught him to read a trail, to see carefully, to watch the wind and to hear the sky.

And now, as usually happened when he was hunting, Jonas was reminded that she was dead.

Two yards off the trail, he spotted a blurred

pawprint in the mud. The rogue priest must be very close. As he watched, the sucking ooze closed over the mark, rubbing it out.

Jonas slid through the reeds, fast and silent as a blacksnake, following the broad cat-Kind tracks even as they vanished.

He tried not to think about his mother.

The priest had chosen a clever place to hide. Once, in a better time, this might have been a rice farm. There were a few signs of the old life here and there. A shattered wall around a swamped paddy. An overgrown orchard. Tall stones that might have stood over graves.

Now it was a maze of sticky bogs, reed thickets and leech-infested pools. A good place to hide.

But Jonas was good at hunting.

He felt her nearness before he saw her. Or rather, he sensed the terrible danger that she represented. It made his heart race and his blood flow quicker.

He saw: *her sharp claws slashing his throat. Her iron staff breaking his head. Her strong arms driving him under the mud to drown.*

A dozen visions of his own death flashed through Jonas's mind. They made him careful. They made him stronger. He grinned a black grin and stepped out into the clearing.

Filthy moss covered the soft ground, broken only by a few stunted reed thickets. The cat-Kind priest was waiting for him, standing ankle-deep in a puddle.

Hunter and hunted stared at each other for a long moment. A month of dodging and dancing had come to this sharp point.

Jonas's keen eyes were hungry for details. The priest's robes were torn and mud-stained, but had once been very fine. Her leopard face looked lopsided. She'd lost some of her whiskers in the chase.

Jonas knew he didn't look any better.

His sodden tunic tugged heavily at his body. His neck itched because the bristles of his fur collar rubbed at his neck, the fabric starched needle-dry from days of sun and wind, from his own rushed breath, from smatterings of mud, food, blood, smoke – remnants of the hurried trail.

The moment dragged into another, and another. Still, Jonas and the priest watched each other. There was usually not much to say when he caught his prey. Not much worth saying, anyway. Nothing that couldn't be said with steel and blood.

Scents and memories came flashing back to him now, as the battle urge took him over.

A thousand clues had led him to this moment –

and to what was coming next.

His fingers reached inevitably for the worn bone hilts of his twin scimitars.

The arced blades slid out willingly, singing, twinkling from their mirror-bright edges. Jonas might have looked a mess, but the Swords of What Was and What Will Be were always well kept. Smelling nice wouldn't help you in a battle, but a polished blade, a dry handle, a dirt-free scabbard just might. Jonas knew better than anyone that death was detail, a force of chance that must be worshipped with each stroke of the sharpening stone, each buffing of the sword rag. He could feel its force gathering in every fingertip, in his roaring heart, in the prickling follicles of his scalp.

"Grand Protector Rahziin," he said finally, giving the cat-Kind her full title. He bowed low – as any human should when addressing one of their betters, no matter how disgraced.

The cat-Kind snarled but said nothing.

As Jonas dipped, his dual scimitars crossed his chest, rising up from his back like wings. For the tiniest instant, his thoughts flashed somewhere else: somewhere high, somewhere across the skies, where skeletal wings beat and empty eye sockets watched on. Somewhere above, death was watching.

Somewhere above, his twin was approaching.

Jonas heard the cat-Kind twitching, the scuff of a paw, a ruffle of robes. Jonas *dared* her, *willed* her to make a lunge for his vulnerable neck.

In his own time, Jonas straightened, the Swords of What Was and What Will Be dangling loosely by his sides. His voice was steady, blank, almost as if it were coming from somebody else. Almost as if it were coming from the sky. "You have been expelled from the Order of the True. You have been convicted of treason and sentenced to death. I have been sent by Grashkor, Gaoler of the Pinnacles, to bring you to your punishment. Resisting is unwise. Will you come with me?"

Suddenly the cat-Kind's snarling mouth transformed into a wide grin. She laughed – a cackling sound that did not sound right in the hushed clearing. "Not a chance. 'Unwise'! Who do you think you are speaking to?"

She gripped her long iron staff with furred fingers. The staff jangled with many bronze rings – a sign that she'd held high rank in the Order of the True. Each ring represented a human abomination that she had wiped out.

"Did they try to insult me by sending an *Empty boy* to fetch me back?" There was no laughter in her voice now. No smile in her eyes. No snarl either, or anger. Only determination, and a sureness in herself. A confidence in her own powers. "I am strong. Water-blessed. I have chosen this ground to fight on. The wet suits me well. Are you not afraid, weak one?"

"No," said Jonas. "I left fear behind long ago."

"Then you are as big a fool as my masters. I have killed many humans stronger than you, pitiful Empty child!"

Her muscles tensed as she gathered her long legs to pounce. She squelched her toes into the mud for better purchase. Her whiskers twitched as she drew in power from the dirty water with a deep breath. Jonas's skin prickled with the static of magic in the air. The priest was indeed water-blessed, and powerful. This might be a harder fight than he had thought. But, like it always did, his own body reacted instantly to the threat of magic, his own blessing taking over.

His was a blessing of death.

His senses heightened. He closed his eyes for a split second, letting himself sink into the crispness of it. The flutter of leaves so clear to him, the tiniest shuffle of a snake in the undergrowth, the smell of rotting wood, of blossoming flowers. He savoured it all. Once more, he heard the cat-Kind fidget. Perhaps she could sense his magic too.

Attack me! Jonas thought. Killing never felt as bad when his opponent made the first move. He could tell himself he was fighting in self-defence. He could lie to himself that he did not enjoy it.

His fingers squeezed tighter around the grooves worn into the scimitars over decades. And with it came his father's voice: *Never touch a weapon unless you mean to use it.* Jonas's father had taught him to fight before he could talk. Fighting was a language that ran deep in Jonas's blood.

The Swords of What Was and What Will Be had been his father's before him. The fingers that made the grooves his father's fingers.

He too was dead.

Death was everywhere. Jonas could feel it leaking from the yellowing reeds and singing in the brief lives of the bog flies. But he sensed his own death-song most strongly right now. It could come in so many ways: a blow, a slip, even a poisonous snake in an unlucky place. Each fight was an infinity of death. A maze of dead ends.

It brought everything into focus.

He could see a vein in the cat-Kind's throat throbbing with life. She sprang forward, howling.

The water gave her strength and speed. She moved fast.

Jonas stood still.

Her staff hummed through the air towards his temple.

Still Jonas didn't twitch.

Now.

At the last possible moment, he brought up his scimitar to block the blow.

The crash and screech of steel on steel sent a marsh heron screaming into the sky. The curved sword stopped the blow stone dead and held it, quivering.

This should not have happened. The cat-Kind knew it. Ordinarily, the staff would have smashed through the sword's weak parry and taken Jonas's head with it.

But Jonas was not ordinary.

The cat-Kind's eyes went wide with shock. She snarled and sprang away – flipping upside down like a dancer. Her water-strength gifted her balance and poise and also a terrible cunning. The tumbling was just a distraction. As she flew backwards, she gracefully flicked a knife straight at Jonas's heart.

This time it was Jonas's turn to be surprised. He hardly saw the blade until it was upon him.

His own gifts took over once again. An ordinary

human would have been dead in an instant – but Jonas felt the moment stretch out like a lazy afternoon by a swimming hole. The way it made sense to him was that the closer he got to death, the slower time passed. Now, he felt he had time enough to admire the way the dagger – which was speeding towards his heart – had been crafted, the gold thread that wove up the steel of the blade like a spider's web. It was a beautiful weapon. Fit to kill any man – or any Kind, for that matter.

But Jonas was not about to die. He felt the familiar heady rush surge inside him – an overwhelming, glorious sunglow feeling. Nearly dying always felt so good.

He twisted whip-quick to the side, impossibly fast, and the murderous knife merely glanced off his shoulder. Its edge was sharp. It sliced his skin. He felt the hot blood flow, and with it his power grew. This felt even better.

Time sped up as Jonas sprang forward. The cat-Kind stumbled. Her yellow eyes danced with disbelief, black slits still focused on where Jonas should have been. She could not believe that he was not dead, but she was even more surprised when she felt how hard he hit. His first blow shattered her iron staff. Brass rings flew in every direction.

"What *are* you?" she screamed as she threw her useless weapon to the ground.

In truth, Jonas could not have answered her rightly, because he did not know the answer himself. But he did not speak when the death-song was in him.

He was afraid of what he would say.

He came forward, smiling, exultant, and saw the fear in her snarling, spotted face. Though she did not understand what he was, she knew her water-strength was no match for the terrifying joy inside Jonas. The fight was over then, though she tried to keep him off for as long as she could. Jonas, with the death-song in him, was as unstoppable as the tide.

He knocked her down with the bone pommel of the Sword of What Was. He slapped the side of the Sword of What Will Be across the cat-Kind's head. It took all his will not to swivel the sword and cut the Kind's head from her body. While she lay gasping in the mud, stunned by the blow, he slapped the Gaoler's manacles on her wrists.

There would be no killing today. The disappointment sank through his body like a dull weight.

The manacles clicked home with a twist of the slim gold key that he kept wedged down his boot. The manacles matched those fastened around his own wrists – although those he could not control. And the only one who had a key was the Gaoler.

The cat priest saw the glint of metal under Jonas's sleeve. "You are a prisoner too. Let me go. We can both flee. There is no one to stop us."

If only it was that easy, thought Jonas.

"Up," he said. Her manacles rose into the air, lifting the cat-Kind with them by her shackled wrists. She was standing now, but her head hung heavy.

"You will come with me to the Pinnacles," he said.

Jonas recognised her panic, and her confusion. This was not the way things were meant to work. He had seen it many times before when he'd defeated a new-Kind in battle.

Humans were weak, and the new-Kind were strong. That's the way it was. How it had always been.

"Who are you?" she said again. "*What* are you?"

"You don't want to know," he said.

He felt a great emptiness as the death-song left his body. And with it, Jonas could no longer feel the watchful eye of death somewhere in the skies above.

He was alone once again.

2

His True Name

"But I was framed! You *must* believe me," said Grand Protector Rahziin, her whiskered face crumpled in fury.

Jonas turned the springhare on the spit to crisp up its back. Little drops of fat fell from it and fizzled in the fire.

They had been trekking for several days, heading towards the Ferry of Solek. Moored at a remote point along the shore of the desolate, battering South Sea, it would carry Rahziin to the Pinnacles of the Damned. The ship was aptly named. Solek, the monstrous shark old-Kind, was said to feed on the souls of the treacherous and deceitful. But where Rahziin was from, the gods of the south were little worshipped.

Rahziin tried again. "Not one of their accusations was true. I am innocent."

"Grand Protector, you do know every Kind I catch always says that, right?" said Jonas.

If he were to believe their excuses, none of the criminals that Grashkor sent him to hunt down and bring to the Pinnacles had so much as sneezed the wrong way.

Jonas understood why they tried it. The Pinnacles of the Damned was the worst prison in the world – a few bleak islands filled with murderers and thieves thrown away in the middle of a storm-tossed sea. No one had ever escaped from the Pinnacles.

No one in their right mind would want to go to the prison in the first place.

Jonas himself had suffered there – he still *was* a prisoner, in fact – and he was never-endingly grateful that his special abilities as a bounty hunter allowed him to leave sometimes.

"But I am innocent!"

Jonas did not reply. He stared into the fire, relishing the warmth. Despite the danger in the Borderlands, he had chanced lighting it. He needed to get the wet chill of the swamp out of his bones. The risk was small enough. They hadn't seen any insect-Kind or spotted tracks from a raiding party. Even so, Jonas had taken pains to choose a well-hidden campsite and keep the fire small.

The logs crackled, sending sparks up into the starry sky. The nicely crisped springhare flesh smelled good. It was nearly ready to eat.

"Pshaw! Humans!" Rahziin snarled her displeasure at being ignored. Jonas could feel her yellow cat's eyes burning at him from across the fire, matching the colour of the flames. Jonas was used to being hated. He tossed the charred springhare to Rahziin and began to skewer another he'd caught in a snare. The cat-Kind ripped the springhare from the skewer with her fangs, tossing the stick away and chewing noisily.

Rahziin had remained mostly silent on the journey – no doubt concentrating on finding a way to escape. Or maybe she had been too proud to speak to a human. In any case, Jonas had found the silence pleasant. *If only she didn't eat so loudly,* he thought. The annoying thing was that Rahziin *tried* to eat loudly – or more 'purely', as she had described it when Jonas had commented on the sheer violence with which she tore her food apart. She had told him that the Order of the True devoted themselves to continuing the legacy of their ancestors, the great beasts called the old-Kind who carried the magic of the natural world in their veins.

"Delicacy is a pitiful human trait," Rahziin had scoffed through her mouthful of food.

Jonas had heard a little about the Order of the True from rumours passing through the Pinnacles, as well as reports from his contacts across the Four Kingdoms. Word had it that the Order of the True were gaining influence over the Emperor. But clearly, Rahziin had done something to upset the ageing lizard-Kind ruler. She would be spending the remainder of her life behind bars – a life which would likely be not very long considering the conditions on the Pinnacles, as Jonas knew only too well.

Why not just use the skewer! Jonas wanted to say to Rahziin as bits of precious meat fell, wasted, from her slobbering jaws. What did her principles matter now? Jonas thought better of it, slicing a piece of meat from a rocksnake which had finished crisping over the flames. He didn't want to encourage Rahziin.

He could tell that Rahziin's silent determination to find an escape was gradually breaking. She probably could smell the sea air, and would have noticed the rounded, weathered rock where the Southern Ocean had once flowed, before it had retreated many thousands of years ago. They were nearing their destination. She had begun to threaten, plead, wheedle, moan, promise. She'd tried every trick to get him to unlock her manacles.

Jonas ignored her. He was long past listening to the pleas of his captured fugitives, especially those who would turn on him in a second. He had to harden his heart. It was the only way. She was a grand prize. He needed to bring her in to shrink his own thousand-year sentence. It was that simple. Maybe then, one day, Jonas could be free. Maybe then he could do as the sea had done and leave this land behind, journeying on a far more pleasant ferry, not surrounded by prisoners, ending up perhaps at a place where the sun shone and nobody knew him as Slayer – the name that he had earned from his years working for the Gaoler.

If only it was that easy.

The truth was Jonas was far from free, even without the magic manacles that bound his wrists. He was a captive of his past, and the terrors and unanswered questions that lay there.

Rahziin slumped on the other side of the fire, picking at the scraps of springhare on the rocky ground with a razor-like claw. "I was a seer, you know," she mumbled. "Valued. I had high-caste friends. The Mothers of Fate saw me as a future Arch Protector, someone who could unify the three points of power – the Mothers, the Court and the Order."

"That's all dust," said Jonas. "Better not to think of that life. What's behind us is dead." *If only I believed that myself.*

"That is not what the Order of the True believe," said Rahziin. "They say the past is alive – and dangerous."

"I have never understood the ways of the Order of the True. Why destroy the Empty when they have many skills to offer, much knowledge to pass on? Knowledge of magic, of industry, of history."

"You speak of the Old Ways. The Old Ways are blasphemous, bounty hunter. They must be persecuted. I would expect nothing less than this humanish idealism from an Empty such as yourself. You do not have the magic of the old-Kind flowing through your veins, the magic of the natural elemental forces of the world."

Jonas looked straight into the cat-Kind's eyes. "You think I am an Empty?"

The cat-Kind frowned. "True, you have some magical blessing – enhanced speed and strength. But even with your magic you are still only one rung above the Empty in our hierarchy of nobility, alongside the mages and other magically-blessed humans. If it was up to me, you magic-Kind would be treated like any other humans. The Order of the True have always believed magic in humans is dangerous. That is why I did not agree with what our Arch Protector was doing. It is a disgrace."

"I have no interest in the inner workings of the Order of the True. That is not my business."

It was better not to know too much – those who knew too much, especially humans, were a threat to the Order. Once, in Whitestone, Jonas had seen an owl-Kind burned alive by the Order for the crime of possessing a book written in ancient human script.

The memory of the burning owl made him lose his appetite a touch. He offered his skewered rocksnake to Rahziin. "Do you want some more?" At least it might stop her talking.

Rahziin wrinkled her nose. "Noble-Kind do not eat reptile."

Jonas shrugged and cut away another morsel with his knife.

As Jonas finished off his meal, Rahziin muttered on about the feud within the Order that had led to her downfall. It was hard to follow, with different factions taking sides, and power plays that sought control over various feudal lords who managed estates across the Four Kingdoms. Then there was the powerful group of female prophets called the Mothers of Fate, and, of course, the Emperor himself. Ultimately, Rahziin seemed to have got on the wrong side of the new Arch Protector, the recently appointed leader of the Order of the True – a lizard-Kind named Malachai.

"Malachai feared me," she growled. "Feared what I knew. I looked in the water and scried the truth. I saw what he had been up to in secret. That is why he condemned me. He wanted me silenced. It is corruption! Malachai holds too much power, and he is dangerous. He thinks *he* is emperor."

Jonas's ears perked up.

"D'you say you saw his past? How did you do that?" he asked, licking his fingers.

"I look in the water and I see visions," said Rahziin. "I have that gift." Suddenly she bared her fangs in a snarl-like grin, as if she'd had a brilliant idea. "Perhaps, hunter, there is something about your past that you would like to know? Maybe we can make a deal. Do you have mysteries that need clearing up? I will see them."

Jonas nearly choked on the bone he was chewing. The truth was he had a heaped plate of mysteries and a brimming soup bowl of unanswered questions on the side.

Jonas tried to keep the curiosity out of his voice. "Show me what you can do," he said carefully, "and we'll see."

Rahziin was too desperate to bargain. She waved her hand slowly over the muddy puddle beside her. Her fingers twitched and curled. A swirling disc of water rose up and hovered in front of her face, shimmering like a mirror. Jonas's heart thudded, partly out of fear and partly out of wonder, and he felt the static charge of magic prickle his skin. He felt his body react instinctively to the power, his blood thumping, his eyes widening in hunger, his fingers itching for his blade, his mind broadening into one vision of the past and future, seeing all the times he might be killed, the many branches of possible death.

Jonas held his breath, trying to focus his mind. He had heard of magic like this, but had never seen it. Seer magic.

Rahziin looked through the lens of water directly at him.

From the other side, Jonas saw her eye shiver, distorted by the lens. Then flickering, shadowed shapes began to shimmer on the surface of the water. He could not make the shadows out. He thought he could vaguely hear something too – it sounded like . . . screaming. He could hear voices, familiar ones, people from his tribe, but their words were too muffled for Jonas to understand.

All of a sudden the disc of water dropped to the ground and shattered into droplets. The cat-seer stared at him in horror.

"I know who you are now," she said. Her voice trembled.

As the aura of the cat-Kind's magic faded, so did Jonas's heightened senses. He was swallowed back into the desolate, disappointing present. The wind howled bleakly in his ears. He felt a great tiredness. "I told you you should not have tried to resist me," he said.

"I have heard of your name. There are whispers of you among the Order – Grashkor's pet, the unnatural one. A hybrid who should not exist, who does not fit into our genealogical categories. A boy linked to a monster, to the force of death itself – a spirit-monster that flies free and watches over its twin. You are the one they call *Slayer.*"

"Yes," breathed Jonas. "That is what I am called now. That is who I am."

"It looks like we can make a deal, then, Slayer.

My freedom for your mysteries. I must tell you, I cannot simply stare into any water and find what you want to know. My scrying only works if I can see for myself the place where your mystery occurred."

Jonas nodded. Inside he felt a mixture of anticipation and dread. The deal meant returning to the Pinnacles empty-handed and facing the consequences. But Jonas had never truly feared Grashkor. This feeling was something else. Jonas would be returning for the first time to where it had happened; the last camp of his tribe, the scene where all his nightmares had come true.

"We need to go south-east," he said. "It's three days from here. We must go deeper into the Quarg basin, in the far reaches of Morta. It's a dangerous journey. The Borderlands is lawless territory. The new-Kind lords claim power over this land but really they do not venture there. They are too scared. The great plains are ravaged by the raiding insect-Kind clans, barbarians who are encroaching more and more on my homelands."

"Ah – your homelands. You intrigue me, Slayer. What place does a force of death call home? I will do what must be done. I trust you will protect me."

"I give you my word."

"The word of Slayer?"

"The word of Jonas, nomad of the great plains, son of the chief of my tribe."

Jonas knew he could trust her. He could see the fear in her eyes as they spat on their palms and sealed the deal with a handshake.

Now that she knew who he was, she was going to be very careful. For a moment Jonas thought he heard a faint shrill cry carry through the clear windy skies above him. The truth was, Jonas could vouch for himself but he could not vouch for the other part of him. He could not vouch for Seth.

That night, Jonas dreamed he was flying in the body of another. On silent wings he threaded the clouds above the misty paddy fields and the small shattered towns of southern Morta. He saw everything in the tiniest detail: his eyes picked out in impossible crispness the individual hairs of a vole as it scurried for cover, a delicate lace of mushrooms growing on a collapsed timber roof.

And all the while he knew those same eyes searched for Jonas himself, who waited asleep in his own body.

The dream was exhilarating, but better still was knowing that it meant his spirit-twin was returning to him. Their minds had connected as their bodies drew nearer. They had shared visions like this many times – always strongest when they had been separated. It was almost worth the pain of being apart.

Inhabiting the flying body, Jonas gloried in the strength and power of his wings. He swooped faster than the wind and was just as invisible. The speed was exhilarating, but there was a purpose to it. He felt his twin's mind drawing him across the landscape.

There was something his twin wanted him to see.

Up ahead was a mossy, muddy clearing with two small figures facing each other.

One was a cat-Kind priest, dancing in to strike a blow with her heavy iron staff.

The other was smaller. A human boy, standing very still. His hands rested lightly on the hilts of his swords. His clothes were tattered, and his boots had holes.

Jonas knew what it meant. His twin had been watching him. He had seen the fight with Rahziin. Jonas felt a glow of happiness. He knew he had sensed his counterpart in the skies above, during the battle!

As the iron staff screamed towards his face, Jonas,

through his twin's eyes, saw the boy's brown eyes turn fully black. He saw him move with frightening speed and stop the blow dead with his blade.

And then, from his twin's perspective, he felt the power and the glory of the death-song, and he exulted because he shared it too.

Jonas woke. It was the black hour before dawn. Nothing moved. The fire was dead. Rahziin slept, curled up in her coat against the autumn chill.

Jonas stepped carefully towards a thicket of stumpy trees. He always knew when Seth was approaching; it felt like his shadow had returned. He was drawn to his twin like iron to a lodestone.

"You fought well," said a deep voice from the leaves. "That cat-Kind priest is no weakling, but you bested her."

"Hello, Seth," said Jonas. "You were gone a long time. Why did you not show yourself?"

"Sometimes I like to keep back and watch you work," said Seth. "Apologies for my absence. I had business. I was convening with the ghost world – you know I need to visit my own Kind once in a while. It gives me strength. The spirits sense a great change coming." He pushed his huge head out of the shadows. In the darkness, the great ghost-form of the wyvern shimmered a pale green. His horned reptile skull dipped and bobbed, as large as Jonas's torso, and the black eye sockets watched Jonas from the translucent green of his ghostly shimmering flesh. Slivers of light danced across his see-through body like bursts of lightning.

Seth had been around for as long as Jonas could remember, since his earliest childhood memories – and for just as long, he had *not* been around. His departures could last hours, or several moons, and there was never any warning when he would leave or when he would return.

"I have wings, child. I must fly," Seth had once said, as a young Jonas beat the wyvern's flanks with his small fists. Each blow thumped an echoing blow against his own ribs. Jonas and Seth shared a life force – if Seth was hurt, so was Jonas. If Jonas was hurt, so was Seth.

"But why did you leave?" Jonas had sobbed. "Why do you go away for so long?"

"My spirit was tied to yours at your birth, Little Fury, pulled from the Land of What Was. I shall stay in this world until our time is done. But what I do in my own time is my own concern."

Jonas had stopped pushing Seth too much. He hated admitting it to himself, but he was afraid that if he carried on Seth might leave him for good, might cut the bond that connected their life force, though Jonas had never dared ask if that was even possible. Seth had been everything to Jonas – parent, brother, guardian spirit – but he had been everything to the tribe too. The shamans said Seth was a gift from the ancestors, the vengeance of all their dead warriors brought back as a weapon to defeat their enemies. They said Jonas, with Seth at his side, was destined to unite the tribes, as Jonas's great-grandmother had once done, leading the united tribe in victory against the insect-Kind to the east and the Emperor's armies to the north. Without Seth, they were *all* nothing.

Seth stepped closer to Jonas from the clump of trees. "As ever, I am sorry for my absence. But you have bad business of your own."

"You know about my deal with Rahziin," said Jonas.

"Did you think I wouldn't? We are linked, brother. Bonded since birth. You are my second life. I feel your heart – even when we are very far apart. I feel the foolish hope inside you. Do not walk that path."

"I must find out what happened to my people, to my family," said Jonas. "Who killed them? Don't you want to know as well?"

The wyvern stooped his head so that his eyes

were level with the boy. "Death walks along that path. If you walk it, there's a good chance you will never come back. Surely you see it too. Surely your death-sense *feels* the great possibility of your own destruction. It is safer to leave what is done behind you. Think only of what is ahead. Of what our destiny could hold once we are free of Grashkor."

Jonas pulled back his sleeves and touched the chainless manacles wrapped around each wrist like thick silvery bangles – the same as the magic manacles that he had placed on Rahziin. The manacles could only be removed by the ruthless gaoler of the Pinnacles of the Damned himself – Grashkor, the Terror of the Sinful. Jonas could barely remember what it was like to be free of the restraints that, at any moment, could lock together and drag him back to the Pinnacles at Grashkor's command. "I feel the many deaths that await me if I journey back to the camp," said Jonas. "But I see death with every step I take. There is always danger on any path."

"This path is *much* more dangerous," said Seth. He did not hide his irritation. "This is a bad risk you are taking. You should not go to that valley. Change your mind!"

"You flew all this way to tell me to stop," said

Jonas. "And yet you claim that you know what is in my heart?"

"Of course I know," said Seth. "I feel you. We are brothers. That's *why* I tell you to stop."

"Then you will know why I must go," said Jonas. "I'm not turning from this path."

3

The Keeper of Worlds

The sky through the portal was as red as the distant mountains, whose peaks jabbed out of the crimson horizon like sharp wolves' teeth in a bloody mouth. No rain seemed to have ever fallen in this land. There were no trees, no bushes, no grass. The scarlet dust was scoured by the wind into massive teardrop-shaped dunes.

As Gael examined the parallel world through the portal gateway – his feathered head tilted to one side – his view shivered ever so slightly. He'd noticed that Type Three portals like this often had an odd, waxy character to them – as if the boundary that separated the two dimensions was actually a thick membrane. He knew better than to go poking his beak through it to see what would happen.

He glanced down at his oscilloscope. The readings were steady, but this was clearly a flux of great power, and it was leaking dangerous amounts of energy – pure volatile magic channelled from the Netherplane itself.

"Fly, Felix," Gael instructed. A jewelled beetle flew out of one of the many bottomless pockets of his cloak. It hovered by his beak, whirring gently.

"Record this," Gael croaked. "Type Three portal. Readings show good stamina, cycleflux about ninety, rising to a peak of . . . one-twenty. Stable now, but signs of recent eruptions. Take visuals of surrounding area, Felix."

The memory-beetle buzzed in the air, capturing images of the area around the portal in its lens-like eyes that Gael would watch again later. Looking away from the portal, Gael followed the beetle's gaze and took in the familiar landscape of his home world around him – if a Gateway Keeper could ever call any world a home. A thousand years ago, when Gael had made this world his base, it had been known as *Havanthya* in the ancient human tongue – funny he thought of that name now. Like much of the history of this place, the name had been long forgotten – or, rather, intentionally destroyed, along with the great spell books of the ancient human civilisations, tomes of written history, art, buildings, even spoken fables treated as blasphemy by the new-Kind. So much knowledge lost. You could not tell that a great imbalance plagued this world, as it did many others, disrupting the quiet beauty that had entranced Gael and kept him here when all the other Gateway Keepers had wandered back to the Netherplane, where they had come from. Even now Gael could hear that timeless dimension of pure magic calling to him through the aura of the leaking portal, whispering things long forgotten, making him yearn for the past, yearn for peace. But he had a job to do. Some disruption was causing pure magic to be channelled from the Netherplane and blast open new gateways – it was unnatural, dangerous. It had to be sorted. And only he could sort it. He was the only one left.

Gael closed his eyes for a moment. The thick woodland smelled of damp pine needles. Squirrels chirped at each other from their nests. A frog croaked a love song. *So far, so very normal,* the great crow-Kind thought to himself. Perhaps the effects of the leaking portal were not as bad as he thought. Nature always surprised him with its resilience.

Felix began to whine through the air, taking

close-up recordings of features near to the portal opening. This was very clearly a dangerous spot: the concentrated, unfiltered magic had caused unnatural, alien mushrooms to grow on the trees and rocks. Several pines had been sliced neatly in half as if cut with a giant pair of shears. Fish floated belly-up on the surface of the pond, which seemed to have an odd rainbow shimmer. Explosions of volatile magic had left large craters in the earth.

A dozen birds and a drift of insects lay dead at Gael's feet. They must have died trying to pass through the portal, poor creatures.

Gael stepped carefully away from the arch where the portal had opened. It was better not to stay very close for too long. Quite apart from the danger, the Netherplane magic was making him feel tired, spreading through his hollow bones and making him long for rest.

Once he was at a safer distance, he looked back. To the untrained eye – and it was lucky that Gael was possibly the most trained eye in any of the Many Worlds – the arch might look like a man-made ruin, covered in vines and lichen. You had to look very carefully to see the remains of teeth lining the top, and the buried lower jaw, and the smooth bone of the upper skull.

"Record this: portal appears to have opened within the jaws of a . . . giant lion's skull. Only fragments of the snout remain attached to the jawbones. I have made note of large incisors and the gaping size of the creature's jaw. This must be the skull of an *enormous* old-Kind, now only petrified bone. Dead five hundred years or more. I do not know the old-Kind's name, but it clearly possesses some latent power. I believe there was once a portal that opened here long ago, and a flux of magical energy has burst it back open."

The memory-beetle gave out tiny clicks to show that it was recording all of Gael's words as it followed behind him. It was a neat little toy. When he was younger, Gael could have remembered all the readings but now that he was getting older he could do with the help.

"Record this: check for the identity of a lion old-Kind." Gael was certain he could dig that information out of his library. "From the dry landscape and blood sky on the other side of the portal, it looks like it leads to the Dark Realm, Gorgonya."

From another pouch in his blue cloak he took a map and scratched at it with his scribing stick. It was marked with the locations of all the other portals that had somewhat mysteriously opened in the past few years.

This one, like almost all the large Type Three portals, had appeared in the northern lands of Anoros. The only exception was a mysterious outburst that had been recorded some years ago in the Quarg basin in the Borderlands, far away in southern Morta, where the human nomads lived. That had been a truly horrifying sight. The memory of all those tribal people's bodies still troubled Gael. At some point, it might be worth returning to find out what had really happened there.

But before he could think any more on this, a line of golden glyphs appeared in the air in front of him. They were sharp and jagged, like teeth and claw marks – the saurian-Kind language of the noble-born Kind. They continued to spool out, as if written by an invisible pen.

"What's this, what's this? A *summons,* from the Order of the True?" Gael began to scowl as he read the noble-tongue writing. "Hm! It seems *Arch Protector* Malachai is getting a little big for his boots."

Gael clicked his fingers and Felix buzzed back inside a pocket in his cloak. "Jumped-up botherers," Gael muttered darkly to himself. "Foolish interruptions . . . No respect for the proper pace of science . . . Knew I must be out in the field." Gael set about closing up the wild portal. After checking that all was as it should be, he drew a large purple jewel from yet another pocket in his cloak's lining.

"Scalx," he growled.

The purple jewel began to glow, a dim light throbbing deep inside it.

"ASCLERAX!" shouted Gael, holding the jewel above his head.

He closed his eyes tight.

The light burst from the jewel, blinding bright – he could feel it wash all around him like a great golden wave. The spell rejuvenated his body the way such intricate, meticulously crafted magic always did. Dancing lightness prickled down every spur of every feather on his body. He never got tired of that feeling.

When Gael opened his eyes again, the portal was gone.

He clacked his beak together in satisfaction at a job well done, then swirled his cloak around his body. There was a sound of crackling static, a feeling like his body was being pulled apart in every direction, and around him there was only the yellow glow of the between-places.

Gael popped back into reality, coughing.

Teleportation always gave him a tickly throat.

He glared at the brightly patterned mosaics and heavy velvet curtains that adorned Malachai's antechamber. He'd never liked the white marble of the great palace at Whitestone, but whoever had recently redecorated this place had no taste at all.

Why have just one golden statue of some poor human being tortured, when you could have five?

"Don't worry, lads. Your boss, Malachai, finally decided it was time for us to meet," Gael croaked at the guards, who were looking slightly surprised that a dusty old raven in a faded blue cloak had suddenly appeared before them. The guards wore the red-mail armour of the Emperor's Own, the personal fighting force of the Emperor. "He summoned me here. I wouldn't stand in my way if I were you – he was very clear I needed to come immediately."

Gael strode through the high doors without waiting for their permission.

Malachai's private rooms were as diabolically decorated as the antechamber. Gael hurried towards the tall figure standing near a table filled with papers at the end of the room. He had seen Malachai a few times before, usually at royal events, when the lizard-Kind was climbing the ranks of the Order, showering the Emperor with flattery and fuelling his paranoia over the danger of the humans. Last time Gael had seen Malachai, the priest had only been a Grand Protector.

"Stop! You can't . . ." a guard yelled as the two Emperor's Own soldiers trailed Gael ineffectually into the room.

All the gilding, expensive fabrics and really horrible pictures were clearly meant to make you feel like this Malachai was rich, nasty and terribly important.

"Pshaw!" Gael had seen a thousand of Malachai's type before – megalomaniacs, fanatics, the lot. He had no time for them. He arrived at the table. The Arch Protector still had his back to him. He was eating chunks of meat from a golden plate held by a shivering human servant. The girl could be no older than eighteen, with dark hair falling about her bowed head. Another power play. As the girl looked up at Gael's sudden entrance, the plate she held tipped slightly and the meat rolled off. She scrabbled to pick the pieces up.

"Do not defile my food by touching it, Empty!" Malachai hissed. "Who are you, anyway, servant? I do not recognise you. I do not appreciate imbeciles serving me, though what can I expect from an Empty?"

"So here I am, popping in double-quick, just as

requested," said Gael quickly. He didn't bother to bow. "What d'you need me for, Arch Protector? I am very busy."

Gael studied the lizard-Kind's face carefully as the priest pivoted towards him. Rudeness could be a wonderful distraction.

The only sign that Malachai was annoyed was a faint hiss as his black tongue flicked out between his heavy, grinding teeth. His eyes were black too, and gave nothing away. They looked small in his large, flat skull. He was a powerful, well-built lizard-Kind – bare-chested with golden rings and ivory circlets on his scaled arms.

"Welcome, Gael, the Gateway Keeper," he said. "It is good to meet you at last. I appreciate your haste. I summoned you so urgently because of important and troubling news. It seems there is a traitor on the Council of Magic-Kind, one who we believe has been helping the human rebels steal powerful spell books from the Tower of Forbidden Knowledge, among other treasures. The Tower of Forbidden Knowledge is an institution of which you are a prominent member, I believe."

Now it was Gael's turn to feel observed. Malachai's black eyes were peeling the skin beneath his feathers, watching to see how he moved and where he looked. He was clearly suspicious, which was strange because Gael had nothing to hide.

Gael kept his voice steady. "A traitor? On the Council of Magic-Kind? Unlikely. And the Tower of Forbidden Knowledge is a fortress. No human could enter without detection."

"It is the only credible way to explain the recent success of the human rebels. Our enemies communicate over vast distances. They hide from our eyes. They spy out our secrets. They must be using powerful ancient human magic – spells meant to be hidden away in the Tower of Forbidden Knowledge. They must be getting help from a skilled human magic-Kind, not some village druid or cheap trickster. All the most powerful human witches and wizards are members of the Council. That is the law. It helps us keep an eye on them. Ah! These so-called magic-Kind are barely fit for the title of 'Kind' at all. Yes, they are magic-blessed, but they still have their weak, frail bodies, their nasty, conniving minds. It is believed the traitor on the Council goes by an alias: 'The Reader'."

"The Reader? I've never heard such a name. And every member of the Council of Magic-Kind has sworn many oaths to protect peace and order. Aiding rebellion is against a lot of rules. The magic of the Old Ways is blasphemous. We only *study* it at the Tower, never use it," retorted Gael.

"Of course it is blasphemous! We think the Reader could be responsible for masterminding the theft of a powerful item from the city of Skin-Grave, too. Foolish humans! No matter, we have Grashkor on the case. He is tracking down the thief as we speak. We have interrogated some human rebels we captured for answers about the Reader."

"Interrogated or tortured?" Gael asked.

"Whatever makes you feel more comfortable," snarled Malachai. "You have always been too soft on the Empty, Gael. I have heard how you treat our inferiors with respect. The Emperor does not look kindly on fraternising with our natural enemy. They must be kept in line!"

"Of course," said Gael. "Small talk with servants can be EXTREMELY dangerous."

Malachai glowered. "Well, our interrogations revealed that the Reader is intent on leading insurrection. This is not how it should be, Gael! They are human scum. We are their superiors. We carry magic in our blood. The magic of the great demigods of the old-Kind, fashioned in the beginning as overlords of our world – great beings driven to extinction by the very enemies you wish to exchange pleasantries with!"

"You know what they say about legends?"

"What?"

"They are *legends*. Not history. Look, Arch Protector. Rather than jumping to conclusions about traitors in the Council, is it not possible that the humans have found these things by themselves? *Without* breaking into the Tower? They have their own culture. They have their own magic. They remember their history, as much as you try to destroy it. They are quite clever, you know." Gael raised a warning finger, as if teaching a slow pupil. "You've heard of the Law of Bad Assumptions, Arch Protector? I can think of a dozen explanations for your little human problem. Perhaps the most obvious is that you are making mistakes. I would not be so sure this Reader even exists – prisoners will say anything when they are being tortured. Sorry – *interrogated*."

Malachai hissed again, and this time he did not hide his irritation. His tongue flicked out and stayed out, tasting the air.

"You should show more respect, Keeper," he snapped.

"And *you* should be careful throwing accusations about," said Gael. "Isn't crushing the humans your responsibility?"

Malachai blinked, as if he'd been struck. "I can crush humans very well," he said, and turned to the servant girl beside him. "See?"

He waved his hand gently and the girl began to choke, as if an invisible attacker was clutching her by the throat.

Malachai watched Gael closely to see how he would react. The girl's face turned red, then purple.

Gael felt guilty. His bad temper and hasty words were going to get this innocent girl killed. But he knew this was a test too.

Quickly and carefully, Gael reached for a pocket, one of the many bottomless compartments sewn into his cloak containing wards, charms and spells. With a silent word of command, he summoned the star-shaped crystal inside it. He felt the faint thrum as soon as he touched it, the static charge of magic flickering over his fingertips. Inside his pocket, the crystal would be glowing grey-black. The colour of storm clouds.

A fierce gust of wind blew the window open. This knocked a lit oil lamp on the windowsill into the curtains. The oil spilled on the heavy fabric, and flames rushed up the fancy brocade.

Malachai cursed and released the girl from his grip. He held his clawed hands high and ripped them back, and the brocade tore magically from the wall. With another sweep of his hands, the fabric was thrown out of the window.

The girl stumbled away from the priest. Stepping forward, Gael threw his cloak over her head and teleported her out of the palace in the blink of an eye. His movements were so sharp that by the time Malachai turned away from the window, Gael was standing innocently in exactly the same place as before.

"Where is the girl?" said Malachai.

"She scampered from the room." Gael shrugged. "Far too quick for an old bird like me."

"And you did not think to use your magic to stop her?" said Malachai.

"Magic should not be used to play silly games," said Gael. "Any real magic-Kind knows that." All the jesting was out of his voice now.

Malachai seemed to feel the rebuke. He clenched his fists and took a step towards the old raven.

"Do not think I am playing silly games," he growled. "The Order of the True does not play games. We have been watching you, Gateway Keeper. You are up to something."

He took another step closer. Now Gael could smell the rotten stink of his breath. *That's what comes from only eating weeks-old meat,* he thought.

"So listen closely. *Hunt down* the traitor in your Council. This 'Reader'. Do not fail me. If you do, I will assume that it is *you* who is betraying us to the accursed humans. After all, isn't the Tower of Forbidden Knowledge in the Hallowed Vale, where you reside, human-sympathiser? You won't be so full of yourself when it is you that our torturers break on the wheel."

The Arch Protector turned away.

"Now get out of my sight."

Gael did not waste any time in doing exactly as he was told. But his gaze was distant as he hobbled down the endless stairs and corridors of the palace.

Such was his distraction that he did not realise he was being followed until it was too late.

"Keeper!" cried the voice. "Stop!"

A small hand grabbed his wrist.

"What! What?" croaked Gael, turning round as he reached inside his cloak for a defensive charm.

"I wanted to say thank you," said a human girl with dark hair and large, luminous eyes. "My name is Roshni, and I owe you a great debt." It was the servant girl. The one he'd saved.

"Say nothing of it," said Gael. "That priest is a creep. He has no right to act that way – to you or anyone else. You owe me nothing, Roshni. Good luck to you."

Gael turned to go, but the hand had still not released his sleeve.

"Sir . . ." Roshni looked up at him shyly. "Might I perhaps serve you? I would make a fine assistant. I speak all the tongues and I know the written languages of all the new-Kind. I even speak fish-Kind, sir!"

"That's very impressive, but I have no need of an assistant."

Roshni lowered her voice to a whisper. "That is not all. My grandfather taught me Havanthyan, the language of the ancients, sir. I can read it too. Surely that might be of some use!"

Gael looked again at the girl. Malachai's new law meant that it was forbidden to even speak the word "Havanthya" out loud.

Strange that a human who spoke Havanthyan would be employed by Malachai. There was more to this girl than met the eye. Even more reason to leave her well alone.

"I'm sorry, my dear, but I really have no need of an assistant."

Still her hand had not released his sleeve. "Sir Keeper. I have nowhere to go. If Malachai finds me again, he will surely kill me."

There was truth in this, Gael recognised. What was the point in half-saving someone? And the girl was nothing if not persistent. He sighed and cursed his soft heart.

"Can you handle a duster, Roshni? I have many old shelves that could do with a polish."

"Yes, sir! Thank you, sir!" Her eyes looked up at him, shining with gratitude. They were swimmingly dark, like an ocean after the sun has fallen deep enough to get lost in its depths. For the second time that day, Gael had the strange sensation that he was being peeled apart and examined right down to his very soul.

He shivered, wondering if he would regret this decision.

Ah well, it was too late for that now.

"We will teleport to the Hallowed Vale. Come under my cloak." He held up a wing to tent the fabric.

"Will Malachai know, sir?"

"I'm sure he's watching us right now. I'm sure he will be annoyed."

This thought was cheering. After they vanished, Gael's last laugh rang out over the empty courtyard.

4

A Vision of the Past

Jonas saw the first curse marker when he and Rahziin were still half a day's journey from the last campsite of his tribe. He had only ever returned to the camp in his memory, until now. He could finally find answers to the mystery that had plagued him since he had discovered the massacre of his tribe three years ago: the bodies of his slain family and friends spread over the ground and decorated with blood. A place, it seemed, where not only Jonas feared to venture.

The curse marker was a totem made of sticks and string. It hung from the dead branch of a tree. As they went past, it twisted in the wind, as if it was watching them.

"Whatever that is," Rahziin muttered, "I don't like it."

Jonas did not explain, but he knew very well what it meant. The other tribes had hung the totem there to declare this land black ground. It was a warning. It meant the grass here was cursed by evil spirits. It meant that it would be unwise to bring herds to this valley. It meant that this place was unlucky.

Jonas wondered if the warning was right.

They had been travelling south for two and a half days now. They had made good time, trekking with long strides across the close-cropped steppe lands. The rolling hills were not hard going. Far off in the distance, the snow-capped peaks of the Quarg kept watch.

Somewhere, Jonas knew, Seth, his wyvern twin, was also watching out for him – though he had flown off angry after their hard words. *Let him stew,* thought Jonas. *This is my path, and I must walk it.*

The way Jonas's tribe had told it, for as long as anyone could remember, his people had grazed their herds in these sheltered valleys. On their trek, Jonas had seen nomad fires at night, though he had avoided coming close to any camps. He knew how careful the tribes of the Borderlands were with strangers. The Quarg basin was a hard land. There was little foliage other than grass, winters were harsh, and droughts sometimes lasted for years. And then there was the never-ending threat of insect-Kind raiders from the east.

As they passed deeper into the valley, the going grew more difficult. The grass had gone ungrazed for three years and now rose waist-high. They passed more curse markers hanging from branches and balanced on rocks. Worse still, as they drew closer to the camp every step, every stone and even every tree became painfully familiar to Jonas. This land was his home, where he had been taught to hunt and ride and run and fight. They had come to this site often.

He tried not to think about his mother and father.

Rahziin sensed his unease. She stopped talking. The only noise was the moan of the wind in the grass.

There were too many ghosts here.

"And there it is," said Jonas, stopping suddenly as they came over a small rise.

The camp lay sprawled out below him. For some reason the grass was lower here, and the camp looked eerily undisturbed, as if the people who lived in the round hide-covered tents had just got up and vanished all at once. Three years, and the camp looked just the same as Jonas remembered it.

The doors of some of the yurts still hung open. Flat stones for hearths were arranged in neat circles in front of each of them. There were pots and pans still out – sitting ready for meals that would never be prepared.

Everything was just as it had been . . . almost.

All that Jonas knew about the most important moment of his life was this: three years ago, he had returned to his camp from a hunt to find everyone dead, including his parents and his beloved cousin Fran. They had been massacred. All of them, slaughtered. The odd thing was, none of the cattle or the horses had been killed. That counted out insect-Kind as the culprits – they were barbarians who destroyed and usually ate any living, moving thing in their path. None of the tents had been taken, nor any of the carts that the tribe used to travel through the plains.

Dazed and distraught, Jonas was found by a rival tribe who took him to the feudal lord who owned the territory where Jonas's community had been killed. The lord was a fat old walrus-Kind, full of his own self-importance, though he knew nothing of the lands which he governed in name only. The rival tribe told the Kind lord that Jonas was cursed, that he had killed all his people. Jonas tried to explain how he was out on a hunt when the killing happened, that the dead had been his friends, his cousins, his parents, his life. Jonas was sentenced to a thousand years for the slaughter of human vassals on land owned by a Kind. Seth had tried to intervene. He had caused quite a shock. But all Seth did was make the walrus-Kind lord rule that the bond between boy and spirit defined Jonas as a type of Kind, and that Jonas should therefore serve his sentence in the Pinnacles of the Damned, where Kind were incarcerated. Jonas had been twelve when he entered the Pinnacles, the only human inside. For three years he had just managed to survive. For three years, he had been obsessed over the same question: what person, army, human or Kind did he have to track down to gain vengeance?

"Let's get this over with, Slayer," said Rahziin, setting off down the slope. "I don't want to be in manacles any longer than I have to be."

A few cattle – the remnant of the herd – munched slowly amongst the tents. That explained how the grass had been kept back. Some of the yaks, Jonas noted, still had their horns painted with the tribe's markings.

There were a few signs of panic and slaughter. A long splash of dark blood sprayed across the hide of a tent. A savage tear that had collapsed another. But there were no bones. The wolves, or the insect-Kind, must have taken them. Jonas was grateful for that.

In the centre of the camp rose a great totem root. Carved pictures of the Earth Father and Sky Mother chased each other around the stump of the upturned tree, meeting only in the directions of sunrise and sunset. The carved images told the story of What Was, What Is and What Will Be, twisted around itself in spiralling layers, just as history, present and future run in parallel with each other – or so the shamans would say. Jonas had never much cared for listening to those wizened old blatherers – he'd much preferred watching the chisellers work. He let his eyelids sink closed for a moment. He could still *hear* the *snick snick* as their fine edges carved new patterns in the hard wood.

"*Jonas! Pay attention.*" His father's voice came almost as clearly. "*These stories are your past, and they are your future. You know the story of this totem?*"

Jonas had heard it many times: how his great-grandmother, the Chief of Chiefs, had felled this great sangwar tree when she was not yet fifteen seasons, a similar age to Jonas now, using only a single-blade hatchet.

It was the last of the totem roots. The sacred sangwar from which they were carved only grew around the mild shores of the Nara Lake far to the south-east, but no tribesfolk had travelled to those waters to glimpse their spirit-self reflections since the summer of death, when the lake was invaded by the Thrashers – giant beetle-Kind larvae, all lithe powerful bodies and saw-like teeth.

"Jonas! You must remember. You carry with you the blood of the past, and we are relying on you to carry it into the future. You must remember!"

Jonas's eyes snapped open. They rested on the ancient stories of What Was, when men and beasts worked together to keep harmony in the world. *I am the* only *one who remembers now, Father,* Jonas thought.

Rahziin wrinkled her nose when she saw what he was looking at. "What is this filth? Your people do not believe this nonsense, do they?"

"I don't have people any more," he said. "They're all dead."

Rahziin spat on the ground to avoid the bad luck. She picked up a dusty clay bowl and pulled her water skin from her belt.

"This will do. Are you ready to find out what happened here?"

Jonas nodded. His mouth was too dry to speak.

"And when I reveal your true past, you will keep your word and set me free." She watched him carefully. "Swear it again."

"I swear," said Jonas. "I swear over the graves of my parents at the totem root of my ancestors."

As he spoke, a tickle at the back of his mind told him that Seth was close. Jonas wondered if the wyvern would try to stop him at the last moment.

Rahziin nodded. "May you walk under the bleak curse if you break your oath," she said. "So . . . Let us see." She poured a slug of water from her skin into the bowl. Then she made the same curling gestures over the surface as before. It began to bubble and froth.

A disc of whirling water rose up. The disc was bigger this time. Rahziin controlled it with delicate twists of her fingers as she lifted it up and looked through the water at the camp.

"I see the life your people had here," Rahziin said. "I see your mornings, rising to the herds in the mist. I see your meals." She laughed. "You ate a lot of soup."

Jonas shut his eyes. He could picture it all so well. This place even smelled just like he remembered.

Rahziin was still turning her gaze around the

camp, peering through the water at the yurts and describing what she saw. "I see your ceremonies and your little joys. I see births and deaths. Tool-making and the passing of seasons. It was a good life you had."

"That final day," said Jonas. "Look for that."

"As you say." Her lens shimmered. Suddenly he saw her frown. Her eyes went wide, as if transfixed by something in the far distance. She began muttering, her voice strained, and Jonas struggled to make out the breathy words. "I see . . . your people . . . I see them dying. They fall before a tide of rippling air."

Jonas's chest tightened. "What is killing them? Kind?"

Rahziin did not seem to hear him. Her body had stiffened like a corpse. "A beast with six limbs and no sides. It stalks through your people, slashing a prophecy in blood. I see them die . . . I see too much!"

Jonas stared as Rahziin's fur began to stand on end, wavering in an invisible current.

"I am drowning in blood! I cannot take it."

"No, don't stop!" urged Jonas. "What is this creature?"

When Rahziin spoke again, her voice was muffled and hollow as if she was underwater. "A creature of the past! The shamans chant a music of death. It is the only way! They are destiny's sacrifice."

"I don't understand," said Jonas. "You speak in riddles!"

Drool slithered from Rahziin's mouth and a strange smile spread across her face. "The Mothers said I would glimpse the purpose of the Creator. It is the start of the Cleansing! One of three branches of fate designed in the Netherplane. But which sacrifice will bring terrible renewal?"

Her turn had taken a full circle. Only now did the cat-Kind priest look through her water wheel at Jonas. Rahziin's mouth dropped open. She started backing away from him, almost stumbling. Her expression contorted into a frozen rictus of overwhelming terror and limitless despair that was beyond anything Jonas had ever witnessed even on the faces of those he had killed.

"Slayer!" she stammered. "You . . ."

"What?" he shouted. "Tell me!"

The disc of water collapsed from her trembling hands. Before she could reply, there was a tearing screech overhead.

"AMBUSH!" screamed Seth. The wyvern was calling his warning from the sky. There was desperate panic in his voice. "INSECT-KIND!"

Then a buzzing, chittering scream exploded around them.

Barbarian war cries shattered the air. The insect-Kind came out of nowhere – jumping, flying, bursting from the ground. The death-song blazed up in Jonas.

He reached for his swords as he ducked beneath the swipe of a huge black axe. The muscular wasp-Kind wielding it grunted in surprise when Jonas wasn't cut in half.

Savage raiders were thudding down all around. Their rank stench filled Jonas's nostrils. They wore no armour because no true insect needed protection. Their shields were covered with human skin.

They were hungry.

The danger of many deaths was so very close that the death-song took Jonas over completely. He roared as the power rose within him.

The insects around him took a step back. They could smell the strange magic inside him. Their fear made him stronger.

"Kill the defiler!" The wasp-Kind rose into the air on her stubby wings and dived, screaming, at Jonas's head. She was a chieftain – Jonas could see the scars she'd won in battle and the tattoos that covered her striped body. Each mark was a victory.

In his mind he saw his death. He saw her rip his head off and carry it up into the sky as a trophy.

He started to laugh.

Then he took two neat steps to one side. He brought his sword up in an elegant curve as she passed. He cut her off at her fat abdomen. She was dead before she hit the ground.

"No victory today," said Jonas.

The barbarians screamed in horror as their leader fell. They chittered and snapped their jaws – and then they attacked together.

"Foul HUMAN DEFILER!" A mantis jumped high in the air and swiped at Jonas with scythe-like arms.

Jonas was in one place then another, moving so fast that he might have been three people. The mantis lost both arms. Now insects swarmed in ever greater numbers, desperate for vengeance. Their corpses piled at Jonas's feet as his twin blades rippled and arced around him like a dancer's ribbons, slashing at insect-Kind as he ducked their crude weapons and bludgeoning body parts. Countless visions of his own death fragmented before him, like reflections in a cracked mirror – *mandibles crushing his skull, an axe made of cattle bone raking his chest, a dragonfly-Kind lifting and then dropping him from the air.* But Jonas was always one step ahead.

The death-song gloried at every near miss and every kill. Jonas felt as if his blood was boiling. He revelled in the power and the speed rising inside him. He had never felt this good. The black joy was incredible.

With everything around him happening so slowly, he even had time to look around the battlefield for Rahziin.

Several wrecking balls had burst from the earth and bowled the priest over. The armoured louse-Kinds were grabbing at her with hundreds of tiny arms. Jonas saw Seth land, invisible beside the cat-Kind who did not even realise that the ghost-wyvern stood behind her. Suddenly the wyvern's ghost-form turned solid, the shimmering green translucent flesh losing its glow and turning a dark, leathery moss colour. The skeleton of the ghost-Kind could no longer be seen, but his eyes burned red and his fangs looked suddenly giant as he snarled and pulled a louse away with one rip of his mighty jaws.

Then half a dozen ant-Kind swarmed in and the battle became too intense to think of others. Jonas was grateful that the wyvern was protecting the cat. He knew he could deal with the rest of the army.

Jonas lost track of the insects that he had killed. The death-song was so pure and so powerful that there was nothing but killing.

He wasn't really thinking any more. He was two swords, spinning through space, a waltz of life and death, destiny itself, forging his own way at the expense of his enemies.

When the insects fled, leaving their dead and dying behind, Jonas pursued them out into the grass. Their fear made them fast – but he cut down a few stragglers before they could escape. He never wanted this feeling to end.

"What are you doing? That's good food you're spoiling. Tenderised meat is a human taste."

Seth's voice pulled Jonas out of his frenzy. He looked down at his hands. He was drenched in blood and sticky juices. His swords were slick. He was breathing hard.

The creature beneath him – a moth-Kind, though it was hard to tell – was long dead, but he had still been hacking at it.

"I felt your joy in that battle," said Seth in ghost form. "Glorious! You truly lost yourself. You are special, you know."

As the joy of the killing faded, Jonas found himself returning. He did not like what he saw or how he felt.

"Did you not see the insects approach?" he said. "We had no warning."

"I saw them only as they attacked," said Seth. "Their

ambush was well done. Just a pity they decided to pick on you. Today was a fine day for killing."

"Where is Rahziin?"

Seth shook his head. "She is dead. It is my fault. I lost her for a moment and when I turned to her again . . ."

Jonas did not know what was worse: the fact that he had turned into a monster again and loved it, or the fact that all of this had been pointless. A hollow pit of dread and worry opened inside him at the thought of so much death, his broken promise to Rahziin that he would protect her, and the lies he would have to tell Grashkor.

Seth had been right. This was a foolish path to take.

The wyvern turned from ghost to solid form, skeleton – other than his dark, gleaming skull – disappearing beneath scaled flesh, the aura of green dying instantly like an extinguished lantern. He bent his head down and took a great bite out of the dead insect at Jonas's feet. He threw his head back and swallowed the flesh without chewing.

"Did she give you your answers?" asked Seth.

"No," said Jonas. He thought of the terrified look in the cat-Kind priest's eyes, her strange words. "Only more questions."

5

The Fallen Princess

Quartz was an easy rock to shape. Something in its crystal structure stored a lot of magic, which meant it just needed a little prod to get it to move the way Lana Shadowscale wanted.

The floor of the mine was littered with tiny quartz figures that Lana had shaped out of the stone while she, her sister and Jun had been taking a break. Birds and monsters, friends and family. Some of the figures were still marching or crawling around, animated by the magic Lana had unleashed from the stone. They would carry on until they used up all their magic.

"Just make one more, pleeeeease!" Lana's little sister, Shahn, begged. She did good googly eyes.

"No, little egg," Lana sighed. "Time for work now." She had a hard time saying no to her sister.

"For rock's sake, Shahn!" Jun gave a mock scowl. "Some of us have a quota to fill! D'you want me to be punished?"

If there had been anyone else there, they would have been surprised to hear a human serf talk to a Kind like that, even if Jun *was* eighteen years old – a woman, or so it seemed to Lana. Lana was four years her friend's junior, still only a child – as Jun always liked to remind her.

It was even more surprising because the blood that flowed beneath Lana and Shahn's scaled skin was as noble as it got. Their great-great-broodfather, Mordrid, had been the last emperor of the Shadowscale dynasty, ruler of all the Four Kingdoms – even if the dank depths of the mine where his descendants now worked were about as far removed from the Marble Palace of Whitestone as you could possibly be.

But Lana and Jun had been working together down here for years, and had developed a healthy respect for each other's talents as well as a warm friendship. Jun loved Lana because of her incredible ability for sniffing out the most valuable rock seams, letting her magical sense for the properties of the mountain guide her. It made everyone's job so much easier. Plus, as Jun had remarked once, Lana's impish sense of humour made a hard life a little easier to bear. Lana loved Jun because she had never seen her back down from a challenge or lose her cool. They made a formidable team.

In the dark danger of the mine, it was hard to tell human from Kind. All that mattered was whether you could be trusted.

"Shall we try that rock face now?" said Jun, pointing with her pick to a blank expanse of wall.

Lana nodded from beneath the hood of her cloak. With her hands stretched out before her, she peeled the heavy granite slab aside in long, smooth strips. She did it so easily the hard stone wall might as well have been a banana.

Shahn watched, entranced, as the rock shuddered and groaned. The lamplight revealed a pure seam of white crystal underneath.

"A motherlode!"

"You did it again, Lana!" Jun set to work clearing away the granite and shoring up the walls.

Lana reached inside the seam and drew out a heavy lump of quartz the size of her head. The stone melted in her fingers like butter.

"This is good," she said, feeling out the structure

of the stone with her mind. "Good enough to send to the palace."

"Jun, why do you always use a pick?" asked Shahn. This was her three hundredth question today. She usually managed a thousand before she went to bed.

"You mean, why can't I magic rock about like your clever sister?" Jun laughed and wiped the sweat off her forehead. It was hot down in the deep seams. "Well, us humans can't do magic so good. We used to, once. But I guess we just forgot how. You heard of Dalthek?"

Shahn shook her head.

"You lizards. He was an ancient human wizard – a conjuror, just like your sister. Conjuring is the rarest of all magic-blessings. Conjurors are touched by pure magic, which is known as shadow when it's in its stable form. Pure magic is powerful and can be dangerous. Just as the Creator used raw magic to shape the Many Worlds into existence, conjurors can draw out the natural elemental magic contained in all things. They can turn one element into another, shape and manipulate materials. But Dalthek was far better than your sister, of course. He lived a long, long time ago. I heard he was the most powerful wizard that ever lived."

"Ooooooh!" Shahn loved stories. "Can you tell

me about him?"

Lana laughed. "Don't believe everything Jun says. She told me once that Dalthek could create objects out of nothing – even though that's completely impossible."

Shahn frowned. "But isn't that what you do, Lana?"

"Not a bit!" said Lana. "I can only shape what's already there. My magic works best when I try to find . . . what something *ought* to be. What it's . . . sympathetic to."

The little lizard-Kind frowned.

"It's hard to explain," said Lana. "Let me show you. You'll need to understand this when you start working down here."

Shahn had shown a few signs of a conjuring talent – though not as strong as Lana's. They'd both inherited their powers from their mother. The Shadowscale broodline had long been known for carrying magical talent. It was said the first Shadowscale empress, Elrith the Living Shadow, had been shadow-blessed, her body covered with fire-like wreaths of shadow. Such an elemental blessing was once admired as a sign of rare power. But these days elemental blessings – whether fire, air or water, metal or stone, ghost or shadow – were seen as dangerous, unnatural, even a curse.

That was why Lana always kept the right-hand side of her body concealed beneath her tight-fitted, hooded cloak. She couldn't always control the flickering shadow that consumed all the way from her right foot to the right side of her head, dancing over every scale of her right leg, the right of her torso and neck, even her face, just as it had once lit the scales of her ancestor. Sometimes, when Lana could tell other people were watching her with curiosity or wariness or hatred, she felt angry at her family – angry at her mother for passing down her ancestor's cursed characteristic to Lana, and the gift of conjuring to both her daughters. Angry, because it put both Lana and Shahn at risk. Even though Shahn was not shadow-blessed, her conjuring power would still draw suspicion and mistrust, anger and hatred. Lana felt angry because the Shadowscale talent carried with it a greater danger than the ignorance of strangers. Hiding behind her cloak could protect Lana from others. But it couldn't protect her from herself. It couldn't protect her from the madness that had ended up destroying her mother, when she became too obsessed with the visions. In the end, her brain had simply switched off, overloaded with the magical disease, and she had died. Lana had been just eight years old. It had happened only three years after her father's sudden murder by human bandits while on the road.

Lana thought if she could teach her sister to channel her magic, then her gift wouldn't get out of control like their mother's had done. This was Lana's duty – to teach Shahn so she would be protected from being a danger to herself. It was a duty that their mother, too self-obsessed, too enchanted by the possibilities of her power, had failed at. Lana knew on some level that her determination to protect her sister was also an attempt to protect herself. Lana had to remind herself every day to study her craft, understand her power, not get lost in the possibility of what feats she might be able to accomplish. After all, Lana was shadow-blessed, with far more potential than her sister or mother.

Lana held out the shining lump of crystal in her hand. "You see this crystal, Shahn? You see how there's little threads of red deep inside it?"

Shahn nodded.

"What do those threads make you think of?" asked Lana.

"They look like . . . whiskers."

"Good! That's just what I was thinking." Lana enjoyed teaching her sister. "Now, who do you know who has long red whiskers?"

Shahn considered this. "Well . . . there's Groesh. But he's so nasty."

"He's perfect," said Lana. "Watch."

In her mind, she pictured the cruel mine overseer, Groesh. She thought of his burrowing claws, as long as carving knives. His huge, white, sightless eyes. His fleshy pink nose and his spindly, twitchy whiskers.

"Wow," said Shahn, watching her sister work.

The clearer the picture, the better the shape. As Lana concentrated, the crystal in her fingers warped and melted. In seconds it had become a perfect mirror image of Groesh. The little figure had delicate red whiskers and ribbons of colour picking out the muscles of his huge body.

It was strange that someone so horrible could be made to look so beautiful.

"Will you teach—" began Shahn, but she never finished her sentence. Lana sensed it just before it happened, the scream of the rock as it was pulverised into dust, and she pulled Shahn away as the floor of the mineshaft suddenly collapsed with a great rumble, forming a hole the size of a cart. From the collapsing rock, a huge, fleshy pink nose poked out of the rubble, sniffing and snorting. Twitchy red whiskers frisked the edges of the hole.

"Careful, you oaf!" shouted Jun. "You'll bring the shaft down!"

"How dare ye!" With frightening speed, the huge mole jumped for Jun and tried to grab her.

Jun dodged out of the way and held her pick in front of her, ready to strike. Shahn started crying. Lana hid the sculpture behind her back.

"Try that again, and I'll cut off your nose," Jun snarled.

"Empty scum," said Groesh. "I'll gut ye for that. Ye have it coming."

Before he could attack, Lana stepped between the snarling mole and her friend.

"Stop, please, Groesh," she said. "Jun is right, you endanger us all! What were you thinking, tunnelling in here?"

"Not my fault ye can't dig yer way out," said the mole. "But all right, I won't slice yer little chum to ribbons YET, *yer highness.*" The mole did not even try to keep the derision out of his voice. His pearlescent eyes – though almost completely blind – still seemed to rest on the points of flickering shadow escaping from Lana's cloak. "Not that I'll have to wait long."

Lana didn't like the pleasure in Groesh's voice – like he knew he was about to deliver bad news.

"I tunnelled in fast cos you've got a fancy visitor, a *royal* messenger from the Emperor's palace itself."

It was bad news. Ever since her mother's sickness and the disgrace it had brought, the Shadowscale broodline's reputation had been destroyed. For months now, rumours had been swirling that her family's control of the mine was to be taken away by the Emperor. If that happened, Lana's brood would be left utterly destitute.

Lana shivered. The mole couldn't have seen that, but he must have sensed her dread.

"That's right," said Groesh. "I'd be afraid if I were you. All of yer. I think this is the end fer yer little crew. And all the wasters you protect." The mole spat at Jun. "Enjoy living while you got breath, human scum. It ain't lookin' good for them Shadowscale freaks. Once the Emperor throws you out of your palace, you won't have anywhere left to go. About time, too. Tonight I'm leavin' for the Ruby Isle to fetch more scum workers, but when I get back I expect things will be very different round 'ere."

Lana held Shahn's little hand as they walked through their nest.

"Did he mean it? Are they going to throw us

out?" said Shahn. She had stayed quiet for most of the walk back.

"Groesh did mean what he said," said Lana. "But that doesn't mean it's going to happen. Not if I can stop it, little egg."

She wished she felt as certain as she was trying to sound.

Their footsteps echoed in the long, empty corridors and drifted away through openings in the ceiling into the limitless blue above – beautiful skies you could only find in desert country. A palace this size should be teeming with servants, but their brood had no lands or vassals any more, no resources or coin to trade. Lana looked about her, trying not to think that she was seeing her nest for the last time.

She had known this home, Whardox Hall, since she was a little girl. The grand building was once one of many that the noble Shadowscale brood had owned across the Four Kingdoms. During the colder winters Lana, her mother and father, her baby sister and her uncles, aunts and cousins would travel out here to the Sunrise Valley to get away from the bustle of Whitestone and to soak up the revitalising rays. Back then, scurrying about the corridors with her cousins and the servants' children, Lana had been unaware of the strife that began to plague her brood. Lana knew her mother had not been the same since her father had been killed – a father who Lana barely knew.

Lana remembered one winter when her uncle told her that her mother needed a long period of rest away from court at Whitestone. Lana and her family never returned to their great mansion in the capital. Whardox Hall became their permanent home – their only home. Lana had never complained. Even when the servants began to be dismissed. Even as her extended family left, never to be heard of again, leaving behind only fearful mutterings of betrayal by the Emperor. Even after the building fell into silence and disrepair. Even after her mother made one final trip to the city to restore their fortunes but came back a ruin. Even after all that, Whardox Hall remained Lana's home. The rooms carried memories, both good and bad, some distinct, some blurred – feelings of hope, feelings of despair. The memories were part of her – just like the feeling of the magic in the quartz rock walls. Her favourite spots were the suntraps, spaced at regular intervals along every corridor. They were open to the hot sun and perfect for basking. At least she could still use those. Once, splashing fountains and gardens had scented the air with flowers and cooling mists, but now the plants were dead and the fountains had failed.

On every wall the polished mud plaster glittered, sculpted long ago by insect-Kind mine constructors. Their hardened spit gave it an iridescent sheen, although it was dull now. There was no longer anyone here to sweep away the dust or polish the walls.

You could see Lana's brood's glorious history everywhere: in the brilliantly coloured rugs sewn from shed scales by her long-dead broodmothers; in the clawed engravings on the walls that illustrated scenes from the time when her ancestors had ruled the whole world. But the Shadowscale dynasty's sharp decline was also visible in the damp, peeling patches on the walls and the insect-chewed corners of the tapestries. In the mining equipment and tunnel plans scattered about. The Hall of the Clear Skies, as Whardox Hall had once been gloriously known, had formerly ruled over a paradise of pristine rock and sand, where great winter parties would be thrown, attended by the most noble of Kind, who got drunk on the glorious purity of the sun and the honour of being asked to attend. Now the palace was used as the headquarters of mining operations which had gradually spread across north-western Morta. The beautiful, bright desert countryside was overrun with worker settlements, shafts and warehouses. No one called this area the Sunrise Valley any more. They just called it the Burrows – a term for the dangerous quarries and mines dug deep below ground.

As they passed beneath the enormous, empty shed skin of Lana's great-great-broodfather, Mordrid Shadowscale, towering in the great hall, she could not help thinking of the shame he would feel to see how things had changed. Moths had chewed their way into the empty shell. Spider webs criss-crossed his body.

Lana guessed her uncle had received the royal visitor in his office. He preferred it because the small room was open to the sun, and more comfortable in size than the larger, more formal chambers. As she entered, Lana saw the familiar papers and maps of mining sites scattered across her uncle's desk – along with her his half-eaten lunch: a puréed larvae soup served in a horned ram's skull, with red beetle bread on the side. If her usually ravenous uncle left just one morsel of food, it meant he was worried. *We're in deep trouble,* she thought, eyeing the cold, half-filled skull.

The messenger – perfectly dressed in the latest court fashion – had black lace at his collar and a horrified expression on his face. He was a slim snake-Kind with hard red eyes.

"Aha! There she is!" Lana's uncle, Bart, had clearly been struggling to entertain his visitor. He was a bluff, cheery Kind who was getting on in age – he had been the oldest of Lana's mother's siblings, and now, the only one left. Bart was a dear, really, harmless – part of the reason he had been spared by the Emperor during the purge that had wiped out the rest of his siblings. He was totally unsuited to making polite chit-chat with a courtier.

"Come here, Lana, let me introduce you – and my younger niece, Shahn. This is . . ."

The snake bowed. It was a complicated manoeuvre – like the unfolding of an uncomfortable chair.

"Councillor Rissok," he lisped. "At your service, Lady Lana."

The elaborate formality did nothing to hide his contempt. His eyes turned towards the dark, flickering shadow spread over the right side of Lana's head.

"We are honoured to receive One Who Speeds Words to Ears," said Lana, managing to remember the correct formal title for an emperor's messenger. She and Shahn curtsied, demonstrating perfect etiquette.

The snake's eyes widened in surprise.

Lana smiled. Before her mother had lost her mind, before the madness had claimed her life, in the rare early days when she was bright and happy, Lahara Shadowscale had taught her daughters how to behave. It was the only thing she had taught them.

The courtier cleared his throat by coughing into a black handkerchief. "I am here to tell you that a recent shipment of rock from your mines caught the Emperor's eye – joy and long life to our monarch. Amongst the slabs of anthracite that we requested was a rogue rock."

Lana's heart began to beat a little faster.

"This rock was beautifully decorated. Magically augmented – very fine, very clever work. The Emperor wishes to know who was responsible."

Everyone looked at Lana.

"It was me." Lana couldn't believe her plan had actually worked. She had caught the Emperor's eye. Maybe she would be able to save this family after all!

The snake nodded crisply. "The Emperor – joy and long life to our monarch – wishes that whoever was responsible for that rock be brought with me back to the palace. He has a project that needs your rare and *particular* skills. He wants to decorate a new palace."

"I say," Lana's uncle broke in. "You can't take Lana. She's needed here in our mines. Production will fall. Can't build a palace without any rock."

Both of them knew this was a lie. The work that Lana did could easily be done by others.

The truth was, her uncle was trying to protect her – from the same dangers that her mother had encountered in Whitestone.

"Are you disobeying a direct command?" lisped the snake.

"No, no. Thank you for telling us. I am deeply grateful for the opportunity." Lana smiled at the messenger. "Could I possibly talk to my uncle for a moment in private?"

"Very well," said the snake. He melted out of the room.

"You can't go!" said the old lizard. His jowls wobbled as he tried to control himself. "I forbid it! The Emperor is a stark raving loony. The court is a foul nest of tricks and intrigue and that Order of the True are crazed fanatics. They have gained too much power. It's *far* too dangerous for you there."

"Uncle—" Lana tried to stem the flow.

"Just look at that messenger sneering at us because he interrupted my lunch. What's wrong with eating a skull of larvae soup, I ask you. I know it isn't fine dragonfly soufflé or rib of wild foal, but do you see many forests around here? They used to say larvae was a delicacy. Tastes change in an instant in Whitestone! The people are fickle. They cannot be trusted."

"Will Lana be like Mama?" said Shahn. She hardly remembered their mother, but she had heard a little of the stories of the madness that had led to her death. "Please don't leave me, Lana."

There were tears in Lana's eyes as she hugged them both.

"I have to go. It's the Emperor's command."

Bart snorted. "Joy and long life to that maniac. I forbid it!"

"Unky," said Lana softly, using the pet name she hadn't called him in years. "My parents are dead. Only I can make decisions about what I do. And I *must* go. If I refuse this, the Emperor will take our mine away and give it to another brood. He will ruin us for ever. But if I succeed, I can restore us to our true standing. Back where we belong."

Her uncle sagged as he accepted the truth of what she said. "I swore I would protect you."

"I can protect myself," said Lana fiercely.

Her uncle looked at her.

"Oh, Lana . . . You remind me so much of Lahara.

You know she swore that she would save us too. And she was standing right there when she said it. That was her last ever trip to Whitestone. When she came back, her illness had consumed her. That city took her soul. It ruined our family. Ah, it all feels like it was only yesterday . . ."

Her uncle never talked about their mother, his sister. Suddenly he looked so much older and frailer than before.

"But I will save us." Lana hugged her family tight. "I promise. I will do what Mama could not."

6

The Pinnacles of the Damned

That night, Jonas dreamed once again of flying. And killing.

He killed with his ghostly claws, so sharp they were practically invisible.

He killed with his jaws. He felt bodies crunch beneath his large, sharp teeth. He tasted the hot, fresh blood of the insect-Kind, and the rush of sweetness that followed.

In this dream, Jonas was here and not here, a nightmare hunter. A ghost wyvern one moment, living death the next. His enemies fled before him – but there was just one he really hunted. He had her scent. He smelled her terror.

The cat-Kind was nimble, even with her manacles

on. As Jonas stalked her, he admired the way she deftly avoided the insect barbarians. She ran between the tents, ducking and twisting, eager to escape.

But she could not escape this doom. Jonas waited, invisible. She slammed straight into his scaly body and fell. Now, suddenly, he found himself looming over the cat-Kind, enormous and hungry, as she sprawled in shock on the ground. He spread his wings and opened his mouth wide.

Rahziin screamed and held up her paws, pleading for life. But there was nothing she could do to save herself. Jonas was inevitable.

"Aaaaaaaaaaaaaargh . . ."

The screaming continued for a long time. An awful cry of pain and despair.

". . . eeeeeeaaaarrgghHHH!"

The scream dragged Jonas from his terrible dream and back to his grim reality on the Ferry of Solek. He opened his eyes to see a fox-Kind on fire. He was beating at his burning shirt with his hands, and his fur was black and singed. The rower next to him did not try to help his benchmate. Instead he carried on pulling at his oar, in a frenzy.

"Row harder, you mugs!" shrieked the skinny salamander-Kind who was standing over the rowers chained to their benches. Small licks of flame twisted about his mouth. "Row harder or I'll scorch the rest of you too."

Huge waves rocked the boat as they ploughed west. The salty air was cold and the icy wind sliced through the rag-blanket that Jonas had tried to wrap around himself. Everything was soggy.

Jonas was awake now, but he was still in a nightmare.

The singed fox-Kind put out the flames. The prisoners rowed hard for the next hour. Periodically, Gruk, the fire-blessed salamander overseer, would breathe fire over another rower to encourage the others to try harder. Jonas crouched near the prow and kept to himself. There were other passengers travelling to the Pinnacles – new prisoners, by their snivelling look – but there was never any point in chatting to fresh meat. They probably wouldn't survive their first night.

Besides, Jonas had too much else to worry about. He hugged his knees and stared at the green water, unseeing.

Had that dream been real? Did Seth actually murder Rahziin and then lie about it?

The dream had felt true. Jonas looked up into the sky. Somewhere above the mists, Seth was circling. Jonas could feel him up there.

What would he say if he asked him?

What did Seth really want? And could he even afford to ask? Jonas knew that the only reason he had survived so long in the Pinnacles was because Seth had been there to watch his back.

"Prison ho!" shouted the tillerman.

The Pinnacles loomed out of the mist. The new prisoners, who had never seen the cursed place before, moaned in horror and fear. Jonas felt for them a little: the Pinnacles of the Damned really was a place that lived up to its evil reputation.

In its awful way, it was spectacular. The craggy, castle-like prison crouched on top of several towering fingers of rock that thrust up from the churning sea. Exposed walkways jabbed across the space between the towers. The buildings were squat, black and rimed with rust.

There was no joy here, and no hope either. There had never been, and there never would be.

"We're late, you hoofed scum," screamed Gruk, and lit up one of the rowers – a scrawny horse-Kind – just for fun.

The exhausted rowers put on a final burst of energy and the boat surged across the sea. The singed horse-Kind moaned in agony until they tied up at the dock. Gruk threw him into the water.

A few enormous bear-Kind guards were handling the fresh meat. They spoke the command words and the prisoners were dragged by their magic manacles on to the dock. As they were taken away, one of the guards nodded to Jonas.

"Hey, Slayer, Grashkor wants a word."

Grashkor the Gaoler's chambers were in an isolated tower known as the Eyrie. It was separated from the main prison by a retractable bridge. In theory, if he ever lost control, the Gaoler would be safe here until help arrived.

In practice, Grashkor did not look like he would ever need help. He was an enormous skin-Kind, his hide a mottled green, almost like a toad, but there must have been some bull-Kind in his ancestry. He had to be ten times the weight of a human, each leg as thick and gnarled as a sangwar stump, and his monstrous arms were riddled with lumpy muscle. He wore a helmet with two huge curved horns, and he never went anywhere without a sword bigger than Jonas strapped to his back.

"Come in," rumbled a deep growl when Jonas knocked on the door.

Grashkor was standing before a huge window,

sipping from a silver goblet filled with warm blood. Beyond him the vast South Sea stretched to the horizon as long waves rolled in and crashed against the prison.

It was an impressive view. You could see all of the Pinnacles from up here. Many cells and common areas were open to the elements – so Grashkor could keep watch at all times over his domain. The prison teemed with struggling life, like the world's most miserable ant heap.

"You have not brought me the cat, Jonas," said Grashkor. He did not turn round. "I saw when you arrived. Where is the priest?"

Jonas tried to keep his face impassive, his body relaxed as he told Grashkor the lie. "She resisted," said Jonas. "She would not come, and she died." Well it wasn't entirely a lie. Jonas just left out the part where he had taken Rahziin on a detour to carry out his own personal objective, and that she had died while helping him on this mission. Also, that he had been planning on freeing her. The less he said to Grashkor, the less chance the Gaoler had of reading his lies.

"Died?" growled Grashkor.

"I was . . . forced to kill her."

For a brief instant he was a wyvern again, sinking

his teeth into Rahziin's neck. He shook his head to clear it. Had that really happened?

"Not good!" Grashkor turned to face him, nostrils flaring. "Not good. You had orders to bring her alive! How do I know that you are not lying to me?"

Jonas was ready for this. "I brought proof."

He threw a cloth sack on the table in front of Grashkor, who emptied it out. A severed paw thumped on to the table. On the back of the hand, still visible despite the dried blood, was the distinctive tattoo of the Order of the True.

Grashkor picked it up and licked the stump with his red tongue. He closed his eyes, savouring the taste.

"It is hers. You have not tried to deceive me. On *this*, at least."

He snapped his fingers. At once the manacles around Jonas's wrists rose into the air. They lifted his arms above his head and dragged him across the room. He was helpless to stop it happening.

Grashkor pulled him in so close Jonas could feel the hot stink of his breath on his cheek. The reek of blood and death was overpowering.

"Slayer. How many years did I say I'd give you off for the cat?"

"Eighty," said Jonas.

"You can have five," said Grashkor. "For the kill. And that's generous. But next time you bring in a hand, when you were meant to bring a living body, you die too. Do I make myself clear?"

"Very," said Jonas. "It won't happen again."

"That's right. Now then, shuffle off . . ." Grashkor paused and leaned closer. "Heh. What's this? What's this?"

He took a long, searching sniff up and down Jonas's neck.

"I smell the dust of the plains. Quargish herbs. Insect blood. Fresh. You've been a naughty boy, haven't you? Did you think I wouldn't notice? DO YOU THINK I'M A FOOL?"

"No, Lord Gaoler, I really—"

"So why were you running about in your homeland? Why did you visit the cursed graveyard of your slaughtered people? It's written on your face clear as day. You know I can see everything. You know that."

"I'm—"

"This isn't a pleasure cruise. You're *lucky* to be a bounty hunter. You are a criminal. A murderer. You will die here."

As Grashkor's anger flared up, Jonas felt his own death sense rising within him at the danger. As time slowed down, he smelled Grashkor's foul breath so intensely he wanted to be sick.

Grashkor stuck his face very close to Jonas's. The reek was overpowering as he crooned in Jonas's ear. "I could kill you right now. Just bite your head off and crush your brains into my goblet. Shall I do that? Seems you don't like doing what you're told."

"I'm sorry," said Jonas. "It won't happen again."

"Make sure of that. Now get out of my sight."

Jonas felt his meeting with Grashkor had gone about as well as he could have hoped. At least he hadn't been whipped this time. Or sent into one of the ocean caverns – the punishment cells where chained prisoners were constantly slammed by giant waves. Maybe the old monster was going soft.

Not likely, thought Jonas. Being back here was punishment enough.

Jonas did not receive a warm welcome when he returned to his cell; a dozen pairs of eyes watched him from around the chamber. Slayer had a mean reputation in the Pinnacles. His cellmates had learned a bloody lesson to leave him well alone.

They all fell silent as he crossed the room.

"Evening," said Jonas.

No one returned the greeting.

At least their superstitious fear extended to leaving his stuff and his "bunk" untouched while he was away. No one had claimed the slab of stone as their own bed. Jonas sat down on it with a sigh and turned to the wall.

"How did it go?"

This time, it was Jonas's turn to ignore a greeting. Seth was here already, invisible to the others. Waiting for him by his bed – like a giant invisible dolly that killed people. Jonas just shook his head. It was Seth, after all, who wanted to keep his presence secret from the other prisoners. Seth claimed it aided Jonas's reputation if they didn't know that Seth watched over him. The other prisoners simply thought Jonas could see things no one else could – could sense danger approaching, or overhear plots to murder him with some kind of arcane human magic – or could cause talon and bite wounds with dark magic, the lost arts of the Old Ways. Now, Jonas started to wonder if Seth just liked to get Jonas to do the killing, to rile him up, to make the death-song sing through him. Or maybe he didn't want to reveal himself in his bodily form because it might make him vulnerable. So many doubts flooded Jonas's mind, making him question everything he had ever thought about his twin, his protector, his guardian.

His deceiver.

The death cry of Rahziin screamed through his memory.

Jonas turned away to face the wall, wishing he could place his hands over his ears or shout to drown out Rahziin's voice.

"Did he reduce the sentence?" Seth asked. "Slayer, why are you not talking to me? Just whisper. No one in here will care. They will think you even scarier. They will think you are putting a spell on them. Tell me, how many years do we have left now?"

Jonas didn't reply. He reached up a hand and swiped a finger across five gouges marked on the wall. On his first day in the cell, Jonas had asked Seth to scratch a thousand lines into the stone above his bunk. His cellmates had watched in awe as the invisible marks appeared on the wall. Jonas's terrifying reputation started to grow from that moment. A human death-mage, a worshipper of necromancy.

Each gouge on the wall represented a year of his sentence. Two hundred and eighty of the thousand years were crossed off.

"Grashkor took off another five," said Seth. He

scratched off five more marks. "Only seven hundred and fifteen to go," he said cheerfully.

Jonas closed his eyes and tried to sleep. He tried to put thoughts of Rahziin's screaming face out of his mind. He couldn't bring it up here. It might be beneficial to make the prisoners think he was a mad necromancer, but having an argument with himself felt a step too far. Any emotion he showed was weakness.

"Sleep," was all Jonas whispered.

For now, he knew Seth watched over him, as he always did.

But for the first time since Jonas could remember, the thought wasn't entirely comforting.

When the bell was rung for the evening meal, Jonas moved, head down, in the flow of the other prisoners. Seth moved with him, always watchful. But Jonas hardly needed an invisible bodyguard now. There was always a space around him, and a silence, even as the crowd grew thick. Any fool knew to keep their distance from Slayer.

The eating hall was a cavernous open space. Troughs filled with foul-smelling food hung from the ceiling. When the second bell rang, guards winched the troughs down to the waiting prisoners. The system was more orderly than you might think. Prisoner gangs controlled each trough and if you weren't a member of one of them, you were unlikely to get fed.

Jonas wasn't a member of a gang, but he ate where he liked.

Today, without thinking, he decided to eat at the amphibian-Kind trough. There was a groan as the troughs were lowered to the chamber floor. Insect mash again.

As Jonas raised a handful of foul-smelling slop to his lips, a gruff voice growled a warning.

"Slayer, you ain't eating here. This is toad territory now. Under new management."

Jonas turned to see a hulking toad-Kind creature glaring down at him. The gangster had giant webbed hands and feet, and a muscular tail like a newt's. His long tongue hung out of the corner of his mouth.

"You know my name," said Jonas. "But I don't know yours. You must be new here."

"I'm Orok the Crusher," said the toad. "I killed three for control of this gang. And no human, no matter how scared everyone else is of him, is going to feed at *my* trough."

Everyone in the prison was watching this

conversation. Enjoying it, even. Jonas could hear bets being made. He sighed. This wasn't the first time a tough new inmate had come in, heard the stories and decided to make a splash by toppling the most feared prisoner in the Pinnacles.

Jonas's death-song flared up, mapping out the threat. The toad could gobble him up, or crush him, or drown him in the trough of insect-mush . . .

Really, what would happen next was that Jonas would kill him. He felt weary and disgusted by this truth. He hadn't slept well. Seeing Rahziin's face had left a faint tremble through his body, a weariness, a guilt, and the last thing he wanted was another fight – though fights just seemed to come to him whether he liked it or not.

"That's fine," he said, holding up his hands. "No problem. I'll eat somewhere else."

"What are you doing?" said Seth as he landed with a screech of talons scraping across the flagstones. Seth never liked to intervene if he could help it. He preferred to let Jonas handle things. But then, Jonas never usually backed down. The truth was, backing down was a sign of weakness. It only gained you more fights in the future. "Destroy him!" hissed Seth, his shimmering green skull snapping towards Orok. "He is nothing but a puffed-up balloon."

Jonas turned his back on Orok and walked away. He just wanted to get through today without killing anybody. And maybe he didn't want to do what Seth wanted for once. The terror in Rahziin's eyes as Seth's mouth came down towards her flashed into Jonas's mind and he squeezed his fists.

"Yes!" said Seth. "I feel your rage, your thirst for punishment. Let it build. This business must be taken care of, Jonas. The whole prison is watching you."

"No," said Orok, who was unaware of Seth's proximity. "That's not good enough. You've disrespected me. You're scared." His tongue flicked out and glommed wetly on to Jonas's shoulder. With a sticky twist the tongue pulled him back so he fell at the toad's feet. "And you're weak."

There were gasps of surprise from the prisoners. The betting intensified. The crazy few who had backed the toad cheered.

"Kiss my feet, human scum," said Orok. "Demonstrate your inferiority. My power is so much greater than yours."

A huge, rubbery toe poked at Jonas's face.

"Fine," said Jonas, and puckered his lips.

"What are you doing?" screamed Seth. His great wings spread wide, bones blackening and shimmering a faint emerald light over Jonas and Orok.

Jonas kissed the toad's foot. The skin was surprisingly dry and rough. It didn't even smell bad.

There were shrieks of amazement and groans from prisoners who'd lost their money. Slayer had never backed down like this before.

Slayer had never lost.

Orok the Crusher raised his arms and flexed his muscles. "I am the strongest!" he roared. "I will rule you all. Orok the Crusher is my name, and I am might— Ach!"

Seth attacked without warning. He curled his long tail around the toad and flipped him in the air. Seth was only material for an instant – moving so fast that you could just see him for a split second, before he vanished again. But the shouts and gasps erupted around the prison. It might have only been for a split second, but the inmates *had* seen Seth. And part of Jonas's mystery, his threat, his protection, had gone – they knew now that Jonas was not a death-mage protected by mysterious forces. He was protected by a Kind – a ghost-Kind, true – but still a Kind. A Kind who could touch, kill others – and could, maybe, be killed himself. It was all there, in that moment.

Orok crashed to the ground, ready to kill Jonas. And he would want to kill Seth too. Already his followers were circling Jonas and Orok, a host of slimy, large amphibian-Kind – on the lookout for the ghost wyvern if he tried to help Jonas again. Some brandished knives. Finally, Slayer had a weak spot. They knew his secret. They knew how to defeat him.

Jonas could taste each prisoner's hunger for blood. Their joy and surprise, their anger and their fear.

He needed to put an end to this quickly, to show them that he was as dangerous as ever.

He just felt tired.

He willed the death-song to take him over. He stabbed his fingernails into the palms of his curled fists. He let the flashes of his many possible deaths riddle like fragmented reflections in his mind's eye.

He saw: *Orok breaking his ribcage to fragments with his thick arms. A darting frog-Kind gangster stabbing him in the back with the thrust of a blade. Slipping in a splattering of spilt food, falling to the ground, Orok's great webbed foot stamping down on his head.*

And it took him over, just as Seth wanted. Time slowed and murder surged within him.

Moving with supernatural speed, he whipped the chain that held up the trough. All those years herding cattle had taught him a few tricks with ropes.

The chain wrapped around Orok's body like a

lasso. When he fell, the tangle held him high in the air, dangling like rotten fruit on a branch.

"Kill! Slayer!" Jonas's supporters were cheering. "Kill! Slayer! Kill!"

They all expected Jonas to end the fight.

"What are you waiting for?" said Seth. "Finish him! They have seen me. You need to show them you are ruthless."

"No." Jonas shook his head and turned away. "Not today."

"ORDER! ORDER!" The Gaoler's terrifying roar silenced the prisoners. Grashkor appeared on the balcony above the chamber. He sneered down at them, disgusted by what he saw.

"Get that toad down."

The bear-Kind guards lowered Orok the Crusher to the floor in a puddle of spilled insect mulch. As his gangmates untangled him, the toad glared daggers at Jonas.

Still no one spoke. Grashkor was likely to cut off the head of anyone who interrupted him.

"I have a job. A bounty hunter mission, open to the whole prison," he growled. "The prize will be your freedom. Your full sentence revoked, however many years you have left. Step forward to the line if you wish to take part."

A murmur of excitement passed through the crowd of prisoners despite their fear of Grashkor. This offer was completely unprecedented. The vast majority of the prisoners crowded towards the yellow line that divided them from the guards. Jonas was among them – although the crowd kept their distance from him even in their excitement.

Grashkor waited until there was silence again. "The prize is so great because the target is so dangerous. The fugitive is a human rebel who recently stole a powerful magical item from Skin-Grave."

The crowd at the line thinned instantly. Almost all the prisoners were having second thoughts. Being alive in the Pinnacles was still better than a horrible death. Any fugitive strong and wily enough to steal something from that cursed place was not worth messing with.

Grashkor chuckled. Only Orok the Crusher and a tall, thin dog-Kind called Brynn the Sly remained, along with Jonas. Brynn had once been the Emperor's Chief Hunter. The Hunters were scouts, spies and assassins. They were crafty, clever and ruthless, even towards each other. It said a lot about Brynn that he had risen to the top of the division. That is, until Brynn had done something to upset the mad ruler. He had probably just been too good at his job, and the paranoid Emperor, seeing enemies all around, had thrown Brynn in prison. Grashkor considered Brynn to be a better bounty hunter than Jonas. It helped that Brynn had a canine sense of smell and was able to sniff out a fugitive miles away on the wind, or pick up a scent trail weeks old.

Grashkor looked at the three of them. There might have been a hint of amusement, even satisfaction in his cold eyes shining beneath his great horned helm.

"Just one of you can win the prize. Retrieve the prisoner. Retrieve the treasure. I am intrigued as to which of you will succeed. As for those who fail me – you know how I treat my hunters who come back empty-handed." His fingers slid to the monstrous broadsword strapped to his back. "If you are lucky, you will get an execution. If you are not . . . if I am feeling hungry . . . Well, you all know that I have a taste for the flesh of other new-Kind. Good hunting!"

7
The Tower of Forbidden Knowledge

"What in all the worlds happened here?" said Gael. "Eek!"

He just about managed to avoid tripping over the severed ant head, but had to put both his boots in a puddle of green ichor instead.

Roshni wrinkled her nose. Gael didn't blame her. The smell was very, very bad.

"A fight?" she said.

"Tsk! No. Use your eyes," said Gael, unable as usual to resist the impulse to lecture. "There was not much fight involved. Rather, this skirmish was so one-sided it was more of a massacre. See? None of these dead insects' weapons have been used. They are clean, untouched. The creatures were slaughtered, never even landing a blow."

Gael looked at the devastation. The collapsed tents. The flies. The blood. In the centre of the tribal settlement he spotted the carved root of a sangwar tree he had spotted last time he had come to this accursed place. Even that was decorated in the remnants of the butchered insect-Kind.

"It was the same the last time I was in this godforsaken camp, three years ago. But then of course the dead were all humans."

"And now it is full of dead insect-Kind?" Roshni wrinkled her nose. "I do not understand why we have come here. It is horrible."

"Because the sensors that I left here three years ago detected a magical flare-up three days past." Gael pulled his oscilloscope out of a pocket and held it up. "Hmm. But if a portal did open, it has already closed . . . Strange – so much power released, twice, in the same place, and so far from the usual lines."

Gael bent over the bodies to look at their injuries. "Record this, Roshni . . ."

In the few weeks that Roshni had been with Gael she'd proved so invaluable that she had replaced his treasured scribing beetle. He enjoyed her quickness and her eagerness to learn, and it was convenient to have someone on hand to lecture whenever he felt like it. The fact that her employment would also irritate Malachai was an added bonus. Roshni had even dealt with the continual camping without complaint. They had managed to visit a number of sites where portals had opened, to track the magical radiation levels.

"Why don't you just teleport us to a luxurious lizard-Kind basking suite so we can get a good night's rest?" she had asked him good-naturedly one night.

"Do you think teleporting is a mere whim or cheap conjuring trick I can call on whenever I want to? Magic *is* energy, my dear. The more you use, the more you must revive in yourself. I do not have an inexhaustible supply. Why do you think I always sleep with no tent over my head, as nature intended? It connects me with the world – the sounds, the smells, the *feel*. From all of these natural currents I draw my power. Remember, magic is a framework, not a force – it is the very structure of our worlds. It connects us all, and we must earn the right to wield it."

"I see," Roshni had said, nodding. "So the velvet pillow that I see you sneaking under your head . . . Does that help you connect to nature?"

Gael had scoffed. "Do you *know* how old I am?"

"As old as the mountains, I think you said."

"A stiff neck does not aid my magical capabilities either."

Now Gael gave a small smile at the memory of Roshni's arched eyebrow. She was sharp, that girl, and sometimes he thought she was sharper than she let on. That velvet cushion really was the most valuable artefact he carried in his cloak. As Gael surveyed the butchered insect-Kind, he was pleased to see Roshni with her tablet and stylus ready, hardly put off by the unsavoury aftermath of the violence.

"These bodies show deep scratches and some bite marks. A few have been injured with weapons. It is possible that a portal bursting open could cause these types of wound . . . but not likely. There is no other evidence of the landscape being affected by a flux of pure magic. The bodies are not as injured as the previous incident. Then, the human corpses were almost . . . obliterated. These are at least recognisable. Have you got all that?"

"Yes, teacher," said Roshni, scribbling fast.

"Hmm?" said Gael. "What's this? A dead cat-Kind, here amongst all the insects?" He bent down to examine the body. "She has been bitten to death. Her hand is missing – it has been cut off. What was she doing here, I wonder?"

Roshni leaned in. "She wears the robes of the Order of the True."

"Malachai's people?" Gael chuckled. "She's a long way from home. Perhaps I should cut off her other hand and send it to Malachai as a present."

Roshni shook her head and scowled. "You should not make fun of him. He is dangerous and very powerful. The Order of the True should not be crossed."

"Pah! They are fools. Always seeking a fight. It is entertaining to tweak those noses."

"Master, you are being foolish. At least do the investigation Malachai asked for," Roshni reminded him for the seventeenth time. "It has been two weeks and you have done nothing."

"My work on portals is not nothing. It is everything, Roshni."

"It won't be if Malachai throws you in prison and executes me."

Roshni fixed Gael with her deep glare. Even the ancient crow found it hard to stand up to such a disapproving look.

"Fine, fine," he conceded. "But we will gather samples before we leave. I need tubes of soil and at least four heads. Get those for me, Roshni. Nice fresh ones. We can boil up the brains to find out what they saw. Then we can jump to the Hallowed Vale and look for Malachai's traitor. But mark my words: it will be a wasted trip!"

The Tower of Forbidden Knowledge loomed over the City of the Hallowed Vale like a warning. Part of its intimidating presence came from its position at the crest of the steep valley that the city was built on. It wasn't the tallest building there – the great University Spire was taller – and it certainly wasn't the most beautiful – the Great Tree, where the aristocratic families had their ancestral nests, was probably the most elegant building in the Four Kingdoms. But the Tower was the most . . . eye-catching. Once a great human fortress, now the Tower was a giant mass of rubble, filled with underground passages and held together by sticky bird-Kind saliva. It was like an oversized ants' nest.

"Happy now, Roshni?" Gael said. "There she is. I give you . . . THE TOWER OF FORBIDDEN KNOWLEDGE!" He swept out a feathered arm dramatically. The grand gesture was somewhat undermined by the coughing fit that followed. "Ach! Clurph! Curse this teleportation! Wretched tickly throat."

"Impressive. I think," Roshni said. "Hard to know

where the building begins and where it ends. What with all the rubble lying around. And it's not really much of a tower any more. More of a pile. I'd like to take a closer look."

"Most new-Kind residents of the Vale avoid looking at the Tower of Forbidden Knowledge, if they can manage it. And by the way, it is considered extremely impolite to mention the building by name. I, of course, have no time for such niceties."

"It has more guards than windows," said Roshni. Her eyes scanned the hulking vulture-Kind who loped across crumbled battlements carrying giant halberds. "Didn't you say we could simply climb through a window to get inside?"

"Yes, that might have been a joke. You won't find any glass in a new-Kind structure. Glass is a human affectation. And most of the holes where the windows once were have collapsed. Besides, the broken ramparts are razor-sharp, with some added spikes for good measure."

"What do they say about a vulture-Kind guard's instinct for intruders? As keen as their beaks. I heard that once."

"Did you? They are mostly nice enough, especially if you offer them a bit of carrion now and then. Non-human of course. Don't concern yourself, child, I have an easy fix for getting you into the Tower. No windows necessary." He reached a talon into one of his cloak's many bottomless pockets and with a quick thought summoned what he was looking for.

"Put this on," he said, presenting her with a bronze ring carved with a repeating pattern of laughing faces. "The Trickster Ring will camouflage you against all forms of detection – sight, sound and even magic."

Roshni's eyes lit up as she took the ring. "It's beautiful." She took a breath and slipped it on. Instantly she vanished. All that was left was a very faint blur, like a heat mirage, and it could only be seen if you looked very closely and kept your eyes on Roshni's position for a long period.

"The only way you will be visible to anyone is if you move too fast," cautioned Gael. "Try waving your hands about."

Two faint blurs appeared in the air where Roshni had been standing.

"See? It's an effect caused by the magical nuclei of particles in your body interacting with other elemental particles around you. Hmm, it's actually more pronounced than I was expecting. Funny. Perhaps some latent magic from the teleportation has rubbed off on you."

"Ah. Sounds about right. I do have a tickly throat. Hey, this is amazing."

"Look, just stop waving your arms and you'll be fine. I said, STOP. There, fine. Don't move too quickly, and stick close to me. My dark cloak will cover up the blurring a little. Right, let's get on with our little wild goose chase, then. Remember, Roshni, this was *your* idea. I am sure Malachai will be most pleased that we are on the trail of these terrifying and dangerous rebel humans who have somehow managed to break into the most secure place in the Four Kingdoms – other than Skin-Grave, of course. Frankly, I think the idea of a human finding a way into the Tower is completely preposterous."

"I'm going to get in though," said Roshni. "Aren't I?"

"Well, yes, of course. But then, you have me on your side – a timeless being who wields magic far beyond the understanding of any human or Kind in any of the Many Worlds."

"Comforting," said Roshni. Gael couldn't tell if she was joking.

He marched towards the Tower's giant arched entrance, crossing a winding pathway that was cut into the valley. He was waved inside with smiles and jokes – well, smiles and jokes from him. The hulking vulture-Kind guards leaning against the cracked columns barely moved a muscle. He swore one day he would get one of them to laugh – the greatest of all his achievements, no doubt, considering he had never even heard one make a noise except for chewing and slavering over a rabbit or deer carcass. Sometimes Gael wondered if they breathed.

Inside the cavernous entry hall, a small sparrow-Kind with eyeglasses sat at a cracked stone desk. He was shaded by a makeshift mezzanine raised on stilts of interwound tree branches. To one side, a section of floor had fallen away, and bird scholars fluttered through the gaping hole to the basement storage room housing scrolls vulnerable to sunlight. "Master scholar," chirped the library porter. "Most wise of all bird-Kind, most noble attendant of our sacred libraries, how are you this morning?"

"Lucian!" Gael replied. "I am well. And you? Busy as ever? How many scholars in today?"

"Twenty, at least."

"Gosh. How *do* you keep on top of things? Cheerio for now, best head up to my offices. Urgent work to see to!"

Gael led Roshni on through a courtyard lined by a row of carved figures, their feet and hands broken off, their faces and hair scratched away. You couldn't tell the sculptures had once been humans – legendary rulers, wise mages and heroic warriors. That was the point, of course. Gael rarely noticed the sculptures any more, but he found himself wishing Roshni could have seen this place in its glory. Somewhere, buried deep, a memory surfaced bright and clear as a reflection on a sun-kissed lake: a courtyard filled with colourful human markets, with bartering and the smell of food, with soldiers in gleaming silver armour and the great war machines of the ancient human world. What had been the name of that civilisation? Something beginning with "G". Gael had been friends with the head wizard, a jovial fellow. He was the plumper sculpture at the end of the defaced figures, the one with the robe. Fred, was it?

Enough! Gael told himself. The problem with all civilisations is that after a thousand years they tend to be little more than rubble and ruin.

"Hold up," Roshni whispered. "You're going too fast. I'm supposed to be moving slowly, you said. I don't want to trip over and shout out in pain."

Gael's talons danced over the uneven floor, and he had to wait for Roshni to navigate the loose pavers with her cumbersome human feet. "Didn't realise. Lost in memories. Now stop dilly-dallying, girl. No more speaking! And certainly no tripping!"

Gael ducked through a partially caved-in corridor, then carried on through a disorientating labyrinth he could navigate blindfolded. Funny how some things stay with you while other things fade away. Some of the walkways were only held up by makeshift struts of crystallised bird spit. Other passages had been newly tunnelled through collapsed sections of the old human fortress. This place was a mish-mash of times and cultures, rather like Gael, which was why he liked it. But what was that wizard's name? Not Fred – Felix! That was it.

"Morning, Gael! You are in a hurry today!"

Gael was snapped from his foolish reminiscing by a passing owl-Kind scholar. "René!" Gael replied warmly. "I trust the Library of Early Havanthyan Language is in good order? Of course it is, with you looking over it. Wouldn't catch one feather out of place in that glorious red plumage of yours. How is your mate? Cassie, is it?"

"She's well! I was wondering if you could help with—"

"Must be going, René, speak soon!" Gael was a regular and popular visitor. He knew every scholar and porter and made it a habit to ask after all their families. But he made sure never to get too close. Friends also had a habit of turning to dust and ruin after a thousand years.

"Ornus!" he screeched to a glowering bird covered in sparkling jewellery. "My good magpie-Kind, how are you? I might need your help with a piece of research I am doing into ancient human runes!" Gael swept on before Ornus could reply. He couldn't stand that self-important blusterer. He nodded to a goose-Kind smoking a pipe. "Artemis, you old devil! I told them you'd never retire. I promise everyone *I'll* drop dead before you do – and I'm immortal! Oops, keep that a secret, will you?"

The goose-Kind grinned back, the inside of his beak blackened from pipe smoke. "You think we didn't know? You look younger than me! Your secret is safe. But please, no necromancy in the libraries."

Once they'd turned into the Lower Spell Library, Gael checked they were alone, then reached into another pocket of his cloak. He pulled out a snout-shaped stone carving. "If any humans have been in this part of the Tower, this will sniff them out," he announced. "The Nose of Detection was created by a new-Kind conjuror during the Hundred Years' War. Fine work. I do sometimes wish I had the gift for magic-moulding myself."

"What was the Hundred Years' War?" Roshni asked.

Gael glanced down at her with a mock gasp. "The

Hundred Years' War? The conflict that defined our age? No? Nothing? It's depressing how much of your own history is lost to you – but then I suppose I can't hold any human to blame. They don't like you knowing these things – those new-Kind who hold the power. They think you will get ideas. The Hundred Years' War was the uprising of the new-Kind, when they took control of the Four Kingdoms from the last great human civilisations of Havanthya, Tengalha and . . . Gwylder! Yes, that was it. I've been trying to remember. A lesson for another time. The Nose of Detection was used by the new-Kind to sniff out enemy positions. The Nose has a bloody history, but still has its little uses now."

"Master," said Roshni. "I'm a human and it isn't sniffing me."

"That's because you've got a Trickster Ring on, obviously," said Gael. "Keep your voice down. People will think I'm mad, talking to myself."

"They think you're mad already," said Roshni.

Gael chuckled. "Yes, they do think me rather mad – sort of common knowledge around here."

"Like you being immortal. Should you be telling people that?"

"Scholars are good at minding their own business."

"Why *are* you immortal?"

"You've asked me this before, Roshni. I've told you, it's not technically correct to call me immortal. It's more that I exist on all possible planes of time and space at once. Do you see?"

"Er . . . yes."

"Such a keen mind you have in that lovely human skull of yours. Anyway, enough questions for now. Onward!" He nodded at a passing hunch-backed pigeon-Kind scholar whose name he never remembered. "Hello, Martyn, or is it Mervyn? Sorry, my brain these days! Yes, in case you were wondering I am talking to myself."

They traipsed up and down the stairs in a number of crumbling towers surrounding the central spire as Gael held the Nose in front of him, but the device found no scent. After the Lower Spell Library, they tried the Upper and then the Middle Libraries (which were above the Upper Libraries, oddly enough). There was a vast number of interesting books nesting on the shelves, but no sign of any humans. The Stacks for storage of less used books were next, then various offices and artefact depositories, but there were no humans there, either.

"This is a complete waste of time," grumbled Gael. "Just as I predicted. Will you listen to me next time, Roshni? I am always right, you know. There is no human spy in the Tower."

"Apart from me," said Roshni.

Gael laughed. Each day he spent with this girl he enjoyed the experience more – true, he wasn't sure she was always trying to be humorous, but she was a reliable source of amusement nonetheless.

Throughout their tour of the labyrinth, they had barely heard a sound other than Gael's small talk with the porters and an occasional scratching of quill or turning of pages. But when Gael and Roshni moved on to the Myths and Fables section of the Archives they heard voices.

Raised voices.

Gael's smile slipped. He winked a silent warning to Roshni, then padded forward.

Two turns and a long stretch of scroll-shelf corridor took them to the commotion. Three members of the Order of the True were standing over a poor elderly goose-Kind who Gael recognised as Metap, an archivist and the life-mate of Artemis the goose-Kind scholar. Both Metap and Artemis were part of the furniture of the Tower and seeing the poor old bird in such a desperate state injected a flood of fury all the way to Gael's feather-tips. Metap lay sprawled on the ground, her tawny feathers splayed and her large yellow owl eyes unfocused. She was bleeding from a wound to her head. She looked like she had a broken wing too.

Two of the robed fanatics – both snake-Kind, one thick-set with dark triangular patterns, the other thin and bright red like a corn snake – were arguing about whether it was better to kill Metap now or take her away to be disposed of later.

The third, a smaller, shifty saurian – perhaps partly a gecko-Kind – was grabbing scrolls off the shelves with her sticky half-webbed claws, glancing at them before tossing them aside. Finally, her yellow eyes gleamed with triumph and she stuffed a thick brown scroll into a large canvas bag.

"INFAMY! You can't steal scrolls from the ARCHIVES!" bellowed Gael.

He didn't wait to attack. That was the mistake always made by the heroic, the young, the inexperienced – for some reason they believed in fighting fair.

Gael was too old for such amateur silliness.

With the star crystal in one hand, he sent a hurricane of wind that slammed the muscular snake-Kind thirty feet back into the wall.

With the other hand he threw a giant fang shaped like a boomerang, which he'd drawn from yet another inside pocket. The fang knocked the corn snake-Kind out cold and would have taken out the gecko too if she hadn't shifted position with surprising speed.

She must be air-blessed to move with such lightness, thought Gael, with the rational part of his mind. The other part was screaming that he was about to die.

Why did he bother to *shout* as he was attacking? For all his experience, he always allowed his emotions to get the better of him. He should have attacked without any warning at all. Never underestimate an opponent. He'd heard that once. Seemed like a reasonable statement. A little too late to pay heed to it now though.

The lizard had somehow crossed the space between them.

A frontal assault is a terrible plan, Gael's rational mind added helpfully, as the gecko-Kind's sharp claws came right for his neck.

But the lizard stumbled. Roshni, invisible, had reached out a leg and tripped her up. The gecko-Kind slammed face down on the library floor, dropping the canvas bag with the stolen scroll.

"My thanks," said Gael. "I purposely left myself vulnerable so you had to step in. You passed the test. Congratulations, Roshni. Remember: NEVER underestimate your opponent." No messing around now. Gael was already pulling out a green orb, feeling the fizz of its powerful displacement magic tingle up his arm.

"*Vaequo,*" he muttered as he pointed the orb at the snarling Kind.

The lizard disappeared. Just like that, Gael made the other two priests disappear as well. The bursts of magic left a faint burning smell in the air and made Gael's heart palpitate.

"Where have they gone?" asked Roshni.

"You don't want to know," said Gael, frowning. Suddenly things had become very complicated. He'd just transmuted three members of the Order of the True straight to the Netherplane, where their bodies would no doubt have been pulled apart into billions of particles by the unimaginable force of the pure, unfiltered magic. Or rather – their bodies had *always* been pulled apart into billions of atoms. There was no linear time in the Netherplane: everything that would ever happen, the timeline of fate, was happening at once.

It was better not to think about it.

He grabbed the fang boomerang off the floor and tucked it back inside his cloak.

"How much stuff do you have in that cloak, exactly?"

Gael shrugged. There was no point in revealing all his secrets to this human, even if she might just have pulled his porridge from the fire.

"I'd like to help this poor old bird," said Gael, nodding with concern to the downed Archivist. "But I think Metap will live, and we have to get out of here before she wakes up. A witness would be a problem."

"What were they doing?" said Roshni. "Wait – do you see that?"

The Nose had fallen out of Gael's hand in the fight. Now it was huffing across the floor towards the scroll that the priests had been stealing, which had rolled out of the discarded bag.

"Curious," said Gael. "It must sense a human touch. Let's see what it sniffs out."

The Nose dragged itself to an old scroll made of stained brown parchment and nuzzled at it like a hunting dog. Gael grabbed the scroll and the Nose, and hustled Roshni away. Although he was dying to get to the bottom of this strange coincidence, it was better not to risk being discovered. With a whirl of his cloak, and another retching cough, Gael teleported them to his quarters. Conveniently, these happened to be high in the Tower's main turret – far from the scene of the crime. "You can take off the Trickster Ring now; no one will disturb us."

Roshni reappeared, and cast her gaze around Gael's quarters. The crumbling series of rooms took up a whole floor of the central turret. In his office was a desk made of twisted branches and decorated with glittering charms, as well as his simple stitched-twig bed, along with a typical sprawling mess of his instruments scattered over the floor. Wind whistled through the gaps in the stonework. Gael appreciated a brisk breeze, which helped him think. He hurried to one of the larger gaps in the office wall. "Need to cement our alibi," he muttered to Roshni.

"Avis!" he bellowed from the opening. "Are you on shift today? Please, I am desperate for refreshment."

A flustered pelican-Kind flapped through the air, carrying a food order to another scholar's office lower down the Tower. "I can't have been anywhere near that scuffle with the Order of the True priests if I was sipping tea in my office at the very same time," Gael whispered to Roshni.

The girl was glancing curiously about the room.

"A little bare, isn't it?" said Gael. "I try not to accumulate too much baggage. Other than the precious things that I must keep safely in reach." He jangled his cloak. "But you'll see my personal library through there, and a balcony where I detect atmospheric magic – oh, and a broom cupboard, which is extremely important. I am a stickler for cleaning!"

Roshni looked about the messy room with a frown.

Gael twisted his head out the back of the opening and squawked after the catering attendant. "Make sure to provide cucumber and lemon, you understand? It is most refreshing after a nap. And my usual order of snacks. Fresh eggs and some dried meat slices." Gael gave Roshni a big wink.

The pelican-Kind soon arrived with the refreshments on a clattering tray, while Roshni hid behind a bookcase. Peering round from her hiding place, Roshni was clearly shocked and mildly disgusted to see the tray had been transported inside the attendant's enormous beak. Humans were so squeamish. "I added those biscuits you liked, sir," Avis said. "And a weevil surprise."

"My thanks, Avis!" Gael grabbed a candied maggot and threw it in his beak.

He scoffed the lot then, once the pelican-Kind was out of earshot, turned his attention to the mysterious scroll. Gael sniffed the page.

"Hmm, do I detect magic? Not mine – but someone else's. Whoever sneaked into the Tower to view this scroll had magical talent. That explains how they got in." Gael fetched his oscilloscope and scanned the pages. He checked the readings. "Enchanting magic. Interesting. Malachai is an enchanter, of course. But his magic is different – it has a lower frequency, and more fluctuations, drawing more on elemental ghost magic. This aura has touches of earth magic, perhaps even belonging to a psychic, a rare sub-division of enchanter who can read thoughts. What do they want with this scroll?" The text was hard to read, written in a cramped, crabby script. "Drat my eyes," sighed Gael. "Where are my eyeglasses, Roshni?"

"On your head," said Roshni.

Gael sighed. "Oh yes, I forgot I had already put them there. You know, if it were up to the Order of the True, eyeglasses would be banned. They're a human affectation, apparently. Most useful, mind." He slipped them down over his eyes and began to read the ancient writing.

"Oho!" he said, once he'd got to the end. "Fascinating stuff. It is a legend from the great anthology of human stories called the *Chronicles of Havanthya*. I believe we have the whole set of scrolls in the library. This particular scroll seems to tell the tale of a foul necromancer called Malvale. This evil wizard used spells from the Tablets of the Creator to unleash terrible destruction."

"Is Dalthek in that story?" asked Roshni. "I love his stories the most out of all the myths of the Old Ways."

"Oof! Be careful saying the wizard's name out loud," Gael warned. "And never mention the Old Ways. Even in a place like this where you think you are safe. Malachai has spies everywhere. I wouldn't even trust Avis, despite that pea-brain not being able to remember a single item in any order. Candied maggots? I ordered fresh eggs! And where is the cucumber for my tea? Anyway, yes, this story does involve the famous human wizard you mentioned. The one beginning with 'D'. The legend describes how he joined up with some strange fellow called the Last Master. I presume this refers to one of the Masters of the Kind – a line of elite ancient human warrior guardians who kept balance in the world. Balance! I can barely remember such a notion. Oh, and Roshni, better not mention the Masters of the Kind either, or anything about human heroes and old-Kind working together. And probably not anything about my work keeping the magical fabric of the worlds in balance. In fact, better not repeat anything you ever learn with me to anyone."

"Got it," said Roshni, tapping her finger against the side of her nose. "You can trust me to keep your secrets. Even your special velvet pillow."

"This is no joking matter, girl," Gael snapped sternly, keeping the glimmer of a smile from spreading across his beak. He returned his eyes to the scroll, flicking through the script. "By Anoreth, this script is hard to read. This story claims that the famous wizard – ah, bother it, let's just name him. The story claims that Dalthek and this Last Master – yes, let's just use his title too or we will confuse ourselves. Keep our voices down, mind. Anyway, they teamed up with old-Kind to defeat terrible magic from the Netherplane."

"Wait, let's go back a bit," Roshni said. "So if humans and old-Kind worked together, is the Spawning not true? I thought humans drove the old-Kind to extinction, until the new-Kind were suddenly spawned in vast numbers, and they defeated the humans?"

"Let's just forget everything we've discussed here, all right? Better to live in ignorance than risk the Order of the True catching you uttering such blasphemy. Hmm, what confuses me is that the scroll says the Tablets of the Creator were buried in their master's tomb. It makes no sense. The Creator is the forger of the Many Worlds. He is ageless. He was never alive, nor dead. He has always existed. He can have no tomb."

"Why do you think the humans would be interested in the Tablets?" asked Roshni. "And Malachai as well? He sent his priests to steal this scroll. So he must be interested too."

"As ever, young Roshni, you ask the right questions. The Tablets hold the key. They are immensely powerful. The spells etched on to the Tablets channel the pure magic that exists inside the Netherplane. There are even spells that open portals directly to the Netherplane. In the wrong hands, those spells could destroy cities and level mountains."

"So do you think Malachai wants to find these Tablets? That would be bad, right?"

Gael said nothing. He settled himself into the carved oak seat of his desk, fluffing out his feathers and wiggling himself to get comfortable. He hooded his eyes and stared into the distance, letting his thoughts roam.

"Um, Master, do you want to have a rest? I could give the place a clean, perhaps? Or sort some of these instruments?"

"Nonsense, girl. I am a little drained from the teleportation, that's all. I always close my eyes when considering a good mystery. I am entering a state of meditation where I can allow my thoughts to weave together like a tapestry, trying out many answers, forming theories, delving into my deepest memories for clues. Please do not disrupt me. And certainly not by *cleaning.* I am a Kind, not a human. Mess helps me feel comfortable."

"Of course, Master."

Yes, thought Gael, *there is much to ponder and many strands to bring together.* He was mighty certain he was missing something terribly important . . . but the pattern was so hard to see.

What did the humans want with the Tablets? What did the Order of the True want with the Tablets? Did the Tablets even really exist? Gael had always believed the Tablets to be a myth. They were said to contain the spells of the Creator himself, spells used to fashion the Many Worlds. Spells that could create matter from nothing, bring the dead back to life, destroy the boundaries between worlds, alter time, and turn cities to dust in an instant. The Tablets of the Creator were like the most powerful spell book in existence. And what could the scroll mean when it said the Tablets were buried in their master's tomb? Wretched riddles!

Gael had not deciphered what he was missing by the time sleep overcame his thoughts, leaving only the dreams of forgotten memories.

8

The Ruby Isle

Jonas knew they were getting close to the Ruby Isle when black-finned sharks began to follow the ship. In the last few days, they'd left the cold, green southern waters behind. Now small coral islands dotted with palms began to appear. Their white sand beaches looked inviting as the vessel navigated through the tricky reefs of the archipelago.

The three bounty hunters – Orok the Crusher, Brynn the Sly and Jonas – had all boarded the same supply ship, bound for the famous trading port of the Ruby Isle. The ship's cargo was fine linen and redsteel chain mail produced in the prison workshops using the famous blood ore mined on the Isle. The ship would return with gold to line

Grashkor's pockets, and more redsteel ore too.

Jonas was surprised his fellow bounty hunters had chosen the same route as him – and it wasn't a happy surprise. The quickest route to Skin-Grave was overland, north through Morta. Brynn and Orok clearly wanted to keep an eye on him – or kill him, if they had the chance.

Jonas was almost tempted to change his plan and take the overland route. He knew that speed was crucial when tracking down a fugitive. The quicker you found the trail, the less chance there was of it going cold. But Morta was a dangerous land – and growing more dangerous as the Order of the True increased their power. Morta was the ancestral home of the noble reptile-Kind. A scorched land made up of vast estates belonging to lords of the Kind, where human vassals toiled away on insect farms and in metal workshops, or digging out the quarries and mines of the Burrows. Whitestone, capital of the Four Kingdoms, was in central Morta, where the Emperor ruled from the granite throne. The closer you got to the seat of the Kind's power, the more anti-human sentiment increased – as if the lizard-Kind needed to prove their high-born status by persecuting the lowest born. Jonas had heard of humans being hunted for sport, or rounded up and killed for no reason other than to prove the unquestionable authority of the Kind. No, Morta was not a friendly place for humans travelling alone. He would be foolish to take the risk.

Jonas's best chance of getting to Skin-Grave intact was by heading west, sailing to the Ruby Isle, which was far away from Whitestone and more lenient towards humans. From there he would sail up the coast of Morta, crossing the border into Anoros by water.

But really, there was no *good* option. Even once he reached Anoros, where Skin-Grave was located, he would be in danger. Jonas had only travelled to the kingdom of the mammal-Kind once or twice before. He certainly had never ventured close to Skin-Grave. The Empty were not allowed within sight of that cursed memorial to ancient evil. Skin-Grave had once been a powerful metropolis built by the ancient humans. Now it was known as the city of black magic, where it was said ancient curses were still on the loose and turned the earth to blood, sending any who ventured there mad. The foul practices of the ancient humans could still be witnessed in memorials, wall paintings and books of their dangerous, wicked writing. It was said Skin-Grave was where the ancient humans had sacrificed the gods of the old-Kind to increase their dominion over the land and the power of their evil curses.

Curses did not frighten Jonas.

Not when he himself was a living curse. A walking curse of death.

"That toad is glowering at you again," said Seth, nodding towards Orok while Jonas tossed scraps of food to the sharks.

The ship wasn't really a friendly place either. There were hulking bear-Kind prison guards on board, so Orok had not tried to kill Jonas yet. But it was only a matter of time. When they reached dry land, Jonas was sure that the Crusher would make his move.

"Let him look," said Jonas. "Looks don't kill."

"I could tip him over the side," said Seth. "Give your shark friends a proper meal. No one would ever know."

This might have been Seth's idea of a joke – but Jonas didn't laugh.

"I think you've done enough."

"As you wish, my twin." Seth clearly sensed it was best not to push Jonas in his current state of mind. The wyvern launched himself from the boat, the green light of his ghost-form shimmering across the deck. Only Jonas felt the wind of Seth's great translucent wings upon his cheeks. Jonas watched as Seth soared over the turquoise ocean before diving towards the water, his talons snatching up large, muscular ray fish. Jonas was doing all he could to bite back his anger towards Seth, and yet he could not help feeling in awe of his twin, of the power of his body and the speed of his flight.

Jonas had been angry at Seth before, but he had never felt such a cold disgust as he did now. Not only had Seth killed the cat-Kind in cold blood, he had revealed himself during the fight at the prison. And for what? A cheap victory that meant nothing. Now Jonas's enemies – Orok and Brynn – knew what Jonas was. They knew that he was vulnerable. Seth's actions had put both Jonas and Seth in danger. Jonas closed his eyes and could faintly feel cool water on his feet, taste the flesh of the ray fish in his mouth, sense the world through Seth's body. They were connected, one life force. If Seth was hurt, so was Jonas. Two bodies, one spirit. It only took one of them to be killed and they would both be sent to the afterlife – and this time there would be no way back for Seth, trapped in the Land of What Was for good. In some ways, Seth made Jonas more vulnerable. It was a strange thought – one Jonas had never had before. When Jonas was a boy,

Seth had protected him, was everything to him: his guardian, his hero, his beloved brother. But Jonas had grown up a lot since then.

For the first time since he could remember, Jonas started to wonder what life would be like *without* Seth. Jonas felt mad, scared to think of such an idea. Seth was like another part of him, a part of his body, one of his limbs. But Jonas also felt relief at the prospect of no longer being bound to his twin.

Once Jonas was free of Grashkor's debt, once he no longer required protection in the Pinnacles of the Damned, would he *need* Seth any more? The idea was almost too strange to contemplate: never again feeling the freedom of Seth's flight, the freedom of his merciless will. Sometimes Jonas wondered if the only reason he could live with the guilt of all the Kind he had killed was because, in some ways, Jonas could blame Seth. Jonas told himself that Seth must be the source of his death-song. If Jonas could somehow sever their connection, perhaps he would no longer be cursed with his instinct, his need, for killing.

Jonas cut away another sliver of meat and threw it for the hungry, snapping sharks.

Sometimes, when the wound is rotten, the whole limb must be cut away – that's what the shaman healers of his tribe had said.

Jonas watched Seth as he landed on the gunwale, chewing on a fish. For a brief second, the ghost wyvern turned into his bodily form and spat a chunk of fish out – straight on to the head of Orok the Crusher.

"Arghh!" shouted Orok, spinning his huge, fleshy head back and forth. His large, wet eyes fixed on Seth. But the wyvern had flashed back into ghostly form and was invisible to the toad. "Who did that? I'll teach you for throwing things at Orok!"

Jonas snorted, unable to contain his laughter. Seth flapped over to where Jonas was sitting. Jonas shook his head at his twin. And in that moment all Jonas's anger seemed to melt away. What had he been thinking? How could he ever be separated from his twin? Seth and Jonas were one. He was just tired, that's all.

"So you forgive me, Little Fury?"

The use of the childhood nickname Jonas's father had given him, and which Seth had adopted, brought a tear to Jonas's eye.

"I'm tired, Seth."

"Well, get some rest. And then maybe you will be done with the silent treatment."

Jonas sighed. "Maybe, Seth. Maybe. Now let me

doze. But keep an eye out for Orok and Brynn, would you?"

They arrived at the Ruby Isle as the morning tide was ebbing. The land breeze brought a heady whiff of spices, roasting meats and raw sewage. The saying went that you could buy anything you could ever want on the Isle, except a clean pair of shoes. What Jonas needed was a boat that could take him north along the coast to Anoros. Ships from every port in the Four Kingdoms were tied up in the Isle's harbour. Throbbing music from a dozen bustling taverns competed for the drinking crowd's attention. Traders hawked sweetmeats, strange brews and questionable opportunities.

It was a glorious mess – especially because the thick, warm rain that was falling had turned the streets into a swamp.

"Ah," said Seth, sniffing the air. "I love this place."

Jonas frowned, but didn't bother asking Seth when he had been here before and for what reason.

Still, the Ruby Isle seemed like a strange place for a ghost-Kind to venture – a teeming throb of overwhelming *life*, of riches and ruin, of worldly delights. Jonas had heard all the tales, had dreamed of such things during the long nights spent in his cell – but maybe they had been Seth's dreams.

Let him have his mysteries, Jonas thought. Shaking himself free like a wet dog, he jumped down on to the quay and splashed off into the gluey mud. Seth followed invisibly above, giving directions.

"Take a right after the statue of the clown with a sandwich," said Seth. "There's an ambush spot there if you want to get your companions before they get you. They are following you, you know."

"I don't want to kill anyone, all right?"

Jonas pushed quickly through the crowd, hoping that would be enough to lose Orok. He wasn't so worried about Brynn stabbing him in the back. The dog-Kind didn't have a vendetta against Jonas. But it would be good to give him the slip too.

"Very well. After the Living Temple, you need to go down Purple Street."

"Is that this one with all the purple flowers?"

"No. It's the lane where that big orangutan-Kind is selling chocolate tasties."

The streets were bustling with intriguing smells and startlingly strange faces. It was intoxicating. But Jonas soon realised the best thing about the Ruby Isle: no one took any notice of a human here.

"It's like they can't see me," he muttered in

astonishment to Seth. "It's like I'm you."

"So long as everyone's making money, no one cares what you look like here," said Seth. "Isn't it grand?"

It was like nowhere Jonas had ever been before. The smartest shops sold weapons forged from the famous local redsteel, or curious potions and elixirs brewed from strange jungle ingredients. The buildings bulged over the narrow streets, jumbled all higgledy-piggledy as if houses from a dozen different cities had been thrown up in the air and left to lie where they fell. A mosaic lizard-Kind basking chamber perched next to an owl-wizard's tree shop, which overlooked the muddy pit of a hippo-Kind's bathing house. Jonas could hear a dozen different languages being spoken at once.

But the most amazing sight was a human who was being ferried above the mud on a palanquin carried by two enormous skin-Kind oxen.

"Is he really their boss?" he said to Seth. "He employs them?"

"Great, isn't it?" said Seth. "Turn left here. We're nearly there."

The tavern that Seth guided Jonas to was called the Punctured Lung. It was largely empty, and had definitely seen better days. Its rushes were filthy, its whitewash was brown and it smelled of sour beer and lost hope.

"You sure this is the right place?" asked Jonas.

"Don't you trust me?" said Seth.

Jonas paused. "Yes."

A sleek, eel-Kind barman stood near the taps, polishing the dark wood.

"That's Nightwater," said Seth. "He can get you on any ship."

"How d'you know this?" said Jonas. "When have you been here?"

"Careful – you'll look mad if people see you talking to yourself." Seth deftly avoided answering the question.

Jonas approached the bar and discreetly inquired if there were any berths free on a ship travelling north to Anoros.

Nightwater didn't ask any questions. "I've a ship leaving tonight. She's built to take quarried marble and worked minerals, so it'll be slow. First stop will be Sephronia in north Morta, dropping some new mining lathes at the Burrows. It'll be a hundred silver, mate. Emperor's coin only."

"Make the price sixty and you've got a deal." Jonas had to haggle. He didn't have a hundred.

Nightwater nodded. "That will do."

The fact that the eel agreed so quickly made Jonas think he hadn't bargained hard enough. At least the big payment made Nightwater chatty. "Lots of work in the mines right now. Can you believe they're building another palace for his mad majesty? You'd think five was enough, eh?"

Jonas hadn't heard this gossip. "Any other news?" he asked as he carefully counted out the coin.

"Things getting worse," said Nightwater. "Like usual. Humans getting uppity. No offence to you. Kind slapping 'em down. Rebels been raiding more. There's whispers here on Ruby that some merchants are funding both sides, getting rich in the middle. Then the Order's doing a madness, trying to change things *here*."

"What's that about the Order?" said Jonas. He couldn't help wondering about what Rahziin had told him about the Order of the True before she died. Something about the leader being rotten. What was his name? Mala . . . something?

"Order's decided the way we mix here, human and Kind hand in paw, ain't good enough. They're trying to change the law – enforce their bleedin' hierarchy! Good luck with that, I say. I've no problem with the likes of you. Specially when you fill my pockets with silver."

"Well, I'm glad you'll still work with humans," said Jonas.

"It's a pleasure doing business with you, lad. I'll have a word with the captain of your ship. Remember she's leaving tonight."

Jonas kept his head down that afternoon until he could make his escape. He scuttled about, buying supplies with the few coins that remained in his purse.

It was a shame he could not see more of the Ruby Isle and get to know the place. Jonas liked it here. Were he ever to gain his freedom, maybe he could even make a home here and leave his past behind him. He could start a weapons forge, or find work on the merchant ships; or tend animals in the mountains and sell them at the many markets that heaved along the alleyways, or to the ships carrying produce across the Four Kingdoms. The idea of a life at all, an existence beyond serving Grashkor, was a strange idea – a dream, almost. Yet the teeming island was the only place Jonas had ever visited where it was possible to live without the constant worry of attack from the Kind. It was the only place where humans were practically equals.

Jonas forced himself to stop daydreaming. Daydreaming could get you killed. You had to focus on the here and the now, hone your senses to the slightest possible danger. He was hardly safe on the island, not with Orok and Brynn about. Seth circled in the skies above, keeping an eye out for the other bounty hunters.

As evening approached, Jonas made his way through the back alleys to the docks. Hazy smoke from cooking fires combined with the tantalising smell of sizzling sausages and fiery spices. Through a gap between a chandler's yard and a sail-making shack, Jonas glimpsed masts, black against the setting sun.

Relief flooded through him. Soon he would be free of the danger of the other bounty hunters.

"Thought you could slip me, Slayer?" Orok's voice rumbled from a dark corner.

"To be honest," said Jonas, "yes, I did."

Orok jumped out of the darkness and splashed down in the mud. He really was huge – so huge there was no way he should have been able to creep up on anyone, much less Jonas. He had hidden himself well beneath those tantalising smells Jonas had just been enjoying. Hanging from one large webbed hand was a hatchet the size of a halberd.

The huge half-axe, half-club ground against the flagstones.

With a creeping sense of dread, Jonas felt his death-song fire up. Someone was going to die soon. Visions of all the ways that Orok could kill him flashed through his mind. Some involved Orok smashing the hatchet into Jonas's flesh. But most of them involved drowning in the mud as Orok sat on various bits of his body. The toad wanted to make Jonas's death slow. He wanted to enjoy it.

"It weren't hard." Orok's huge tongue lolled out and licked his lips. "There's only one ship leaving for north Morta for three days. And there's only one of us leaving on it. ME!"

"Have you been practising that line?" said Jonas, playing for time.

The toad had chosen his ambush spot well: they were in a secluded court. The alleyway was cramped and the close-quarters combat would play to Orok's strengths. Jonas's agility and speed would be compromised. While Orok's webbed feet were designed for slippery surfaces, Jonas's boots could easily skid on the muddy stone. No one was about. No one would stop the fight.

Jonas thought of running. But if the toad knew what boat he was planning to take, what was the point? Jonas would have to face Orok. It was only a matter of time.

"Any last requests, Slayer?" snarled Orok, poising to spring.

With a sense of great weariness, Jonas put his hand on one of his swords. "I don't want to kill you, Orok." Maybe if he just wounded the toad, he could get away on the boat and get ahead of the chase.

"Your request is granted," said Orok. "I shall very much enjoy killing *you*. I will crush your puny Empty body, nice and slow."

"Enough of this weak banter," snapped Seth. The shimmering wyvern crashed down between Jonas and the toad, the visible bones of his skeleton clacking together. In the same movement, Seth launched from his crouch and sliced a razor-sharp claw towards Orok's throat. As he did so he turned into his bodily form. Dark scaly flesh rippled with the power of the explosive attack.

But the toad-Kind was ready. Jonas knew it even before it happened. He sensed the sudden danger, his senses screaming as the death-song reached a powerful crescendo.

Orok grinned as he ducked with surprising speed and then launched towards Seth, swinging the hatchet.

At once, visualised in pristine clarity, a new vision of his own death sprang into Jonas's mind:

Seth's skull crushed by Orok's hatchet . . . Seth's limp form falling to the floor . . . his body turning ghostly and then dissolving into nothing but green mist . . . Jonas closing his eyes, awaiting his own death . . . Then . . . opening his eyes. He was not dead. Seth's death had not caused Jonas's. How was that possible? Their life force was linked. That was what Seth had always told him. One could not survive without the other. A hatchet flew towards his face . . .

With a flick of his horned head, Seth managed to turn away a fraction at the last second, deflecting the blow slightly. But still the force was immense, crushing, paralysing Jonas with a sweep of unbearable pain across his own cheek, spreading to his head. Jonas fell to his knees. His thoughts clouded in confusion. *You need to get up,* he told himself. But where was he? *Get up, Jonas!* What was going on? *Get up!* His hands slipped. He couldn't see. His head throbbed.

He smelled a rancid odour close by and sensed a massive form hovering over him.

Jonas looked up into Orok's victorious, sagging face. Orok sat on Jonas's chest. His huge body pressed down with terrible force. Instantly, Jonas couldn't breathe. His ribs felt like they were going to snap. Orok whispered in Jonas's ear. "Feel the life being squeezed out of you, Slayer. Pah! You are no Slayer. You are weak. I'm going to make this last hours. There is no one to protect you now. No sneaky ghost-Kind bodyguard."

Jonas saw his own death in his mind an instant before it happened . . . *Terrible pain across his chest, ribs giving way under the weight, heart crushed, mind empty.*

Then the weight eased. There was light above him. He took a long, heaving breath. His vision came back into focus.

Jonas looked into Seth's eyes. The wyvern's face was swollen on the left side, his yellow eye all but closed up.

Jonas scrambled to his feet. He saw Orok nearby, lying lifeless on his front in the dirty alley. A great gash made by Seth's talon sliced down his back.

Jonas turned to Seth. The adrenaline, the killing power, the death-song faded inside him. He felt drained, weak. Pain lanced through his head and ached inside his chest each time he tried to breathe. Most of all he felt angry.

"Why'd you do that?" Jonas said, trying to shout, though his voice came out in a wheeze.

"Do what?" said Seth. "Save your life?"

"Save my life? You're a liability. I had things covered. You love killing too much. It makes you vulnerable. It makes me vulnerable. If you hadn't revealed yourself in the first place in the Pinnacles, Orok wouldn't have known he could target you."

"You think I am a weakness. I make you what you are. I make your death-blessing powerful. Without me, you would have been dead long ago."

"You're being defensive. Admit that you make mistakes. You don't make me better. You make me worse. Impatience for killing can make you vulnerable. And I can't worry about what you're going to do in a fight. You're too unpredictable."

"We'll talk later. You're hurt. You're tired. You still have the embers of the death-song inside you. What will you do? Fight me? That would be like fighting yourself!"

"Would it?" Jonas let the answer hang there.

"You are a killer, Jonas. The sooner you embrace it, the better. For both of us. I won't have to put up with these tedious guilt-ridden outbursts. You've been moping all day!"

"I don't enjoy killing," Jonas said. "Not like you do. You killed Rahziin too! What did you do that for?"

Seth gave Jonas a long, cool look. His nostrils flared. "She was dangerous. She would have killed you. I had no choice."

"You're lying! I saw her in my dream. She was running away."

"You're right. I killed her." Seth shook his head. "But you're wrong too. She was dangerous because she was distracting you. You have to win your *freedom,* Jonas – then you can look ahead to your great potential, your great destiny. And you won't do that if you go chasing the past. You should be grateful to me. I helped you then. Just like I helped you today." Seth bent down and took a bite out of the toad's leg and chewed. "Yuck," he said. "Too fatty."

Jonas wanted to scream. He hated the way Seth always thought he knew what was best. He hated the way he ate. He hated the way he killed.

"I don't want you to help me any more," he said, just about keeping his voice level. "I don't need you, I know that now. You are also keeping things from me, lying to me. What is my great destiny you always talk about? You won't even tell me. Maybe I don't want it. I know, Seth! I know that I don't need you to survive. I saw it with my death-song. I saw you die, and I lived. I'm going to find a way to sever our connection. Until then, I never want to see you again. I don't want you to come with me to Anoros."

Seth turned solid, his wings spreading large as a sail. The bone of his reptilian skull gleamed. Seth usually only turned into his bodily form in combat. It was rare Jonas could look at him for this long and this close up. He couldn't help a slight shiver – maybe in fear, maybe in admiration, maybe even in pride. The wyvern was a spectacular monster.

Seth laughed, spitting out one of Orok's toes which had been hanging from the corner of his mouth.

"You've been angry at me before. That's why your father called you Little Fury. You've always had trouble controlling your rage. Your hunger for fighting, for death. Yes, I make your death-song stronger, but it comes from you. You were born with the death-song, Jonas. I didn't give it to you. It was this power that brought me to you from the Land of What Was, that linked our life force. Maybe you could survive if my spirit was vanquished. I don't know the answer. But I do know that without me you would be alone. We are family, whether you like it or not. How many times have we squabbled? How many times have you told me to not come back if I left you?"

"This time I mean it," said Jonas. And he was surprised to realise that he did. "I don't want to see you again."

In a green shimmer, Seth's dark, scaled flesh melted away and he stalked around Jonas on silent feet. "You're being foolish. You will never survive without me. You would never have lasted a day alone in the Pinnacles, Slayer. And you won't last a day in Skin-Grave. I am your eyes. I am your ears and I have had your back, always."

Jonas knew there was truth in this. But he was more afraid of what he was becoming than being vulnerable. A flashing image of Rahziin appeared in his mind; the priest speaking her final vision, her wide amber eyes falling on Jonas, full of unimaginable horror, as if she was glimpsing the Land of What Was itself. Had she seen then that Jonas was leading her to her death? Jonas had promised her life, given her his word to set her free. But apparently he was incapable of giving such a promise – even to himself.

Maybe he could change that. All he knew was that he couldn't go on like this any longer.

"No," said Jonas. "I mean it. We are finished." The words felt good.

"Do you think you could survive without me,

Little Fury? How will you cope on your own? What will you do if this time I really *don't* come back? Will you cry again? No one will care! I am all you've got. You are nothing on your own."

Jonas gritted his teeth in a half-smile. "I have wings. I must fly. Isn't that what you told me once, when you left me?"

A booming rumble erupted from Seth's chest, making Jonas's skin prickle. "Jonas, you – you—"

"GO AWAY!"

Seth spread his wings and took off in one great leap. He did not say goodbye.

9

The Emperor and His Advisor

With a final bone-rattling thump the cart drew to a stop. The two harnessed emus cawed with relief and clawed angrily at the ground. It had been a hot, dusty journey across central Morta. Lana had spent the first day fighting back tears thinking of Shahn's face as she waved her goodbye. Her uncle had been there too, with a look that suggested this might be the last time he would ever see her. On the day Lana left Whardox Hall, Bart had taken her aside and told her about Whitestone, about how power was wielded in the capital, which noble families at court were ruthless and to be avoided, where she might go if things went wrong – he still had a few contacts in the capital. The last thing he had said was: "Do not delve too deep into your mother's past, Lana. Sometimes there are things not worth knowing." Lana had frowned. She would rather have known everything about her mother, but her uncle had not said another word on the subject.

Jun was the final person to see Lana off, flagging down her cart as it left. "Lana, I will take care of Shahn – don't worry." Lana had grinned as Jun leaped up on to the cart. She leaned close and whispered in Lana's ear. "This phrase will grant you peace and protection from my people. I will miss you, Lana Shadowscale." And then she had spoken the secret phrase.

Now Lana gazed along the wide, blanched-stone avenues of the bustling city of Whitestone, which spread from its central point like many rays of a blinking star. The main three thoroughfares faced the rising, midday and setting sun at the spring equinox – which wasn't many weeks away. There was no escaping the heat. Even for Lana, a lizard-Kind used to the desert of the Burrows, it became almost unbearable riding the open cart with the sun above her. She could feel her scales drying out as the moisture was sucked away.

She had been young when her family permanently moved from the capital, and Lana only had vague memories of the city – some of which might have been imagined from her uncle's stories. It was one thing to be told family stories about the wonder of Whitestone, but quite another to see a legend spread out before you. The city tumbled across the hillside, vast, shining and pure bone-white. Generations of lizard-Kind emperors had turned the capital city into a haven for cold-blooded creatures. Lana spotted huge basking chambers, elaborate nest-sites raised on delicate arches, clever aqueducts that fed the thousand dancing fountains, and tier upon tier of statues.

"I just wish Shahn could see this," said Lana to herself. The journey had taken three days, and Lana worried she was already forgetting the exact details of her sister's cheeky grin.

"That's far as I takes yer," growled the owl-Kind carter as he reached a huge open square at the centre of the star-shaped map of roads. "Not getting any closer to that mad-nest."

He nodded towards the Marble Palace at the far end of the square. The mountain of curved, snaking pale stone rose up from a swathe of tropical gardens. Around the square were mansions with their own gardens, like smaller offspring. From what her uncle had told her, these were home to noble-Kind courtiers. She wondered if one of the buildings had once belonged to the Shadowscale brood. She didn't recognise any of them, but she had been a young girl when she had lived here and barely recalled anything but the majestic white stone and the ornate golden-thread drapes of her bedroom.

"My thanks."

Lana climbed down from the cart. She set off towards the lush palace gardens, wandering between the towering trees. The breeze smelled of honeysuckle and mistmoss. This was as close to paradise as Lana had ever been. Hundreds of human servants were dotted throughout the garden, tending to the plants.

Sheer determination had carried her so far, but now she began to feel nervous.

"I can't turn back," she whispered to herself. "That way lies only ruin."

Trying to look confident, she strode through the garden towards the main gate. Lana was surprised to meet a handful of guards wearing the robes of the Order of the True. Lana's uncle had mentioned that the Order were gaining more influence in the capital, but still she was shocked that they were seemingly acting as guards to the palace itself. Their headquarters were at the Temple of the Creator, on the other side of the city.

Lana approached the guards, heart thudding. They took one look at her cheap clothes and the flickering shadow that danced over one side of the body, and condescension filled their downcast expressions.

"Off with you, shadow-blessed freak!" snarled a porcupine-Kind, needle-sharp spines bristling. Around his wrists jangled iron bracelets. Lana knew the metal bands showed how many heretics he had killed. "Lucky we don't spit you right here."

"I was requested by the Emperor himself," Lana said evenly, though her chest rattled with each breath. "Councillor Rissok passed on a message to me." She was aware of the shadow-flame licking out from beneath her hood and over her brow. It always became agitated when she was flustered.

"Maybe you *were* invited," said a chameleon-Kind who was clearly the leader. As he strode forward, the other priests bowed their heads. His bulbous eyes fixed their attention on Lana, and the mottled skin on his face changed from green to warning-red. "But how are we to know that? It is hard for us to believe that a shadow-blessed could have been invited into the Marble Palace. I can see you are not from around here. Elemental-blessings are considered dangerous around these parts, by order of the Arch Protector. They are a curse upon the purity of noble-Kind blood. Maybe I tell the Emperor you tried to put a curse on us, so I had to cut your throat. The Emperor is a confused old lizard-Kind with a short attention span. The simplest explanations often go down the best with him."

Lana backed away. "Of course," she said, turning and walking away.

"She wanted to see the Emperor!" the porcupine-Kind snorted. The others laughed.

Lana cursed herself for an optimistic fool. She'd assumed that an invitation from the Emperor himself would mean that she was at least expected. But she had no letter. She had no proof. Perhaps the Emperor had forgotten he had summoned Lana at all. Had this whole miserable trip been wasted?

Lana skirted the gardens, looking for a free spot of shade to cool her rapidly heating body. The midday sun was unbearably hot, even for a lizard. Her blood felt like it was boiling. Lana found a scrap of cover under a fern as far away from the Order of the True priests as possible. What was her next move? She had no friends here. Come to think of it, even if someone knew who she was, they might not be friendly: her mother's disgrace had put paid to that.

In the fierce heat, nothing was moving apart from a steady stream of human workers coming and going by the servants' entrance – there were gardeners as well as kitchen staff and quartermaster's servants carrying supplies into the building from carts parked outside the gardens. The poor humans looked like ants scampering around beneath the giant walls. They were pitiably thin too – even more run-down than the humans she knew from the mines.

And then Lana noticed something else: there were no Kind guards at the humans' gate. Perhaps the Order of the True did not want to shame themselves by getting too close.

Lana scurried down to the human entrance, careful to stay out of sight of the guards. The humans saw her coming and watched her warily. They were too afraid to challenge her, even though this was very unusual.

"Hello . . . erm . . . I'd like to get in . . . to the palace," said Lana. "Can I just slip through here? Please?"

Her request was met with silence. No one seemed to know what to say.

At last an old man in rags was brave enough to speak.

"Alas. I'm sorry, honoured mistress, but we cannot let you in." The humans were too scared to look her in the eye. Some of them were trembling. Lana was shocked. Even the prisoners she knew from the mines were not as craven as this.

"*The blood of the Masters runs through your veins,*" whispered Lana. It was the phrase Jun had given her.

The old man's head snapped up. He suddenly looked a lot calmer and more assured. "Let her in," he said.

Several human hands grabbed her. Before she knew what was happening, the heavy gate was open and she was through to the other side. Still none of the humans would look at her.

It all happened so swiftly and suddenly that she could not quite believe it was true.

What does Jun's secret phrase mean?

"Please, tell no one of this," said the old man. "And go well on your journey."

All the humans carried on with their tasks, coming and going as if nothing had happened. She might have been invisible.

With a spring in her step, Lana walked into a marble corridor. The stone felt deliciously cold beneath her claws. The air was cool and crisp.

Lana splashed water on her face from a convenient copper trough. The water felt even better on her dusty scales.

And so to find the Emperor.

Conscious of her dusty, unfashionable clothes, Lana was careful to avoid crowds and courtiers, but it was not difficult to find a way through the maze of corridors and rooms. It was obvious from the flow of traffic where the centre of power lay. It helped too that this was a saurian-Kind home. Everything felt familiar, even if it was built on the grandest of scales. There were solars for basking, and dark ombral chambers for cooling down, and the rooms grew ever more opulent the deeper she went.

Gradually, Lana crept closer and closer to the Emperor's apartments.

At last, she reached a shaded space so magnificent she knew she must be close. Giant damask cushions dotted the room, which was divided into little chambers by delicate screens made of gold and ivory. A few courtiers in complicated robes were having important, secret conversations in these sheltered nooks. At the far end of the chamber was an ornate door, with two enormous gila-Kind guards in ceremonial armour.

Lana entered the shaded chamber. The air was

misty with the spray from a moss-encrusted fountain carved from a solid block of jade. The chamber was so peaceful, and so well adapted to soothe an over-hot lizard, it took all Lana's strength not to collapse right there and rest her baking bones.

Instead, she sneaked into a corner and set to work.

Concentrating, she stirred the flickering shadow that usually shimmered over the right-hand side of her body. The shadows spread across her skin like flames wicking across dry wood. Soon they covered her entirely, blending Lana into the gloom. It was a trick she had mastered in her bedroom at Whardox Hall – even Jun and Shahn did not know that she could camouflage like this, merging her form with the colours and shapes around her. So camouflaged, in fact, that the human workers overseeing the quarry carts heading from Whardox Hall to Whitestone did not realise when Lana approached and set one of her magical quartz figurines on the cart, hoping the Emperor would learn of the enchanted craftsmanship.

Lana let her eyes drift closed for a moment, letting the shadow merge with the light, blue-veined marble around her. The fizz of magic leapt over her scales – it was a wondrous, exciting, intoxicating feeling.

Concentrate, Lana, she told herself. Opening her eyes, she fixed them on the gila-Kind. Every few seconds, the guards' heavy blue tongues licked out, tasting the air. Even if she was invisible, they would know she was there. She would have to do more if she wanted to get past them.

Luckily, the ombral chamber was not busy. Lana waited as courtiers left, walking past her along the corridor. Soon it was almost empty. Then she gathered more shadows around her. The darkness took shape. This ancient place was powerful; she could feel the energy in the cool stone beneath her feet feeding her strength. To her surprise, the shadows grew faster than normal. She shaped them easily with her mind, crafting a rough human figure out of pure gloom.

Lana had told Shahn that it was impossible to use their powers to craft something solid out of nothing.

But she had been lying.

Lana's powers were far greater than Shahn could understand. Lana didn't understand the limits of her powers herself. And she didn't want to inspire her sister to experiment with her own gifts – gifts Shahn's lesser talent might not be able to control.

She gave her human figure a sword and shield,

and a helmet to hide his featureless face. His black armour was convincing. She saved what little colour she could manage for an eye-catching red cloak.

"Fish well, little friend," she whispered, and sent her lure running.

The two gila guards could not smell the shadow, so they were surprised by the figure that came charging at them. Lana made it curve towards them, then suddenly break away down a side passage.

"Intruder!" roared the guards, and they gave chase, thundering off.

In the panic, no one saw Lana, a second shadow, slip towards the Emperor's chamber. The huge door opened inwards and Lana slid inside.

"I've done it," said Lana to herself, still protected by her shadow skin, but she took a deep breath when she saw what lay ahead.

On a golden bed set on a golden plinth lay a giant, heavy-bellied komodo-Kind. He wore golden robes too, studded with fiery rubies – meant, no doubt, to look like the scales of Fernwing, the great old-Kind dragon god.

The Emperor was snoring, sleeping off a meal that had stained his teeth and jaws with dried blood. A foul stench filled the room. It came from the giant golden bowl beside the bed. The bowl was filled with huge, rancid chunks of raw, fat-streaked meat.

The reflected glow from all that gold filled the room with light. Even the white walls shone yellow.

Lana's shadow-blessing could not cope with the dazzle. It faded.

The human servants saw her at once.

"Intruder!" they cried.

The Emperor woke with a snort.

"Wha— What? WHAT!?" he growled, shaking himself. "I'M NAPPING!"

"O True Dragon, o Scaled Glory, o Emperor who walks with gods," began Lana, stepping forward, bowing at every step.

She'd practised this speech dozens of times in the cart. The Emperor had over a hundred titles, and it was important – and difficult – to get them in the right order. Even an informal greeting like this required at least a dozen complicated phrases.

"Shut up!" barked the Emperor, blinking at her with little piggy eyes. "What do you think you are doing, coming in here? This is my NAPPING ROOM!"

"Ahm, you invited me, O Golden Friend of Fortune. My name is Lana, my brood is Shadowscale. I am a sculptor of stone."

"You BORE me," roared the Emperor. He

reached out a claw and spiked a hunk of flesh from the golden bowl, then swallowed it without chewing. "Where are the guards?"

Lana realised she was failing her only chance. She decided to take a risk.

Near the Emperor's bed was a vast marble bath carved out of a single piece of rock. Settling her feet against the floor, Lana reached out with her mind, drawing energy from the ancient stone all around her. Once again, she was surprised by the rush of power she felt. It was almost too much.

"See what I can make you, O Tooth that Crushes the World."

Working quickly and decisively, she melted the marble bath and remade it. With the power available to her here, it was easy. The hard stone glommed and puddled like molten wax.

"Hey there! What are you doing to my bath?" The Emperor's curious gaze sharpened. "Is that me?"

"I am making a statue of your greatness, O Eye that Blinds All Others."

A towering figure grew in the golden half-light. Lana depicted the Emperor at battle, roaring his defiance with a massive axe in his hand and a headless human at his feet. His belly was much smaller than in real life. He looked like a giant hero of old.

"I LIKE YOU!" said the Emperor. "MORE! I want to see a statue of me and my favourite snakubine, ROTILLA! Someone fetch ROTILLA!"

The doors slammed open. But it was not Rotilla.

"Infamy!" shouted an impressive-looking lizard-Kind in sweeping black robes. "See! An intruder has desecrated the rest-nest of the Foot that Stamps the Fallen! Guards! Seize her! Kill her! Then kill yourselves for allowing her inside! I told Your Excellence that we should use my priests to guard your private chamber. The Emperor's Own soldiers do not have the wits! They blemish your great name."

The shame-filled gila guards lumbered towards Lana. The lizard-Kind in black robes came smoothly behind. His black eyes bored into Lana, utterly without warmth. His guards seized her with heavy hands.

"Ho, steady there, Arch Protector Malachai!" said the Emperor, a little uncertain. "This girl's a talent! Look at this fine likeness she's crafted of me. The teeth are particularly good. It used to be my bath!"

Malachai squinted up at the statue. His tongue licked out and tasted the air carefully. He did not appear to like what he saw. Lana shivered. This was a Kind to be afraid of. She knew that the Arch

Protector was the highest position in the Order of the True. Usually the Arch Protector resided at the Temple of the Creator and rarely set foot in the palace. Religion and matters of court were meant to be kept separate. That was what Lana's uncle had told her. It seemed things had changed.

"Your wisdom is infinite, O Mind that Masters all Matters." Malachai turned away from the statue, unmoved. "But she is a shadow-blessed witch who consorts with human rebels. Like all spies, she will die, painfully and at length – after she has given us all her secrets."

The Emperor shrugged his agreement, as if he was bored of the whole thing already.

"Dammee, Malachai! What a shame that she is a spy. She has a gift . . . Though you're right, she does have that awful skin, too. Sorry, girl. If you were as beautiful as your mother, I would say, 'No, she must live! I'll marry her!'"

"Her mother? What?" said Malachai. For the first time, he seemed less in control of everything. He'd even forgotten to give the Emperor an appropriate title.

"Can't you see it?" said the Emperor, turning back to his cauldron of meat. "You remember Lahara, one of the most beautiful Kind I've ever seen? She was a Shadowscale, just like this one. Shame she lost her mind with those visions. I would have happily made her my wife. I blame the Mothers of Fate for corrupting her with their power. I'll admit those female seers give me the heebie-jeebies! Ha!"

"The daughter of Lahara Shadowscale," repeated Malachai. He looked again at Lana, this time more carefully. Lana averted her eyes, feeling suddenly like she didn't dare to look back.

Malachai nodded. "Again, a thousand apologies for this unwelcome intrusion, O Generous Giver and Taker of All Life." He began to move backwards towards the door, bowing. He made it look easy. "Take her away – but be gentle. Perhaps we should have a more . . . *friendly* chat, my dear. There are renovations being made to the Temple of the Creator. We are adding some more decorative touches. I'm sure we can make use of your special talents. Not only is your magic strong, your artistic eye is sublime. Your likeness of the Emperor is extraordinary . . . isn't that right, O Highest Reptile of Our Most Noble Race?"

The Emperor grunted but did not look up from his golden bowl as Lana was walked away.

10

A Human Song

"*We were on the ship the Talontree,*
when the whale rose up and broke the sea . . ."

The man's clear tenor voice soared high above the creak of rigging and the rush of water against the hull. He might have been a miner heading for a dirty, dangerous job in the Burrows for little pay, but he sounded free and full of joy.

"*We lowered the boats and rowed away,*
never knowing if we'd see another day . . .
ROW, MY BRAVE BOYS, ROW!"

The other humans crashed in, adding their voices in many parts. The great chords of their knotted song boomed bravely out across the ocean.

Jonas kept himself to himself. He did not sing with

the miners. He hadn't sung in years – even though he'd loved chanting in the past. He'd had a good voice, too. Some of his happiest memories were late-night sessions with his tribe, sending bright songs whirling up into the night like the sparks from their fires.

Watching the miners over the four days of the voyage, he'd realised they were also a tribe. They might not have been as free as his people had been, but they had their code and their proud traditions. They kept their dignity.

Last night, on the cramped, stinking lower deck, he'd watched from his hammock as Kolya – a boy his own age – went through the manhood rites. Kolya hadn't cried out as the burning brand scarred his cheeks. Jonas watched him afterwards, celebrating with the other miners. Despite all the pain and suffering ahead, they'd found joy in that moment. Kolya had gone in a boy and come out a man.

Jonas had never had his own manhood ceremony. It should have been two summers ago. He realised he would never know what Kolya was feeling.

There was other differences between them: Kolya had friends, and family. Jonas didn't even have one person he could call either. In fact, for the first time in his life, Jonas was truly alone. It felt wildly strange.

Even after everyone in his tribe had died, he'd had Seth. The wyvern had always been there, no matter what. When they'd had a row, or when the wyvern had flown off on one of his mysterious journeys, Jonas could still feel their connection at the back of his mind, like a second shadow.

But now Seth was *really* gone. In his place there was an empty sensation that Jonas had never felt before. Jonas probed this space, as if he was feeling out a missing tooth. Jonas hadn't realised that banishing Seth would cause them to separate so fully. Was Seth so far away that their connection was broken for now? Would he even come back from the Land of What Was? Was their connection gone, and the death-song with it? Jonas didn't like to admit it, but he felt vulnerable. He didn't know how he would react in a fight. Jonas had imagined many times what it might be like being free of Seth, and never more so than recently, when he had longed for it. But now it had happened, it didn't feel good.

The dreams had stopped too. This was a shame – Jonas had liked flying. He didn't like admitting it, but he even missed the wyvern's awful, bloodthirsty humour. Sometimes a situation was so bad the only thing that helped was a bad joke.

He could just imagine what Seth would be saying

now: "Look at you, boy, moping about like a seasick cat. You want to be friends with these pathetic mine boys? You want to sing with them? They'll all be dead of black lung before they see thirty winters. I wouldn't even eat them. They'd taste of rock."

The singing suddenly stopped.

"Shut yer awful racket!" roared a harsh, rasping voice. The huge, lumpy shape of Groesh, the miners' mole-Kind overseer, had emerged on to the deck. "I didn't travel all the way from the Burrows to the Ruby Isle to bring back singers. It pains my delicate ears. I can tell ye, when ye get to my mine there ain't going to be time for all this pretty chanting."

"But we aren't at the mine, sir," said Kolya. "You've hired us to dig. We will – and hard. But this time is ours. It's in the contract!"

"Insolent clut!" Groesh's fleshy pink nose snuffled at the boy. Without warning, one of his shovel-like paws backhanded Kolya across the deck. The mole-Kind's sharp claws left deep scratches in his chest. The wounds leaked blood – not deep enough to kill, but if they weren't dressed quickly they might get infected. Groesh grinned. "Yer mine now, paper or no paper. I'll show you a contract!"

He lifted up his arm to strike again.

The mole was going to kill the boy. Some miners

cowered in shock. One or two stepped in front of Groesh, including a heavyset woman holding a frying pan, but the mole flung them aside.

Kolya stared at the fallen woman. "Aunt Cleo!"

"I'm going to make an example of you, boy," said Groesh, towering over Kolya.

"Stop!" Jonas stepped forward. The mole turned towards him, blinking with surprise.

Usually, at this point in a fight, Jonas's mind would be fizzing with visions of his own death. He would be seeing a spray of hot blood as sharp claws slashed across his throat, or feel heavy chains wrapped around him as he was thrown into the ocean attached to an anchor.

This was the death-song. If you knew just how fragile the thread of your life really was, it gave you power.

Normally the death-song shrieked in Jonas's mind, but now it was barely a whisper. Jonas felt nothing. He was naked.

Alone.

"Foolsome," hissed Groesh. "Very foolsome."

The mole lunged forward.

Time didn't slow down. Jonas jumped back, desperate, trying not to panic. The deadly claws hissed past him, faster than he could follow.

He could smell the overpowering stink on the mole-Kind's fur. He could taste his own fear.

Another swipe. Jonas dodged again, but not quickly enough. The fist lamped his shoulder, slamming him into the deck. Jonas felt wetness in his mouth. He spat red blood on the wood.

"This weren't your fight, you fool. You aren't mine. But you'll die all the same." Groesh raised his fist high for a final, killing blow.

Jonas saw the sun glinting on the bone-hard claws.

Maybe it was the blood, maybe it was his closeness to real danger, but at last, a little power surged into him. As the mole's fist slammed down, he was on his feet eel-fast, leaping away.

Groesh's claws stabbed into the deck, gouging deep into the wood. He stuck there, fast.

The mole hissed with annoyance. He pulled and pulled.

"I'm fixed 'ere, you sniggle-worm!"

Jonas acted on instinct. He grabbed a vicious, pointed tool and raised it above his head. It would crack the mole's skull like a nut. He felt a savage joy rising inside him. He'd beaten this monster by himself. Maybe he didn't need Seth.

But even half-blind, Groesh saw enough to squeal.

"Enough!" rasped a voice. The rough raccoon-

Kind captain stepped down from the raised cockpit on to the lower deck, the gold of his many chained necklaces and jewelled bracelets glinting in the pristine light reflecting off the ocean. "Human! Drop that marlinspike. Groesh, I'll have none of this roughery on my ship!"

"He cheeked me, Captain," growled the mole-Kind. "It ain't right for a scumming human. They'll get ideas."

"I saw what happened, Groesh," snapped the captain, twirling his magnificent whiskers. "Treat your employees as you like on land, but I won't abide foul handling on my ship. Besides, I liked their singing."

A faint cheer sounded from the humans. Growling more threats, Groesh hauled himself below deck.

"You're a brave lad," said the captain, coming across to Jonas. "But the next time you raise hands against your betters, I'll throw you to the sharks."

He stomped away, muttering about dirt-loving lubbers.

"Thank you," said Kolya. The boy grinned at Jonas. "That was not your fight."

"No problem," said Jonas. He tried to smile back. It came out all wrong.

Kolya didn't seem to mind. "You're a quiet one,

aren't you? I saw you watching us."

Kolya's aunt – Cleo, was it? – came over, dusting off the frying pan that had been thrown from her hand when Groesh knocked her aside.

"Always the quiet ones though, isn't it? Meek as mice, and then taking on giant moles three times their size."

"I've never seen anyone move so fast!" said Kolya. "How did you learn to fight like that?"

"A lot of practice," said Jonas.

Kolya laughed. Jonas tried another smile.

This one worked. It felt good.

Kolya looked up questioningly at Cleo, who nodded. "Hey, how about sharing some mead and dried pinefruit?" asked Kolya. "We've got a load down in the cabin. It's our last stash. You better get it while you can."

Jonas paused. He might have had a lot of practice at fighting, but he hadn't had a lot of practice being with other humans. The truth was Jonas had never trusted himself with others of his race. What if the death-song took over? What if Seth got bored and played tricks on the humans, or even manipulated a fight?

But Seth wasn't here.

Jonas's heart still thudded from the fight with

Groesh, adrenaline energising his muscles. This was a different feeling to what Jonas usually experienced after fighting, when the death-song faded and he only felt shame, regret, tiredness, his whole body aching and sore and tired.

Jonas felt *alive*.

"Pinefruit, you say?" Jonas said. "I don't think I've tried that. Kolya, is it? Nice to meet you. You too, Cleo. My name is Jonas."

11

The Cave of Relics

During the day the breeze was always blowing.

Like many scholars' rooms in the Tower of Forbidden Knowledge, the crumbled gaps where Gael's windows had once been looked out west. As the cool mountain air met the muggy heat of the valley, the winds grew throughout the day. Gael's quarters were filled with the sound of rustling paper, as the teetering stacks of notes, maps, diagrams and charts were rustled by the wind. Thousands of whispering books lined the shelves and were piled up on the floor of the large library adjacent to his study and makeshift bedchamber. A door from the library led out on to a large, crumbling balcony, from which Gael could hear the humming and spinning of his atmospheric instruments joining in the chorus.

"I'll have that tea now, Roshni," called Gael from his study, without lifting his beak from his book. He'd been sitting there for three days now, reading, reading and getting no further.

The human brought his tea almost too promptly. He sometimes wondered how she knew what he would want before he asked. Still, it was better than trying to summon Avis over the gale. Roshni took delight in creating a larder in an old cupboard, filling the shelves with tea, snacks and provisions for light, tasty meals that she prepared on a small stove. After some persuasion, Roshni had convinced him to allow her out to the food market in the centre of the Hallowed Vale, where she bought fresh rabbit, mutton and a variety of insects. Catering to her own tastes, she had even found a small human market in the outskirts of the bird city, where she bought fresh fruit and vegetables, herbs and spices. She could be gone all day, and sometimes she would sleep on the hills overlooking the city. Gael didn't like it when she was gone too long. He got worried. It was a strange feeling; it interested him. Why did he care about this human girl so much? He found himself pacing his quarters when she was gone longer than expected, and had to stop himself jumping with nervous relief when she reappeared – *literally* reappeared. After all her worries about sneaking into the Tower, the girl now thought nothing of using the Trickster Ring to slip, invisible, in and out of the fortress. Gael found himself warning her repeatedly not to carry meat past the vulture-Kind guards. Roshni came up with the idea of obscuring the smell of the carrion with some strong-smelling ointment Gael used to moisturise his feathers, which she spread over her cloak. Against all his considerably better judgement, Gael was even persuaded to allow Roshni to use the striding stone, which allowed the user to teleport – simply a case of waving the stone through the air, and visualising a location they wished to be transported to. "It's really a crude form of teleportation compared to my own methods, and not a little dangerous," he had said to Roshni. "Imagine if you accidentally thought about the ocean and you ended up teleporting yourself to the bottom of the sea. It's *only* for emergencies, hear me? If you are attacked by bandits in the hills, or an Order of the True priest takes a disliking to you."

"Of course," she'd said. "What else would I use the stone for but emergencies?"

As Gael watched her bring him his tea, he wondered, not for the first time, not for the hundredth time, if he just *might* be getting too close to this human girl.

"Ah, that new herb infusion is my favourite. It's the elderberries, I think. Who would have thought, a bird-Kind, enjoying fruit!" Carrying the tray across the room, she braced herself against the gentle sway of the floor as the central turret of the Tower of Forbidden Knowledge rocked like a ship in the wind.

She didn't spill a drop.

"My thanks," grunted Gael.

"Don't drink it straight away, Master," said Roshni. "You'll burn your beak."

The wind caught hold of Gael's notes and threatened to blow them out of the window, into the void. Roshni dropped a rock on top of them to hold them fast.

"What would I do without you, my dear?" said Gael. He still hadn't looked up.

"Shall I check the readings on the balcony, Master?" said Roshni.

He glanced up to watch her working outside on the exposed terrace. She didn't seem to mind the thousand-foot drop, either. This human girl really was a marvel.

It took courage. The balcony was extremely exposed, which was ideal for the delicate instruments he had arranged out there. Several anemographs measured minute fluctuations in magical fields, while various windmill-like devices recorded their power and direction. A large antique barometograph dropped tiny crystal balls into an augury bowl whenever a particularly large flux occurred. Yesterday, Roshni had figured out a way to improve the accuracy of the anemographs using a redsteel needle for the gauge. The metal was lighter than the old lead needle, and resistant to corrosion.

"Anything interesting?" said Gael. "Do I need to come out there?"

"Not really, Master," said Roshni. "There appears to be a small amount of turbulence going on in the north, but I believe it is just background fluctuation. Nothing to worry about."

"Good, good," said Gael – but this was a big lie. The truth was, things were *far* from good.

Ever since he had realised that Malachai was looking for the Tablets of the Creator, Gael had been worried. The Tablets were immensely powerful, and horribly dangerous in the wrong hands. Having met the lizard, Gael was pretty certain that Malachai had a nasty pair of hands – with sharp claws too.

Yes, he might recognise a danger, but that didn't mean Gael knew what to do. He'd read every book he could think of. He'd combed his memory for anything he might have forgotten. But he'd drawn a total blank.

Where were the Tablets said to have been kept? Hadn't he known that once? The pain of this thought nagged at him like a rotten tooth. It was worse, somehow, that he had forgotten. The key to everything was locked up in his head, and he couldn't get in.

Hmm. Perhaps it was time for desperate measures. Jog something loose, that might work, mightn't it?

"You are muttering and staring into the distance again, Master," said Roshni. "You told me to nudge you when you did that for more than five minutes."

"Ho! Hey, what? Oh, yes, thanks," said Gael. "Was pondering hard, you know?"

"Can I help you with anything?" said Roshni.

"Help me?" Gael blinked at her, his eyes still slightly fogged. Roshni's question seemed innocent enough but Gael was still amazed at how much he had let this girl into his confidence over such a short time. After centuries of avoiding close relationships with mortals, maintaining complete privacy, he felt like an elderly grandparent tutoring a fledgling.

Perhaps he was overthinking things. Roshni was useful, there was nothing more to it. He nodded decisively and jumped to his feet. "Well, I suppose you can. Try and ask good questions, eh? You're good at that. Come on."

"Where are we going?"

"To the larder – or the broom cupboard that you have made into a larder. It has a nice big keyhole."

Gael marched through the library, on through the space in an old crumbled exterior wall, into a room filled with black cloaks. Roshni had laundered them and they hung on pegs. Beyond, there were the remnants of a battered old wooden door – one of the few hinged doors that remained in the whole of the Tower. The room was east facing and the coolest in his quarters, with just enough gap in the bricks to allow the wind inside, without being wide enough to attract insects and birds to the food and tea Roshni had stored there. Gael reached inside his cloak. He tried to summon what he was looking for, but the artefact was a stubborn thing – it was powerful magic, among the most powerful in his whole cloak, and often powerful magic had a will of its own.

There!

He felt thick gnarled metal in his talons and pulled

out a large iron key with a flourish. It was ancient and covered with a delicate spiderweb of verdigris.

"The door's not locked, Master," said Roshni. "I've been using it all day."

"Of course *this* door isn't locked, my dear – but then, we aren't hunting *biscuits*."

He shoved the key into the lock and jiggled it about.

"Probably quite stiff, haven't used it in a few decades, you see? Ah, there. In we go!"

With a groaning screech, the key turned. Gael shoved the door open to reveal a space that most certainly wasn't a larder. In place of the neat shelves that Roshni kept well stocked with biscuits, cucumber and banana-nuts (Gael's favourite) was a dark cave lit by glowing fungal light.

"What's going on?" said Roshni, amazed.

"I was hoping you would ask better questions than that, human," sighed Gael. "But I suppose the surprise has got to you. The key is magical. Whatever door you insert the key into will open up to this cave, my archive. It's where I keep my relics safe. My cloak can't house everything I own. I have been alive a long time."

"A dragon skull . . ." Roshni whispered in awe. Gael watched the girl stare about her in wonder, her face lit up a ghostly green by the shroomlight. The cave wall had hundreds of small niches carved into it. Most held a single object, though the dust was so thick it was sometimes hard for even Gael to tell what they were.

"Where is this place?"

"A better question. The cave is in another world altogether. A safe, dead world. No one lives there, so you won't have anyone stumbling in, if you see what I mean. Less to worry about."

"And why are you showing me this?"

"Now that is a much better question still. I am showing *you* so I have to explain things to you. I've often found that helps me to remember. It dusts off the forgotten corners of my mind."

Gael walked forward and picked up a glass sphere; when he blew on it, it began to glow brightly.

"Bit of light will help. Now, let's see." He held the glow-globe high. "These over here are some my most valuable relics. They once belonged to humans like you. Great heroes – legends, even. The Masters of the Kind."

"So the legends are true?" said Roshni. Her eyes were very wide, and she trailed a hand over a small wooden shield with hollowed-out shapes carved in the wood, as if objects had once been embedded there.

"Mostly. They weren't always heroes, for one thing."

"What's that one there?" asked Roshni, pointing at a large curved talon.

Gael picked it up. "This is the Talon of Aephos."

Roshni gasped. "Aephos the Healer?"

"The very same. She was a mighty old-Kind indeed, one of the oldest. I knew her in many of her incarnations. She had a habit of dying, then reawakening from inside that volcano of hers. I suppose you can't blame her. She was phoenix-Kind. The Talon has magical healing properties, I believe, pretty handy."

"So you actually knew Aephos?" said Roshni.

"Oh yes," said Gael absently. His bright, inquisitive eyes were flickering over the nooks, searching for something he couldn't find.

"So you are . . . what – a *thousand* years old?"

"Try multiplying that by itself. Or maybe I'm older," sighed Gael. "You somewhat lose track of the years after a while. Time's endless river rushes on, that sort of thing."

"But what have you been doing for all that time?"

"Watching doors, you might say. I am the Threshold Keeper, the Guardian of the Many Worlds," said Gael solemnly. "I keep balance. I maintain the gateways between the worlds. It has always been my duty and it always will be."

It took a lot to silence Roshni, but this response stopped her questions for a moment.

The truth was, Gael was feeling his many years of life. His memories grew dimmer, not so much because they were forgotten but because there were so many to keep in their proper order. Even answering a question like "How many times has the entire cosmos nearly ended?" was hard.

The answer was too many cursed times. Gael sighed, as he paced through the cave. The dusty objects only made him feel depressed. He couldn't even remember what a lot of them were, and certainly not their history. It was a shame that the splendour of these artefacts was dying as Gael's memory faded. He was no closer to remembering what he had come for.

"What exactly did you do with the Masters?" said Roshni, seeming somewhat recovered.

"I used to help them, when their cause seemed right. It was not always the correct choice. I have since learned that choosing sides only leads to disappointment. It is far better not to be involved."

Roshni considered this. "That doesn't sound useful. What if you knew for certain their cause was right, or good?"

"Most evil is done by people who consider themselves good," said Gael. "This is a hard truth. Better to observe and mind my task. I keep the pathways open, I watch the ways and hold the flux in balance. Let others rush about. Just as day follows night, evil will pass and good will have its time."

"You sound like a tired old bird," said Roshni.

"I am certainly that," said Gael.

"But, Master, you can surely see that something is wrong now!" Roshni spoke more boldly than she had ever dared before. "You fought side by side with humans in their glory. You know how far we have fallen. How greatly we are now oppressed. It is not just!"

"And when humans were the oppressors, was that just?" Gael asked.

Roshni's face was flushed. "Master, you must choose a side. Don't you want to see Malachai thwarted? What of the rumours that he intends to replace the Emperor with a new monarch he can fully control? His puppet? We humans will never have peace if that happens."

Gael shook his head. "I cannot take sides."

"And if the Order of the True take control of the Hallowed Vale, what then?"

"I will move somewhere else, as I have done before. I will continue to mind the gateways. Please stop pestering me, Roshni!"

"Pestering?" Roshni's hopeful expression faded, returning to a plain, unreadable countenance. She masked her disappointment quickly, that girl. She masked all her emotions pretty well, come to think of it. Which was why it was odd seeing her speaking so passionately about the human cause – the rebel cause. Because that was what it had sounded like. You couldn't blame her really – for hoping the humans might rise up, defeat the Kind, and lo and behold perfect harmony would be restored. Peace and justice for all! Pah! True, the world was not just. But then, was it ever?

"So, this Talon . . ." She pointed at the dusty, curved bone. It looked wickedly sharp still. "Can I study it? It could be a part of my . . . apprenticeship."

"Apprenticeship!" Gael was amused by this idea. "Is that what this is?"

"I think you know it is," said Roshni. "I've been learning a lot. And you teach me well. You did not have to."

She smiled, half cheeky, half innocent.

"You are right, I didn't. Ach. Very well," Gael agreed. "You may borrow the Talon. But be careful.

It is a powerful thing."

They returned to the kitchen. Gael watched her cradling the artefact, her face lit up with fierce delight – like a young chick after its first flight.

Gael was surprised to realise he was pleased that she was happy.

Was Gael fooling himself that Roshni was merely a useful presence to have around? Could it be that he actually cared about this human? Certainly, Gael had never before put up with anyone 'pestering' him, as he had put it. And yet he found himself regretting his harsh words to her.

Could it be that, for the tiniest moment while Roshni had been 'pestering' him, he had begun to agree with what she was saying?

12

The Inspection

Within a week, a following wind brought the ship in sight of the northern kingdom of Anoros. Jonas had watched as the sea turned from turquoise to grey, and the colourful ray fish were replaced by darker shoals of mackerel and other cold-water fish.

"Not worth the bother. All bone." That was what Seth used to say about mackerel. Jonas couldn't help but smile at the memory of Seth choking and spitting out fragments of broken skeleton.

Seth was gone.

Jonas had to keep telling himself that.

Still, Jonas thought he had a point about mackerel. He was sick to death of picking rib-bones from his teeth, and while the pickled flesh prepared by Cleo was tasty at first, it had quickly become sickly. It didn't help that Cleo always insisted Jonas finish every scrap on his plate.

"Growing boys need their food," she'd told him, arching an eyebrow at his unfinished plate. "The trick is take the whole spine out in one go. You'll choke on a bone otherwise."

Jonas had watched as the distant coastline changed day by day. By the time they reached the port town of Sephronia, on the border of Morta and Anoros, the cliffs had grown harsh and desolate. Darkness came and went quicker in this land, though the heat was worse than southern Morta in the middle of the day. This was rugged, dry terrain – the lands of the Burrows. Many other quarry ships passed them, carrying loads of rock mined from the tunnels and bound for the corners of the Four Kingdoms. Olive trees grew crooked on the dusty hills and the dry air was spiced with the smoky smell of liquorice grass.

It had not been a happy ship – and not just because of the endless meals of soused mackerel. Groesh had retreated to his cabin to lick his wounds, but his foul temper leached poison through the thin walls. Kolya and his friends' faces were grim too, as if they all knew the fury that awaited them in the mines. They had stopped singing. From what Kolya had told Jonas, through their long talks, long meals together and long days spent lying next to each other on deck, the human workers had been promised better conditions in the Burrows than those they faced in the redsteel mines on the Ruby Isle. Mining jobs were running short on the Ruby Isle – too many humans had arrived looking for work. Kolya said they had been foolish in believing Groesh's promises that they would be treated well. As soon as they had signed their contracts, he had turned violent.

Soon, the ship rounded the headland and the bay of Sephronia opened before them. It was a famous anchorage, protected on three sides by barrier islands, and dotted with the bright sails of fishing skiffs. The hills were scarred by the whitestone quarries of the upper Burrows, and the port looked busy as cranes loaded ships with freshly cut stone.

Their ship had just dropped anchor when a large dark galley came racing out of the port. The ship was heading straight for them. Its sail was black and painted with a crescent "C". Jonas recognised the symbol and realised where he had seen it. The same shape had been carved into the metal rings that had dangled from Rahziin's staff.

It was the symbol of the Order of the True. This wasn't good.

"What's about?" growled the captain, watching them approach, oars churning, through his glass. "I don't like this one sniff."

"Inspection!" a voice roared through a bullhorn. "Prepare to be boarded!"

The captain protested that his papers were in order. "We're just carrying lathes, man. And a few miners, nothing more."

"Stand aside. The Order of the True commands it."

At that name, a chill settled over the boat. A couple of robed priests stepped on to the boat, followed by soldiers whose heavy armour rattled as they stomped across the decks.

The priest in charge was a frilled lizard-Kind with dozens of brass rings clanking on his forearms. The sight of the ornaments brought back the memory of Rahziin, and her body lying on the dusty ground of the camp. Jonas pictured Seth standing over the corpse, and he felt a jab of fury. But he felt a twinge of uncertainty along with it. Jonas was not used to experiencing fear. He never really had when Seth was around.

A part of him could not help wishing Seth was by his side, ready to protect him if the priests made trouble. Jonas made a ward to the moon goddess, praying the soldiers would move on quickly.

He knew more than most that prayers were never answered.

The armoured figures disappeared below deck. Their search was not gentle. Everyone could hear the sound of crates being smashed and machinery breaking. Standing in the crowd of humans on deck, Jonas noticed the glances passing between them. They were right to be scared of the Order, of course – but there was a deeper terror here.

Something was wrong.

His hand went to the familiar weight of his twin swords hanging at his belt. Suddenly Jonas was glad that he had dressed to leave early.

"Found it!" roared a voice from the hold. "The villains!"

Soon, soldiers were hauling out heavy wraps of redsteel weapons sheathed in oilcloth. "They were hidden inside the rollers, Magister. Most cunning."

"So our little tip-off was right," said the lizard. "And these are rebel weapons, intended for the resistance. Fine, expensive work too."

He picked up one of the swords and swished it through the air.

All about him, Jonas could smell the thick fear. Jonas's senses heightened but without the normal clarity and fearless purpose of his death-song. His own death was very near – as was all the other humans'. There would be a massacre soon. The humans were unarmed. The soldiers that surrounded them now carried spears and wicked curved knives.

"What did you know of this treachery?" The leader spread his leathery skin collar as he advanced on the captain. "Why betray your own Kind?"

"I-I didn't. I don't. I know nothin', yer grace," begged the raccoon-Kind. "Believe me! I took it as a consignment, s'all."

"Lies!" snarled the magister. The sword flashed in the sun and the captain fell to the deck, clutching his bleeding arm. "Wipe out the rebel scum. All of them."

The soldiers advanced, grinning.

Jonas tried to let the death-song build in him, tried to dampen the jangling fear swimming in his gut. But his legs felt like lead. He could hear his own breath juddering through his chest.

And then Jonas felt the worn finger grooves on his swords where his father's hands had once rested. He remembered the words his father had spoken to him once.

True courage is not acting without fear but acting in spite of it.

Jonas let the muscle memory of his father's sword-fighting lessons take over.

Although his arms trembled, he forced his hands to remain loose around the hilts of his swords. He picked his moment. As the soldiers pulled out their weapons, Jonas lunged, as swift and merciless as a mountain lion. Before they had even raised their weapons, Jonas had killed two, finding the gaps in their armour between the helmet and chest plate with precise stabs of his blades. He caught the look of stunned surprise in their eyes before they died.

Some of the other soldiers scrambled away in terror, while others gathered up weapons and crouched, ready for Jonas.

After a moment of shocked astonishment, Kolya and his friends and family members grabbed up their smuggled weapons and joined the fight – but they might as well have not.

Thrust by thrust, Jonas attacked the remaining group of soldiers. Usually, Jonas fought in a trance of death, moving without thinking, barely aware of each thrust and parry. But this time, he was aware of every strike. He spun and ducked and danced around the Kind, whose speed was hampered by their heavy armour. Every attack was a leap of faith. The death-song was there faintly, but Jonas could not picture the clear warnings of his own death like he usually could. He had to trust himself, trust his experience, his father's training.

He realised that he was fighting in the style that the tribes had called "the relentless storm", where every movement led into the next, designed to maintain momentum and stop opponents from asserting themselves. It was more like a dance, wearing the opponent down with sustained jabs and thrusts and slices, and very different from the crushing, direct, superhumanly powerful blows that Jonas fought with when taken over by the death-song. His strikes no longer carried the death-song's supreme, unnatural strength and speed.

Jonas remembered something his father had told him once. It was after Jonas had begun to best him in the training circle, when his father had given him the twin scimitars:

"Jonas, my son, here are my blades. The Swords of What Was and What Will Be are the hope of our tribe. In you we carry the hope of our ancestors and the hope of the future. When you fight, you must channel the past, your skill and training. You must rely on it, trust in it – this is what is represented by the Sword of What Was. But you must also be ready to change, to adapt and adjust to each opponent –

this is represented by the Sword of What Will Be. And you, Jonas, you must be the present, the now. Let your instinct guide you. Channel the forces of the past and future into each moment of the battle."

Jonas had never fully understood what his father had said. The death-song had always guided him. But now, fighting with the death-song so faint, and relying on his own skill, on his own training, Jonas finally knew what his father meant. His weapons became part of him and he trusted in himself fully, trusted in the past and what he had learned, trusted in the future and his own survival, and most of all trusted in himself. Jonas noticed everything – every slight movement of his opponents, every time they readied to strike.

After what might have been seconds – though it could have been minutes – of pressurising the group of soldiers with his relentless attacks, striking their armour with a flurry of blows, keeping them pinned back and draining their energy and morale, he forced them backwards towards the side of the ship.

In one sudden dancing movement, Jonas swivelled and leaped backwards, ducking and spinning and slicing the rope that held the ship's mainsail into the wind. The heavy horizontal boom at the bottom of the sail swung across the deck, smashing the soldiers overboard. Jonas did not fancy their chances swimming with armour on.

Jonas looked around for the pair of Order priests, and saw they were back on board their ship, which was sailing away towards the harbour. Jonas knew if he allowed them to escape, they would alert the soldiers at the port. But with the rope holding the boom severed, Jonas's own ship had spun windward and bobbed there, stationary. There was no way they could catch up with the black galley.

"That was . . ." Kolya clapped Jonas on the back. He was grinning like he was mad, utterly unable to believe what had just happened before his eyes. "That was . . . completely . . . terrifying! And sort of beautiful, the way you fought. I've never seen anything like it. Thank you! Thank you! You've saved us all."

There were shouts behind them, and a loud splash. Groesh, the mole-Kind overseer, had jumped overboard to save himself.

Jonas knew he should kill Groesh, but a sudden disgust stayed his hand. He looked at the bloody carnage that stained the deck. There was actual blood washing like sea foam through the scuppers.

Seth was not here, but still Jonas had done this. He'd killed all these people by himself.

And deep down, he'd *enjoyed* it.

Jonas felt better now than he had felt in days – the pressure that had been building up inside him had been released. He felt light, airy – as if he might fly away like a wyvern.

This was troubling.

All around him, people were praising him and asking questions. But he could not really hear them. He watched, half-dreaming, as the ship prepared to sail away from the harbour. Even the Kind among the crew were eager to leave Sephronia. After the massacre, the Order of the True would be coming for them, as would the soldiers of the Emperor's navy. Human or Kind, they were as good as dead if they did not get far away as soon as possible.

They fixed the severed rope and sailed away from Sephronia, further north into Anoros. The winds were behind them and they should get a head start on any pursuing ships. The captain of the ship agreed to moor up in a sheltered cove, and the humans could disembark under the cover of dark. The raccoon-Kind kept giving Jonas fearful glances, and Jonas suspected the sailor would have done anything he asked of him. "I'll probably wreck the ship in the cove, anyway," the captain said, fiddling with the gold chains around his neck. "Pretend all the crew were drowned. Might be my only way of escaping them priests. They do hold a grudge, them Order of the True folk. They'll call me a human sympathiser. I'm just trying to make a living!"

Jonas considered things, sitting alone at the bow of the vessel. With the deaths of the Order of the True priests and the soldiers, he had put his mission in jeopardy. Soldiers would be scouring the land for humans. Not only that, if he could be identified as Slayer, there was nothing stopping the Emperor overruling Grashkor and ordering Jonas's execution. He needed to hide out for a while. Lie low until the Order found something else to turn their violent attentions to.

Jonas knew that had he been fighting with the full power of the death-song, he would never have allowed the priests to get away. And yet, even though the death-song was weaker, Jonas still felt guilt as the adrenaline of the fight wore off. Guilt and pain. More often than not, Jonas came out of fights unscathed. But now he had a cut on his cheek, bruises up and down his body. Without Seth nearby, Jonas was a worse fighter, and yet he was still not free of the guilt of killing.

It was almost night before he moved from his position. The other humans turned to watch him. There was fear in their eyes – but something else, too. Something he hadn't seen before.

Hope.

"You must come with us, Jonas," said Cleo, bringing him a bowl of hot mackerel chowder and a blanket to wrap around his shoulders. "We have a base hidden with magical illusions. Our leader, the Reader, will be keen to talk to you. You could be a mighty weapon in our fight for freedom. I have never seen anyone fight like you, human or Kind."

Jonas blew on the soup to cool it down. He wasn't sure what to say. Part of him dearly wanted to go with the rebels. Actually helping people felt different and exciting.

But he knew he could not run away from the manacles. Sooner or later, the Gaoler would pull him all the way back to the Pinnacles of the Damned. Grashkor would drag him across the bottom of the ocean, if it came to that.

"I have a task that I must fulfil," he said, suddenly conscious of the weight of the manacles on his wrists.

Cleo looked at them with sharp, observant eyes.

"Do you need help with those?"

"Their magic can only be undone by the Gaoler of the Pinnacles of the Damned."

"They say the Reader is as powerful as Dalthek himself. She will know how to free you, I'm sure. We rebels are much stronger than people think. But with a mighty warrior like you fighting beside us, we will become unstoppable."

We rebels.

Jonas had always considered the human rebels far removed from his world. The wars and politics of the Four Kingdoms had been unimportant to his tribe, or to life as a prisoner or bounty hunter.

Jonas's goal for three years had been freedom. But for the first time, he wondered if he could ever truly find it while the Kind ruled over the humans. And things were getting worse for his race. It was clear that the Order of the True were gaining power and that they wouldn't stop until humans were driven out of the Four Kingdoms or wiped out entirely. Did Jonas really have a choice? Once again, Jonas half expected Seth to arrive and convince him that dreaming of a paradise where humans lived free from the terror of the Kind was just that – a dream. Seth would tell him that he needed to find the fugitive human thief so he could finally escape Grashkor – and then he could find out what had happened to his village. He could finally exact revenge.

But what then? Would Jonas return to his village, try to decipher Rahziin's prophecy, find out who had killed his people? What was revenge worth if there was nothing to look forward to afterwards?

Kolya put his arm on Jonas's shoulder. "Please, Jonas. We fight because we have to, not because we want to. We want peace."

Peace? Jonas's heart swelled. It had been a long time since anyone had needed him for anything other than killing. It had been a long time since anyone had touched him.

Jonas had to struggle to fight the tremor of emotion in his voice when he finally spoke. "I will come with you. I will help you. Free me from these manacles, and I won't rest until you – *we* – can have peace."

13

Lana's Creation

This was certainly better than torture.

Lana planted her feet firmly on the scaffolding planks and drew a deep breath. Down below her, important people were watching. She had been told that even Arch Protector Malachai himself had come to see her sculpt and paint the final designs on the roof of the Temple of the Creator.

Their voices rose dimly up to Lana, but she had no ears for them.

It was an extraordinary honour to be chosen for this task, but it was an honour that Lana fully deserved. She was the best – capable of far more already, even after these few short weeks, than artists and sculptors who had trained for dozens of years.

Lana's had been a dizzying rise through the ranks of the court artisans. Her magical talents for sculpting stone and frescoes, and animating the carved images with constant magical movement, earned her more and more duties during the final stages of the Temple of the Creator's renovation. And each task she'd been given had become increasingly larger in scale, and more important. Lana had started with small structural work, binding bricks together in the new sections of the Temple. She had moved on to adding her own motifs to stairwells. Then creating whole sculptures of the gods of the old-Kind – Sephron, Fernwing, Aephos. Finally she had been tasked with adding the finishing touches of Malachai's grand vision on the Temple roof. Lana still found it hard to recall exactly how she had managed to turn her fortunes around. From almost being thrown in the dungeons and interrogated, she now found herself standing one hundred feet in the air at the pinnacle of a rickety pyramid made of ladders, bamboo and knotted twine, about to create on the most spectacular canvas you could imagine.

Lana raised her arms above her head and closed her eyes. She felt the ancient power of the stones far beneath her feet rising within her. She channelled the power up through her body, tightening and tautening the now familiar surge as it came, until by the time it reached the tips of her splayed fingers it was as sharply focused as a redsteel scalpel.

The ceiling of the Great Chamber of the Temple of the Creator was formed of huge slabs of veiny, rose-pink marble. As Lana reached her mind out towards it, its cloudy surface melted like candle wax.

A gasp came up from the crowd below.

Lana began her work.

Painting and shaping with her fingers and her mind, she carved a dreamscape in stone. Her subject was the rise of the new-Kind, and she started with the Spawning, when the Creator had formed the new-Kind from the dying life force of the old-Kind. As she shaped and coloured, traced and contoured, Lana used her magic to give her scene a soul.

A myriad of new-Kind spawned and tumbled in ever-evolving abandon. Lizard and lion, wolf and wyvern, ant and armadillo. All the new-Kind, in all their majesty, danced on the ceiling in the joy of their first steps.

Only the Creator was still. The god's form was obscured by a cloak decorated with groups of oval spirals, like insect wings, and his face was covered by shadow. It was said that the Creator had no single form. Or rather, his form was pure magic, constantly shifting into new shapes; his body was made from the raw creative magic of the Netherplane – the same magic he had used to fashion the Many Worlds, and the old-Kind, before he had finally spawned from those ancient gods the many new-Kind.

Lana worked all morning, without rest, delighting in the task. She was unaware of the watchers below. It was only when she had finished, and was climbing down the scaffolding, her mind half broken by such concentrated effort, that she became aware of the applause that echoed through the Great Chamber.

"Magnificent!" cried Malachai, striding towards her. He clasped Lana's fingers in his own and drew her to him. She had no choice in this. He turned to face the crowd, still holding her close.

"Fine work will be rewarded! The Emperor has already awarded Lana and her brood a new nest. All hail the great artist!"

The cheers rang out again. Malachai smiled down at Lana.

"A word with you, Master Sculptor?" he asked.

Lana could not refuse him.

They walked into a cloister. During the weeks Lana had been working in the Temple, Malachai had admired her work from afar, occasionally interrupting his many meetings to talk with her and express his pleasure over Lana's creations. Lana felt great pride during these moments. She also guessed that Malachai made a scene of praising Lana to show that he accepted her. That, despite her shadow-blessing, she was welcome here. It had taken a week or so for the other artisans and priests to stop looking at her flickering shadow with suspicion. But if Lana was the ward of the Arch Protector, they could hardly argue she was cursed, dangerous or any of the other silly ideas people had about her.

"There is a fine mansion ready for you in the palace square," said Malachai. "It once belonged to a treacherous cat-Kind member of our Order, but she is gone now. A fitting nest for a brood as illustrious as yours, close to the main palace in Whitestone." He smiled at her.

"My thanks," she mumbled.

Malachai continued, "You have probably guessed that I knew your mother. I am sorry I have not been able to talk much about her yet. She had great potential, great power, just like you. It is a shame her visions proved so costly."

Lana paused. She was wary of insulting Malachai, but she couldn't pass up the opportunity to find out more. "My uncle said my mother claimed to have been visited by the Creator himself. I think I have a memory of one of those visions, when she was on her deathbed. She was describing him to me. She said he had come to her many times through her life. She called him the Father. I have based my depiction of the Creator on my mother's dreams of him."

A flash of unreadable emotion passed over Malachai's scaled face – anger, perhaps, insult, and maybe something else. Curiosity.

"I hope I haven't insulted you, Arch Protector."

"Of course not, girl. Yes, I remember the Mothers of Fate talking of what Lahara claimed she saw in her prophecies. But you cannot always take what those visionaries tell you as the complete truth. Fate is constantly changing. It is impossible to entirely predict it. Your mother did not have your talent, Lana. She was a conjuror, but not shadow-blessed like you." He pointed to the wreaths of shadow that flickered over the right side of Lana's body. "It is right to be wary of an elemental blessing, but they can be the sign of the touch of the Creator. You carry pure magic within you – the magic that the Creator used to fashion the worlds. You are even more powerful than your mother. You must not fear her madness. You must embrace your powers. Then think what you could achieve!" He swept his hand towards the images moving across the ceiling of the Temple. "This is just the start."

"Thank you, Arch Protector. I have never met another elemental-blessed like me."

"They are out there. Fire-blessed, metal-blessed, even death-blessed. But I have never met a shadow-blessed. The element of shadow has the greatest potential for power. Shadow is the stable form of the pure magic that exists in the Netherplane and was used to forge the Many Worlds. Shadow can be moulded, can be turned into anything. The truth is you are wasted somewhat on these decorations, beautiful though they are. They are mere distractions for someone with your talent."

Malachai guided her along the cloister. "Conjurors like you and your mother can manipulate the magic that exists in all things, change its properties from one element to another. But if we can channel the magic of the Netherplane, an almost infinite resource, you could become as powerful as a god. As powerful as the Creator . . . That was what I was thinking when I saw that image of the Creator that you sculpted. Of what you might be capable of . . . with the proper training, of course."

Malachai stopped and turned to face Lana.

"I would like you to join the Order of the True, as an apprentice."

Lana had not been expecting this. A dozen thoughts whirled up in her mind like startled birds.

She should accept, surely. She knew that her family would be safe if she took up the offer. Safety was good. She was burning to discover more about her powers, burning to discover more about her mother.

"I . . ." began Lana, and stopped.

"You are unsure," said Malachai.

"No, but . . . my mother, she . . ."

Lana remembered the last thing that her mother had said to her. She'd been lying in bed, eyes wild, muscles straining. She'd grabbed Lana with the full force of her madness and screamed.

"I HAVE WALKED THE NETHERPLANE! YOU ARE HIS CHILD. THE CLEANSING IS COMING."

This horrible memory must have been written plain on Lana's face because Malachai tried to comfort her.

"Do not be afraid. You must understand that your mother was not trained, and she got too greedy with her knowledge. Her mind could not handle it. With caution and practice you will not suffer her fate. Your shadow-blessing means you are more powerful, more able to control yourself. But I must warn you, if you do not learn to wield magic, it can learn to wield *you,* however powerful you are. I know that you have family you need to protect. A young sister, Shahn."

Lana's eyes snapped to Malachai. Was that a hint of a threat? Malachai's tone was not cold, but his eyes certainly were.

"Your new house in Whitestone is ready for your family. But remember, the houses near the palace are required for those most important to the Emperor. Right now, you are important, but all of us, one day, might *stop* becoming important. So, will you join?"

Another face appeared to Lana now, and it made her feel guilty. She imagined the grief and anger that Jun would feel if she were to find out. The Order of the True despised humans. They believed the humans were inferior and, ultimately, should be driven out from the land of the Kind, or even wiped out.

"I do not hate humans," said Lana. "I am not sure I can join your order. There is one human friend in particular who I could not betray."

"You might be surprised to know that I used to have human friends too," said Malachai. He laughed, as if trying to prove that he had once been young and foolish. "Humans, alone, can be good and kind. But together, they are only a force of destruction."

He pointed at Lana's work – the moving figures of the Creator when he fashioned the world, the history of the world up to the modern day. Although Lana had added her own touches, she had been working from Malachai's design. She watched her own work move about – figures fighting in battles, the great monsters of the old-Kind, the swarms of humans slaying the demigods.

"Look at the work you have completed, the messages it tells us. This is why I ordered the renovation – to make the Temple of the Creator the most beautiful temple in the Four Kingdoms, a reminder of our history. Before the time of the Spawning, the old-Kind were almost wiped out by the humans. That cannot happen again. But it *will* happen, if we do nothing."

He pointed at the various images on the walls. All of them showed humans slaying old-Kind or driving them from the magic places that they had been linked to. Aephos from her volcano, Fernwing from his caves, Sephron from the boundless ocean itself.

"Some were murdered, others left diminished and despairing by humanity's arrogant lust for power and their boundless capacity for violence and destruction. Our ancestors' old magic was extinguished. The world was put out of balance."

He turned and looked Lana in the eye.

"That is what we fight. Even now. The human rebels grow in strength. They are everywhere. You know, I have just had word that they slaughtered a boat full of our soldiers in Sephronia. Imagine that, so close to your home!"

Lana was shocked.

"And that phrase that you used to gain entry to the palace." Malachai's voice was ice. "Perhaps you thought I didn't know? It is a code word for the rebels and spies. Those human servants were traitors, feeding information to the rebels. They slipped away before I could capture them. It is not right that the enemy's passwords should come so easily from your lips. Your father was killed by human bandits, Lana! We cannot stop the inevitable. War is coming whether we like it or not. We must choose a side. We must fight for our Kind."

Malachai snapped his fingers, and some disciples stepped forward. They were dragging a prisoner. A struggling, kicking human.

"I did manage to catch *this* rebel . . . She was the human who taught you the phrase, wasn't she?

Our enquiries suggest she is high up in the rebel organisation, planning skirmishes against the Kind in northern Morta and southern Anoros. She also had information on a recent theft at Skin-Grave. She said the theft was indeed planned by the Reader, leader of the rebels, as we had suspected. She said the thief – a girl called Halima – is hiding out, though the prisoner claims not to know where."

Lana gasped. She could not believe her eyes.

It was Jun. Jun was just as shocked as she was. Her skin was bruised and bloodied. Her mouth was gagged.

The shock in Jun's eyes melted away. Now all Lana could see was anger and hatred.

"Please, don't hurt her any more," Lana said.

"This prisoner led an uprising in the Burrows," Malachai said. "Your home was overrun and looted."

Lana felt a sudden surge of terror. She couldn't believe what she was hearing. "What of Shahn and my uncle? Why was I not told of this?"

"Thankfully, I had already sent people to bring your family to Whitestone. They are quite safe."

Lana breathed a sigh of relief. Could Jun have threatened Shahn? It seemed absurd.

Jun was shaking her head desperately. Her eyes bored into Lana's.

"Take the prisoner away," ordered Malachai. He turned to Lana. "You see why we cannot trust humans? That is why you must join us. Together, we can win this war."

Lana watched them drag her friend away. *Was* she still her friend? The look of hatred in Jun's eyes had made Lana squirm. But had Jun felt this hatred all along – had she been trying to harm Lana's family? No, she couldn't believe it.

One thing she did know: she would not be able to help Jun at all if she did not join the Order. And Malachai would not protect her family if she refused.

"Very well," said Lana. "I will join. You have convinced me."

But she knew it wasn't true.

"Good," said Malachai. "Together, we will ensure peace for the great family of the new-Kind."

14

The Reader

The blindfold was hot, tight and scratchy. The narrow path was uneven and stony. Jonas stumbled more than once. Each time, Kolya caught him before he fell.

Jonas swore and carried on trudging.

He had no idea where he was, which was a very unfamiliar feeling. He could sense the bulk of a mountain rising to one side of him as he climbed the switchback trail. The other side felt windy and open.

This made him wonder what the drop was like. But it was better not to think of that. Or what would happen if he really fell.

He stumbled again, and Kolya grabbed his shoulder.

"I'm sorry, Jonas. Thank you for submitting to this," he said. "I would have hated to have had to insist."

"I understand," said Jonas. "It is better I am blind, and right that you do not trust me yet. Still, I have been wearing a blindfold during the day for almost three days now, and I do miss the sunlight. How far north-east must we travel?"

"North-east?" said Kolya, worried. "Who said we were travelling north-east?"

Jonas smiled. "I can *feel* the sunlight too, Kolya."

But he did not say his true reason for agreeing to be hooded. He hoped that if he had no idea where he was, then Seth wouldn't either.

It was another half day's march before they allowed Jonas to remove the blindfold. By that time, they'd crested a ridge and were moving through a dense forest of pine and larch. The air smelled clean and fresh.

The rebels stuck to game paths and took great care to leave no tracks behind, but they also moved with a happy, lengthening stride that showed they were nearly home.

A short while later, they arrived suddenly in the camp. One moment, they were walking through the forest, and the next, they were surrounded by a military encampment.

Jonas was impressed. There were a surprising number of rebels hiding beneath the trees. An army, you might call them – though the humblest army imaginable. Their tents were of woven branches, and they cooked over dry oak and ash timbers so the fires made little smoke.

"Wash in the stream," said Kolya. "I will let Alia know that you are here. She is the leader of our fighters."

The water was bracing, mountain-fresh. It was pleasant to wash the blood and dust away. Jonas kept his eyes down, but he was aware of the curious stares he drew.

Kolya reappeared, smiling. "You come at a lucky time, Jonas. Our council is meeting. Both the Reader and Alia are here. They were glad to hear of what you did. They want to meet you."

Jonas nodded. Most of the rebels were gathering in a clearing. There were perhaps two hundred of them there, men and women, and a few who were barely more than children. Walking among them, Jonas could not imagine how this band could defeat the legions of the new-Kind. The Emperor's soldiers were savage, highly trained warriors. The elite packs of the Emperor's armies were bear-Kind and wolf-Kind. It would take five humans at least to bring down one of those formidable warriors, who were trained from birth to fight with spear and fang. Then there were the regular soldiers – less mighty, but greater in number. There were the Hunters, a division of skilled trackers and assassins. There was the Emperor's navy, a group of fish and amphibian-Kind. And there were the bird-warriors of the skies: vulture, hawk and eagle-Kind.

Some of these humans looked as if they didn't know which end to hold a sword.

At the centre of the clearing was a tall, spreading tree. A ramshackle treehouse was cleverly hidden inside it. Some figures, all masked, were standing on the balcony, looking down.

"Our leaders," said Kolya. "They have gathered in conference. Some of them have come by magic, you know. Thousands of miles in a jump." He sounded impressed.

Jonas was only reminded of the dreadful shackles around his wrist.

"I don't like magic," he muttered. "You can't trust it."

One of the leaders stepped forward and raised her hands for silence. She was obviously a woman, or perhaps even a girl – her frame was slight and frail – but that was all Jonas could tell about her. She wore a crow's mask and a hooded cloak.

The clearing was instantly quiet.

"Greetings, those who worship the Old Ways, loyal followers of the promise of Dalthek, rebels and warriors for the human cause. I have summoned a gathering here today for an important reason. Too long have we lived under the violent rule of the Kind. We have the skills, knowledge and magic to defeat them. We have the numbers, if only we could unite. For many years we have attacked from the shadows, using skirmish forces, thieves and spies. We have been triumphant!"

Jonas couldn't help but feel moved as the crowd around him cheered. There was something odd about the crow-masked woman's voice. It was even, not full of passion or emotion, and yet it seemed to thrum through his blood, raise the hairs on his neck, awaken feelings of confidence and pride – things Jonas had not felt in a long while.

The leader of the rebels continued. "The Kind try to keep knowledge from us. They try to stop us remembering. But the tales of Old live on. Knowledge is power. If we can use the magic of our great ancestors, if we can remember their knowledge, as well as their pride and their faith, then we WILL win."

Another cheer rang out. Humans banged their shields, whooped and whistled. Jonas tried to stay rational. She spoke well, this woman, but still – what she asked was impossible. Humans could not overthrow the Kind. Not without a force of ten thousand.

"We have decided that the time has come for us to show our strength," the leader continued. "We have hidden ourselves long enough. We have kindled our strength in the shadows, growing our hidden flame spark by spark. Now is the time to unleash the blaze!"

All around Jonas, the rebels were tensed, smiles on their faces, listening with knife-keen attention. They didn't cheer any more. They listened. But their fevered concentration was more impressive than any applause.

"We will take the ancient human city they call Skin-Grave. When we claim this holy settlement for ourselves, we will send a message. We belong in this world too. The Kind are scared of Skin-Grave – because they are scared of *us*. We will use this fear against them. Once we are inside that walled city, they will be too scared to fight us there. And if they do, we will use those large walls, the defences and the spells kept there, to keep them out. Once we have this stronghold, we will inspire others. Our enclaves across the Four Kingdoms will grow in number. We will show our tormentors that we are strong.

"It is time that we trust in ourselves. We must not think that we are worse than them. We must forgive ourselves for the failures of the past."

It was strange, but as she said these words. Jonas had the strongest feeling that she was looking right at him. It was impossible to know, of course – Jonas could not see the rebel leader's eyes under her mask – but the beak seemed fixed on him. More than that, the prickling feeling on the back of his neck was heightened, and emotions fired inside his chest.

"You are alive, so you deserve to live. To breathe free air. To taste what has long been forbidden. You should walk in the open and speak your truths. Our cause is not a war of conquest. We do not seek dominion, merely a place of our own, and the right to call it 'home'."

She was persuasive. Jonas felt the justice of her cause – *our cause* – in that quiet voice. It called to him, resonating like a single plucked string inside his body.

Our cause.

I could be part of this.

"War is coming," said the woman, still staring at Jonas. "And it is a war that we will win, together."

There was a silence then. Jonas found himself holding his breath, along with everyone else in the clearing.

In that long, drawn-out moment, he once again had the clear sense that she was looking straight at him, and that her message was meant for him above all others.

Kolya nudged Jonas in the ribs. The spell broke.

"That was the Reader herself!" he whispered. "Isn't she good? You know you've made the right choice now, brother."

The clearing emptied.

When Jonas looked back up to the balcony, the crow-masked woman was gone.

Hours passed. The rebel leaders were still in council and did not want to meet Jonas yet. Jonas was itching to speak with the Reader, to see if she could use her magic to remove his manacles.

Everyone around him was busy, preparing for the march, sharpening weapons, packing baggage. The camp bustled like an ant heap, but there was very little for Jonas to do. He took himself away into the quiet of the forest. Were the humans really planning on attacking Skin-Grave? It seemed they were serious, and it seemed the attack would happen soon. When he agreed to come with Kolya and Cleo, he had not known that he would be walking into a battle. But the words of the Reader had awoken something inside Jonas. The spark of hope burning brightly. The feeling of belonging. Of letting the past go. Of finding a new tribe.

He found a comfortable cushion of pine needles and moss, and tried to relax. But his mind would not permit that.

He knew he was no closer to finding the thief. But Jonas thought maybe he was glad of that. He did not know what he would do if he found her.

"Cut her to pieces," said a voice in his ear.

Jonas nearly jumped out of his skin.

"Seth?" He turned, half expecting that his mind was playing tricks on him again.

It wasn't.

The wyvern crouched before him. He was very real and fully visible. His scales gleamed ghostly green in the dappled shade. His muscles rippled with light as he yawned lazily.

"No need to sound so surprised, Jonas," he

purred. "Did you not think that I would find you? You are not hard to follow. I predict this will soon be a problem for you."

Jonas blinked, started to grin and then remembered that he was meant to be angry.

His confusion must have showed. Seth laughed.

"Go away! I've made my choice," said Jonas, recovering. "I didn't want to see you. I still don't. You shouldn't have followed me."

"Are you sure about that?"

"And what are you doing, showing up like this? And solid as a rock! Someone is sure to see you, glowing up the glade like the world's most terrifying fairy!"

"Good – though I expect you shouting like that is more likely to give us away. We need to leave here, Jonas. You are getting sucked into a fight that isn't your own. It's high time you got on with your task. You can use these rebels to track down the thief who stole something from Skin-Grave. And you need to do it quickly. Do you think once the humans start a war with the Kind that the Kind will care about one silly thief? Grashkor's promise to set you free will disappear."

Jonas shook his head. "Seth, I have found my destiny. I am sure of it. It's with these humans.

Once I see the Reader, she will be able to undo my manacles."

"And you think you will be free then, Jonas? Do you really think you will be able to hide your true nature from your new friends much longer? Like I told you, the death-song does not come from me, it comes from you. I only intensify it. You cannot escape what you are. You are death-blessed. You are not meant to live among the living."

Jonas clenched his fists. Annoyingly, his anger only made the death-song grow inside him. Seth's presence strengthened the feeling. He was about to charge at Seth, just like he used to when he was a small boy, but Seth spread his wings, looming to his full, amazing height.

"They aren't telling *you* the truth, Jonas!" Seth's voice was urgent now.

"What do you mean?"

"I heard the pretty speech. But better still, I heard what their council was talking about *before*. Stupid place to have a meeting, a treehouse, especially when there's an invisible little bird about."

"Tell me! What did you hear?"

"So we're curious now, are we? Lucky old Seth was here, eh? Well, your Reader's an impressive talker. But she's lying too. The reason they are "invading"

Skin-Grave is not to take the city. They've lost their thief."

"How?"

"She's called Halima. She was supposed to exit Skin-Grave via a tunnel network that comes out close to this forest. Skin-Grave is only a few miles south-west of here. But this Halima hasn't appeared. They believe she could still be down there, perhaps captured by the Order of the True priests who patrol the city, stopping anyone going in or out. So that's the real purpose of their raid on the city – to find her."

"Why do they care about the thief so much?"

"Why don't you care?" Seth snapped. "Get Halima, get the item she stole and you will be free. Free to do everything you are meant to do. When the time is right, I can even help you find out what happened to your people. Your only cause is to yourself."

My cause.

Jonas had the uncomfortable feeling that Seth was back inside his head. And that he'd been there the whole time.

Seth stared at him and waggled his eyebrows, as if to say: "I am." And then his voice was in Jonas's head, as familiar and unconscious as blinking.

Remember, Jonas. You are not like other humans. Their cause is not yours. And turn, look, get ready! It was not just me who followed you.

There was a desperate shout from the other side of the camp.

"The Kind! They're here!"

15

The Council of Magic-Kind

"Where have you been, Roshni? We will need to get ourselves sorted. We must call the meeting of the Council of Magic-Kind right away!"

Roshni rushed in, dropping her dusty cloak on the table. She was out of breath. "I'm sorry, Master, the market was busy."

"You were gone all afternoon!"

"I . . . I found tomatoes, though."

"Tomatoes?" Gael harrumphed. "Forget tomatoes. It is nearly time to begin the summonses!"

Roshni bowed her head. "I'm sorry."

Gael's irritation passed as quickly as it had flared up. Today was too important to let emotion make him hasty. Haste was the mother of mistakes.

"No, *I* am sorry, Roshni. I am nervous. It makes me cranky. Can you remember the plan?"

"I should hope so." Roshni laughed. "We've been over it two dozen times!"

"Humour an old raven, Roshni."

"We go to the meeting. I am invisible, wearing the Trickster Ring—"

"And very, very careful. Extreme care! You are surrounded by powerful witches and wizards."

"I'm very careful." Roshni nodded. "I barely breathe. My footsteps are shadow-soft. Then, while you talk to the magic-Kind, I will watch the oscilloscope. I will scan each wizard and check to see which magical aura matches the aura of whoever sneaked into the Tower of Forbidden Knowledge and took the scrolls. We will find out who the traitor is. After we give their name to Malachai, he'll leave you alone. You won't be in danger any more. I'm sure Malachai will be very pleased with you, actually. He might even reward you! Meanwhile, whoever the traitor is will suffer a very slow and painful death. Just for helping the human rebels fight for their right to exist."

"Girl, I do not care about pleasing Malachai any more. And I certainly don't fear him. I simply need to know who is interested in the Tablets of the

Creator and why. I know I am missing something, and I need to know what it is! And I don't appreciate you goading me."

Roshni laughed. "Of course. I can be quite a pest."

Gael clacked his beak. "I think we are ready to spring our trap. Shall we begin?"

He picked up a quill from the desk. It seemed to be made of light, with a curious shivery quality. He scrawled a message on to a piece of parchment.

The ink glowed blinding white.

"There!" With a flick of his wrist, the parchment disappeared. "One hundred summonses sent. They will not be happy about meeting. Magic-Kind rarely enjoy meetings. They are too full of their own importance. We all want to speak at once. Ah – the summons portal is opening for us – just as it will be opening across the Many Worlds at this precise second."

A portal, blurred, translucent and wavering like whirling smoke, appeared in the middle of the room.

"Ring on," said Gael, and stepped through. Roshni followed, invisible.

They arrived instantly in a corridor lined with portraits of ancient leaders of the Council of Magic-Kind – stretching all the way back to when the ancient humans founded the Council so wizards and witches from across the Many Worlds could meet to discuss issues relating to magic. These days only a dozen magic-Kind turned up, five of which were from Roshni's world and were required to attend by law. Magic users from other worlds had become less cooperative over the ages. The floor was paved with rune stones, whose glow gave the corridor a pulsing, shifting feel.

The jump made Gael cough, as usual.

Other magic-Kind began to appear through their own portals. Gael watched Roshni's amazed face as they stepped through into the pocket dimension where the Council met. Some of the wizards were human, some looked like humans but had wings, and there were a couple of new-Kind from Roshni's world. Malachai used to be a member but had boycotted every meeting – he couldn't stand not being in charge. But he still had some magic-Kind loyal to him on the Council. Gael greeted a few councillors as they entered a grand circular hall. Around the edge of the room were a hundred seats carved out of black wood. They looked like thrones.

Gael settled himself into his favourite chair and waited for the room to fill. But it never did. He sighed with disappointment.

"They treat us with mistrust," said Gael. "And rightly so."

Roshni had sat down next to him. Gael could hear her faint breathing. "Who?" she whispered.

"The wizards of other worlds. They do not come to our meetings. Once, this Council united magic-Kind from so many worlds. We worked together to protect all the worlds and the paths between them. It was a sacred duty. But in recent years, our harmony has fractured. Many magic-Kind from other worlds now refuse invitations, even from my pen. Partly this is due to the growing isolation of the worlds, but mainly it is because of—"

"Silence," snarled an unhappy voice. "The Chair of the Council of Magic-Kind calls order for this *unnecessary* council."

"Her," said Gael, sinking lower in his seat.

A wizened old woman had stomped into the chamber. She wore a wolfhide cloak over her shoulders. A wolf's skull with the lower jaw missing, rust-brown with age, rested over the top half of her face. White fangs gleamed in her mouth and her eyes were bright and yellow behind the bone. She carried a spiked wand like a giant thorn.

"What type of new-Kind is she?" whispered Roshni. "Wolf?"

"No," said Gael. "Kezia is human, a magic-Kind. But she wishes she were a proper new-Kind. Those eyes and ludicrous teeth are mere illusions. Of course, that does not stop her being loyal to the Order of the True. She thinks because she is magic she can count herself among the animalian new-Kind whom she worships. Malachai despises all humans, of course, even if their magical talents technically count them as the lowest rung of new-Kind. That's something he wants to change. If it was up to him, humans would be classed as humans, whether magic or not. But he keeps Kezia happy because he knows she is useful and because she treats him like a god. It was an unhappy day that she became Chair."

The chattering in the room slowly died out as Kezia made her way to her throne. It was the biggest and most impressive of the bunch. Gael looked around the room. There were many angry faces.

"It is her they hate," he whispered to Roshni. "She despises wizards from other worlds, where the new-Kind never spawned. Yes, that's right, Roshni. In some other worlds, there are no new-Kind, and in some a few old-Kind even still live on."

"We need to change some laws around here," snapped Kezia, looking directly at Gael. "Especially the one that allows old magic-Kind to call pointless meetings on a whim. This is a waste of all our time. Why have you summoned us?"

Gael stood up. He took his time, as if to emphasise his extreme old age. His bones gave a few theatrical cracks. He cleared his throat.

"Thank you, Chair," he said, with extreme politeness. He bowed deeply and got straight to the point. "I summoned the Council because I believe the Tablets of the Creator are out there, and someone is searching for them. My instruments suggest a great magical power is growing. It makes me wonder if the Tablets have in fact been found already."

The witches and wizards might have been listening with only half an ear before, but they were all interested now.

"Nonsense," snapped Kezia. "They are legends, no more."

"They are being used," insisted Gael. "I have been researching fluxes in powerful magic happening across the worlds, blowing open portals. Yes, there is always imbalance in elemental magic, but only the Tablets could explain the raw magic of the Netherplane that is seeping into the worlds. Only the Tablets of the Creator can force a link with the Netherplane. The fabric of our shared reality is breaking apart."

With a deft flick of his wrist, Gael made a floating globe featuring the Four Kingdoms appear in mid-air in the middle of the council chamber. Each of the fluxes that he had tracked down and closed was marked in red. When you saw all thirteen together, they made a pattern like an oval spiral, similar to an insect wing.

"This is how it looks on this world. And I have seen similar eruptions on other worlds as well."

Another flick of the wrist and more planets appeared – filling the chamber with all the spinning planets of the multiverse. There were fluxes on each one, always in the same oval spiral arrangement.

"Those of you who have travelled from afar will perhaps have seen this too. Note how they always appear in the same pattern. It is a warning."

There were nods of agreement from a few witches and wizards. But there were scowls and frowns too.

Kezia had the biggest frown of all. "Patterns! Supposition! What real evidence do you have, Gael?"

She sounds rather curious about that, thought Gael. *Does she know something? She is close to Malachai, after all.*

"I have no clear proof," he said, "only fears and

worries. And I am sorry for it. But I believe the danger is real, for all of us. It is never wise to be too certain."

"And who do you think has found these magic tablets? Assuming they are real, of course." Kezia's voice dripped with sarcasm.

"One candidate would be the person they're calling the Reader . . ." began Gael.

"The human rebel!" Kezia interrupted. "She is a traitor and a fool. She will die."

"And yet she is powerful," said Gael. "And, I note, still eludes you and your precious Order."

Kezia scowled.

"But in truth, you may be right," Gael went on. "She may not be the culprit. Which brings me to my purpose in calling you all here. I would like to briefly question each of you, individually. It will take only a little time – three questions, no more – but I will be able to satisfy myself that you, my friends, are not responsible, at least."

A storm of outrage broke out then, Kezia's voice loudest of all.

"This is a disgrace!" she cried. "An outrage! You would include me? Your elected leader?"

"I am the Gateway Keeper," said Gael. "And I have been for many an age. The connections between our worlds are fragmenting. It is my right, by the laws that we all swear by, to do everything I can to prevent that. My request cannot be denied."

The magic folk submitted gruffly to the truth of what Gael said. One by one they filed into the little side chamber where Gael set up his inquiry. Roshni waited, invisible, beside him with the oscilloscope in her hand.

He asked them all the same three questions.

"What is your name?"

"What is your world?"

"What did you have for breakfast?"

The last question was designed to surprise. If a magic user was masking their magical aura, they might lose concentration and the oscilloscope would detect it. But Roshni's oscilloscope recognised nothing. It found no match with the magical trace left by the human who had entered the Tower of Forbidden Knowledge.

Kezia was the last witch to come. She refused to answer the questions.

"This is the final indignity, Gael," she said. "You are going senile. You talk of legends. But worse, you think that this Reader – a pitiful human – would be capable of actual power. It is laughable. You are clearly losing your mind."

"Are you not a human yourself?" Gael asked innocently. But although a dark spark of hatred danced in Kezia's eyes, she did not rise to the bait. Kezia was hiding something; he was sure of it. Making her angry might force her into a mistake.

"I am more than that," she said. "And you know it. But it matters little. After this charade, you are finished, and you will never waste my time again. I will ban you from the Council."

She stomped out of the room.

Gael sighed. "Was it her?"

"It was not, Master," said Roshni. "The oscilloscope did not recognise any of them."

"What a waste of time," said Gael. "So I have made trouble for myself for nothing. We should go."

He got up, stretching his long legs.

"Oho!" said Roshni, sounding excited. "Wait! Who is in that picture?"

"What? Where are you looking? I can't see you, remember?"

"The tall shadowy-human, there," said Roshni.

Gael cast about, his eye falling on a strange painting, which he assumed was what she was talking about. It showed a humanoid figure entirely covered in pure flickering shadow – like black flames. Only the red eyes were visible. They glowed.

It was not a pleasant picture.

"That's the God of Magic," said Gael. "Otherwise known as the Creator, who fashioned the Many Worlds from the raw magic of the Netherplane."

"Have you seen what's on his cloak? The design?" Roshni's voice came from right by the picture. She must have been staring very closely at it. She sounded even more excited now.

There was a strange pattern of oval rings, dotted with gold circles, painted on his cloak. The rings looped inside each other and looked exactly like an insect's wing.

"That is the symbol of raw magic, the dangerous unstable magic of the Netherplane, which the Creator used to build the Many Worlds. The symbol is used because this is the shape of the aura of raw magic. It spreads out in waves, mutating all matter it touches. Very dangerous stuff – you should never allow yourself to come into contact with raw magic radiation, and if you do . . ."

Gael trailed off as the realisation hit him. He scrabbled around inside his cloak. His trembling fingers found his map, where he had marked the locations of the portals that had been blown open by the leaked raw magic of the Netherplane. He held up the marked locations next to the shape of the insect wing. "You've done it, girl. You've solved the mystery of how this raw magic is infiltrating the world."

He placed the map on the floor, gathered an inkpot and quill from his pockets, and then began to draw swirling loops over the points on the map. The sites of the portals were all located on the lines of magical radiation. Gael looked to see where the arcs were emanating from.

"Skin-Grave," muttered Gael. "That's where the raw magic is leaking from. The Tablets of the Creator must be in Skin-Grave. Someone has been using them to access the Netherplane. It is stupid, dangerous, ruinous. It could put the very elemental fabric of our world in jeopardy."

"You've cracked it," said Roshni.

"*We've* cracked it," replied Gael. "And who controls Skin-Grave, my dear?"

"It's . . . Malachai and the Order of the True." Now Roshni saw it. Her brow furrowed.

"Troubling, indeed." Gael nodded. "*Malachai* has found the Tablets, not the humans . . . Dalthek save us all."

16

Hunter in Hiding

The battle was over before it began.

The howling, roaring charge of the Emperor's elite battalion overwhelmed the human rebels' camp. The tents burned. The wolf-Kind and bear-Kind soldiers were merciless. Those humans that were not dead laid down their weapons.

Jonas watched it all happen, dumbstruck, from the edge of the forest. He could have run many times, but guilt rooted him there.

"Flee, you fool," urged Seth. "Flee while you still have the chance."

Jonas ignored the wyvern.

Marshal Vanbrink, the huge brown bear-Kind commander, had led the ferocious rampage from the front. Now he towered over the huddled group of captured rebels. His glaive – a monstrous weapon, half spear, half halberd – towered above even the eight-foot bear-Kind, and was dripping blood. Around him, humans crouched in the crimson-stained dust, surrounded by blades, axes, fangs and claws. Beside the bear capered a smaller figure, thin and twitchy.

"Brynn the Sly," whispered Jonas, recognising the Emperor's old Head Hunter and prisoner from the Pinnacles who, along with Jonas and Orok the Crusher, had been recruited by Grashkor for the mission to find the fugitive thief. Jonas had almost forgotten about the wily dog-Kind.

That had been a mistake. A big mistake.

After Orok had been killed, Jonas had assumed he was safe from the threat of his competitors. He had been distracted by the strange freedom of Seth's absence, and then by the hope given to him by the human rebels. Hope for a new life, where he could leave Grashkor's mission, the Pinnacles of the Damned, his old life as *Slayer*, far behind him. He'd been a fool.

Suddenly he had an awful feeling that this was all his fault.

"I told you – I know I shouldn't say it – but I

did," said Seth, reading his mind. "If you'd let me gut the scummer back in the port, this would not be happening."

The Marshal raised his voice to a tree-shaking roar.

"SLAYER!" he bellowed. "We know you are here. Show yourself. I want to thank you personally for gifting us this victory."

"That's nice of him," said Seth.

"Come out, Slayer," continued the Marshal. "Come out now. Else for every minute you don't come, your friend Brynn here will slit one of these soft rebel throats."

"Right, time to leave, Jonas," said Seth. "Leave them to it. They don't mean a thing to your mission."

The Marshal scanned the edge of the forest, waiting to see if Jonas appeared.

"Grab one, Brynn," he said. "Pick a fresh, young rebel. Show him you mean business."

The dog-Kind dragged Kolya out of the pack and held his large, curved dagger to his throat.

The whites of Kolya's eyes showed, but he didn't cry out.

Jonas could not bear it. "Stop!" he called. "I'm here." He moved out of his hiding place, treading softly across the pine needles.

"Curse you," snarled Seth. "You'll die. Those rebels are dead already."

"I can't abandon them," said Jonas. He walked towards the soldiers.

He wasn't sure if Seth followed invisibly behind. He could not feel him.

Everyone was watching.

The huge bear towered over him. His armour blazed with gold and polish.

"So, so! The famous Slayer!" growled the Marshal. "We *finally* meet. Though you are less than I was expecting."

The faces of the humans were hard and cold as they realised who Jonas really was. They had heard tell of Slayer too. The human bounty hunter who worked for Grashkor, who worked for the Kind.

"Look how they stare, Slayer," whined Brynn, his raspy voice surprisingly high-pitched. "Poor things. They didn't know the poison they'd stirred in their tea 'til it was too late, did they?"

Jonas couldn't meet Kolya's stare. But he felt the shame of his betrayal.

"How did you follow me?" he asked Brynn.

"You stink of death," said Brynn. "You always have. All I had to do was follow my nose."

There was no sign of the Reader amongst the

cowed rebels, but all the rest of the leaders had been captured. Their hatred hit Jonas like a blow.

"Now, Slayer." The Marshal took a pace towards Jonas. "By delivering these rebels into our hands, Brynn the Sly has done more than enough to earn his freedom. But have you earned yours? Have you discovered the thief of Skin-Grave?"

"Traitor!" hissed Kolya.

Brynn slapped the boy to the ground. He grinned a wicked toothy smile as he pulled a dagger and knelt on the boy's back. "Any who resist will be killed."

If Jonas hadn't been sure of his plan until then, he was now. He drew his sword and threw himself at Brynn.

The dog-Kind smartly lifted his dagger to block the blow. Their blades rang together. Jonas fell back to the ground, his arm numb.

Brynn skipped away, smirking. "You'll die for that, human."

Jonas tried to summon the death-song, but it was too weak. All he felt was fear and anguish that his friend was about to be killed.

"Time with these humans has made you weak," said Seth.

A great emptiness filled Jonas. He felt heavy and

weak and slow.

He looked up at the laughing faces of the soldiers, at the cold hatred of the rebels.

He had no friends here. He was alone.

He was Slayer. He always had been. He was not human. He was not Kind. He was no one. He was death itself.

The Marshal stepped forward, raising his huge black blade above his head. His armour glittered.

"I expected far more from you, Slayer," he said. "But it seems you are no more than a snivelling boy. Come on, fight me like the terror people say you are."

Jonas got to his feet. He tried to summon the death-song again but it wouldn't come. He was still empty. He had no chance of winning. He was surrounded. The Marshal spun his sword in dizzying patterns that Jonas could hardly follow.

One blow from that huge blade would cut him in half.

"So, Jonas," said Seth, whispering in his ear. "Perhaps now you are finally ready to die? I am not looking forward to my spirit re-joining the Land of What Was permanently. It is a boring place, mostly. I will miss the world of the living. And to think you had such a great destiny."

"Leave me alone," said Jonas.

"What did you say?" said the Marshal, frowning.

"I will not ask again," said Seth. "Are you ready to die?"

Jonas looked up at the sky. It was a deep, almost hypnotic blue.

Somewhere, a bird was singing, completely oblivious to the carnage below.

What did he want? Was he finished? Was this his time?

"Do you choose death?" said Seth.

With a sigh, Jonas made his decision. He let down his guard, defeated.

The Marshal raised his weapon and began to bring it down. But he was already too late.

For all at once, as if a great dam had broken, Seth had flowed inside Jonas, flooding his senses, filling every part of him. Jonas welcomed his brother back with open arms. He had never wanted the death-song more than now. He did not fight it, he urged it on.

The death-song soared. Time slowed to a trickle, but every tiny instant was sheer delight.

"This is good," said Seth. "Being together again. I am glad you let me back in."

And Jonas agreed. He began to laugh and as he

laughed, he danced.

Before the bear-Kind Marshal knew a thing, his head was lopped clean off. It bounced three times on the ground with an expression of shocked surprise it would never lose.

Brynn the Sly was next. Gutted on the half-turn, he never even saw the blow that killed him. His body fell next to Kolya, who watched in horror.

Jonas howled and his enemies were afraid. The song soared higher.

Seth was in him as he had never been before. They were brothers, their souls lashed together in the glory of death. When Seth bit a throat, Jonas tasted the hot blood. When Jonas sliced a shield and took the arm that held it, Seth's claws ripped the flesh as well.

The mighty elite division of the Emperor's army fell back in terror. Their commander was dead; their friends were falling to a foe that moved so fast his opponents in combat stabbed each other in their panic and confusion.

Soon they were running. A rabble rushing down a mountain, pursued by a bloody terror that could not be defeated.

The killing was so sweet that Jonas never wanted it to end.

He had never felt so good before. His brain went black. He could not seem to hear or see or feel. But he knew he was fighting. Jonas felt himself shrink into nothing inside himself, vaguely aware of what was happening, vaguely aware of his body seemingly acting of its own free will, striking down enemy after enemy.

"Stop! STOP!" It was Seth's voice that brought Jonas at last to his senses. He was standing, covered in blood, before the human prisoners. They cowered away from him, utterly terrified.

Although he lowered his swords, Jonas felt a flash of disappointment. He hadn't wanted the killing to stop.

Finally, Jonas managed to say something. Some part of him wanted to explain. To tell them he hadn't betrayed them – not on purpose, anyway. That he wanted to fight with them. But that was all over, Jonas knew.

"Sorry," was all Jonas muttered, though he wasn't even sure if the word had come from his mouth.

"You are cursed, Slayer!" Kolya said.

"He is death!" another voice called.

Jonas did not disagree with them and, he found, did not care. He did not want to care.

They were right. Death was who he was.

"Let's go," said Seth. "Before they do something stupid and you have to slaughter them too. Follow this river. It will take us to Skin-Grave; the thief is somewhere in the tunnels there. Soon we will be free."

Free. At last Jonas realised that the only freedom he could ever feel was the freedom from himself when the death-song took him over.

17

The Thief of Skin-Grave

With Seth scouting ahead, Jonas ran fast. He did not feel tired and he did not slow down.

The trees flashed by, mile after steady mile. He had never felt so alive in his body. Strange that it took truly embracing death to feel this way.

The walls drew close. Seth reported that smoke was rising from campfires in the city.

"There are many priests there," he said. "More than I was expecting. The Order of the True are up to something."

"I do not care how many there are," said Jonas. "They cannot stand before me."

"Ha! Brave words, brother. It is true – you might be able to defeat an army, like you defeated the elite division. But then you would not win your freedom. Those priests on the boat did not hear your name – but once you are known as an ally of the rebels you will be a fugitive for ever. Think with your head, not your sword. Even I acknowledge that killing everything is not *always* the best solution."

Jonas felt a little disappointed.

"So how do we get past them?" he asked. "Those walls are tall."

Now that they were close to Skin-Grave, the city's grim walls towered above the surrounding plain. On the ramparts, the crescent banners of the Order of the True hung limp from their standards. There was no wind and the dust hung heavy in the air. The ruined city squatted like a curse upon the land, black and grim and filled with ancient death.

It made Jonas feel even better. The scent of the tombs was intoxicating. It sang in his blood.

As the stream that they were following approached the wall, it dived into the ground, foaming and roaring.

"This is the secret entrance the rebels used. Jump in. Hold your breath a good spell. The flow should carry us past the watchers on the walls, directly into the catacombs."

Jonas dived into the cold water. The roar of a

waterfall filled his ears.

The death-song was as welcome as a lullaby. He saw himself . . .

. . . *tumbling into sharp rocks* . . .

. . . *smashing his bones* . . .

. . . *drowning in darkness* . . .

He should have been afraid, but the nearness of death made him supremely strong. With swift, powerful strokes, Jonas rushed at the frothing waterfall. For a moment, he was weightless, soaring down, down through the black air, before he plunged once more into the whirling current. But the churning waves could not hold him. He glided through their grasping fingers to emerge in a calm pool, deep underground.

Seth was waiting. All was dark, except where the wyvern's faint glow lit up the mossy rocks.

Only, as Jonas's eyesight grew accustomed to the gloom, he saw they were not rocks but tombs.

Everywhere he looked was a tomb. There were humble niches carved in walls, grand vaults built of marble, carved sarcophagi arranged in ranks and massive bone jars as broad and tall as wine vats.

And all were stuffed with bones.

In some rooms, the bones were arranged in patterns. Pretty collections of femurs winged above doorways like fans. There were walls built of skulls. A detailed map of the world made entirely of fingers.

If the scent of Skin-Grave had been invigorating from the outside, now that they were in the belly of the beast, Jonas was overwhelmed. The stench of death was everywhere. Every breath that Jonas took, each bone he saw – and there were a lot of bones – sent the death-song thrumming inside him.

Even then, he might have been able to stand that, if it wasn't for the voices.

They whispered from the shadows. They called from inside their dusty tombs. Fragments of speeches and half-heard stories. He would not call them ghosts. They were too faded for that.

". . . there was an eel in the garden."

"I called her my lucky charm."

"Did they know, duck, what they were doing?"

It was said that Skin-Grave was haunted, and dangerous, and full of occult evil. But this didn't feel that way to Jonas. These were ordinary people. It was the weight of all that death that was too much. Every inch of him felt sensitive, tumbled in the flood of dead lives more thoroughly than any waterfall could manage.

He moved forward as if in a trance. It was lucky Seth was there to guide him and keep him on the path. There were signs of recent damage everywhere. Walls had collapsed and fresh cracks stabbed across the floors. Several times, he felt a rumbling beneath his feet like an earthquake.

A particularly strong tremor toppled several skulls to the ground. Jonas did not react as they smashed beside his foot.

Seth glanced back. "Are you all right, brother? You've gone a bit quiet."

"I'm fine," said Jonas. "It's just . . . this place."

He found he did not want to say its name out loud.

Jonas was not sure how long they wandered. Overwhelmed by the murmuring bones, he'd almost forgotten why they had come – until he sensed her. A spark of life as bright as a firefly in a dark wood. Surrounded by so much death, she was easy to see.

"This way," said Jonas. He did not need to explain. "Here." The thief was trapped inside a tomb. The entrance had collapsed, blocked by heavy rocks.

Seth phased through the rocks and reported back. "Halima's there, asleep. She's thin. Her fingers are torn to shreds. She must have been digging, trying to get out for weeks. She has been feeding herself on mushrooms and rats and a small stream of water. I think I see how we can shift these rocks."

"Good," said Jonas. "Then we are nearly done."

"Soon your manacles will be broken."

"Halima!" Jonas called, when they were ready. "We are here to help you."

He heard her startled voice through the rocks. "Who are you?"

"The Reader sent us. Don't worry. You'll be safe. We need to get you back to the forest quickly. The Reader is waiting."

The lies came easily to him. So did the digging. Powered by the death all around him, Jonas eased away the heavy rocks.

"Thank you!" Halima's voice came faintly through. "How did you know where to find me?"

"The Reader can sense you," said Jonas. "She has been looking for you, we all have."

That last statement at least was not a lie.

Soon they'd cleared a hole big enough for Halima to peer through. Without Seth's glow to light up the space, it was hard to see anything. In the faint lichen-light, Jonas could just about make out the flash of her smile.

He pushed his arm through. He felt her hand take his.

"Thank you! I'm so hungry."

The hole was growing bigger and bigger. Jonas reached inside again to lever a rock away. It came loose in a shower of pebbles.

"What's your name?" said Halima suddenly. She was a small girl. Though her skin was deep brown and her hair cut short with a blade, she reminded Jonas of one of his cousins, Fran. Halima had the same wiry frame, the same dancing light in her eyes, the same bony shoulders. Though Fran would never be seen without her sable fur hat.

"My name is Jonas." That was a lie too. He wasn't Jonas any more. He was Slayer. He couldn't allow himself to be Jonas, or he might let emotion cloud what he was about to do.

"I am so grateful for this, Jonas. Push just here. I think the hole will be big enough for me then."

With a tumble of rocks, the blockage collapsed.

"I think I can squeeze through now. Oh, but I am hungry! Try eating rats and mushrooms for weeks on end. I could find some kindling down here to cook them, but yesterday I actually thought I might have to eat them raw. Can you believe it?"

Jonas turned and reached back for a set of the Gaoler's manacles he had ready in a knapsack, but as he grasped them, he heard light steps darting past him.

"No!" Then Seth was shouting. "She's running away!"

Jonas scrambled to his feet. He could still faintly feel her life force burning bright, but she was speeding away through the tunnels.

"How did she know?" cursed Jonas, springing off in pursuit. "All she saw of me was my wrists."

And then he remembered his own manacles, whose weight he no longer noticed, and saw what she had seen.

But there was no time for regrets. As they thundered through the dark corridors, the hollow-eyed skulls watched the chase.

"Can't you be quieter?" hissed Seth.

"Why don't you do something? Can't you fly?"

"We're underground, Jonas. Besides, this place is terribly unstable. If I knock the wrong pillar, I could trap us all. There is powerful magical energy coming from nearby – I think it's causing those earthquake tremors. Can't you feel that static on your skin?"

Jonas noticed it now, a strange energy in the air. He wondered if the power was making his death-song stronger. The murmurings from the tombs grew lounder in his ears. Funnily, though they came from the dead, they reminded him of life, of the everyday things he had once known in his tribe.

All that was gone. He had to get the thief.

She was very quick, and her plunging route through

the maze of tombs was calculated to deceive. But Jonas was strong and she was weak, and in a hunt that is usually enough.

He cornered her in a vast chamber, much bigger than any room he'd seen yet. She'd fallen over the shattered rubble of some vast statue. She clutched her knee, her face taut with fear and anger as Jonas placed the manacles on her wrists, and locked them with a twist of the golden key.

"You are a traitor to your people," she said.

"You're wrong," said Jonas. "I have no people. I am Slayer."

18

The Tablets of the Creator

Skin-Grave wasn't just a haunted, eerie place. It had a physical effect on Lana. It made the shadows in her skin come alive and seep from her like a writhing black cloak, thicker than she'd ever seen before. It frightened her, and others. Lana was conscious of the wary stares of the robed guards of the Order of the True who watched her from the streets, and the way they tried to hide their disgust – especially when they thought Malachai might be watching them. But Malachai barely turned his head, scurrying with ferocious intent through the ancient city's streets.

Amazingly, every part of the sprawling settlement had remained intact since the age of the ancient humans – the battlements, the drawbridge leading over the moat through the exterior wall, the magnificent central palace, the barracks, the town square and the small brick homes. The craftsmanship was remarkable – delicate, refined and ingenious. Lana had no idea humans were capable of such feats of engineering and beauty. It far exceeded the subtlety and skill of any new-Kind buildings. Lana imagined what Jun would say: "We humans are so much more advanced than you jumped-up new-Kind, admit it!" The thought made her heart burn. She had managed to persuade Malachai not to kill her friend, but the last she had heard Jun was being kept in the dungeons.

"Can we not simply exile Jun to the Ruby Isle?" Lana had asked Malachai when he seemed to be in a good mood – which was rare. "Or she can help me with my building work. The Emperor has requested I start work on another palace for him, and Jun is very skilled."

"Lana, you must learn to harden your heart. Do you not realise Jun would betray you in a second? It is for your safety that she remains in the dungeons. Focus on your work, on unlocking your powers, and I will think about showing mercy."

The Order of the True guards were everywhere

in the city, patrolling the upper ramparts armed with bows and manning huge catapults. The only damage to any of the human buildings had been caused by bored priests who had taken a hammer to the brickwork or smashed up old porcelain toys with their feet.

What was even more remarkable, even more creepy, were the other memorials to everyday life, left untouched for hundreds of years: there were rotten carts, pails that once fetched water from wells, market stalls and pots and pans for cooking, clothes – and lots and lots of skeletons.

Malachai was far too busy to notice the sly looks the guards gave Lana, or the way they would make sure to spit or smash up piles of old furniture when she passed. From the moment they'd teleported into Skin-Grave, the Arch Protector had been on edge. He hadn't told Lana why they had come here – only that it was time to 'test her powers'.

They'd finally arrived at the city's palace and found their way to the dark tunnels beneath it filled with tombs and bones. Eventually, deep within the catacombs, they arrived at a grand chamber – a tomb the size of Whardox Hall. It was magnificent. But Lana could feel the dangerous, powerful magic seeping through the place. It was like nothing she had ever felt. The shadows across her right side flamed, sending power through her veins. She could sense the magic all around her, in the rock, in the earth below, in the bones of the dead.

Still Malachai said nothing to Lana about what they were doing here, instead barking orders to a group of figures – some human and some new-Kind – who were scouring pages of runes written in ink and comparing them to other ancient human texts. Magic thrummed all around. Some of the figures wrote symbols of light in the air, manipulating them with a flick of their hands. Lana was surprised to see humans working alongside the new-Kind; an elderly mouse-Kind, a tall, bent-backed ferret-Kind wizard, and a couple of reptile-Kind. It seemed Malachai was prepared to put his principles aside when it served his purposes.

"How can you not have the Tablets translated already?" he shouted at a strange-looking human woman in a wolf's-skull headdress. She was snapping orders at the human mages, but turned towards Malachai with a cowed expression. "I have given you far too much time as it is, Kezia. I hope you won't let me down." Her jaw wrinkled in a grimace. She bowed deep, knotting her fingers.

"There have been distractions, Master," she

pleaded. "That pest Gael is poking his beak around. He called a meeting of the Council of Magic-Kind. I had to attend otherwise it would have drawn suspicion. As I have mentioned to you, I think he might suspect us. I've had to work more slowly, with only the mages I truly trust."

"I will deal with Gael, Kezia," snarled Malachai. "The coot has outstayed his welcome. Recruiting him to find the thief was a mistake, for he is too clever for his own good. My spies at the Hallowed Vale believe he is getting too close to the truth. He suspects what we are doing, he detects the raw magic of the Netherplane. But do your job better, Kezia, or I will deal with you as well."

"It shall be as you command, Master. To the glory of the Order."

"Give me the key," snapped Malachai. "I would look upon the Tablets myself."

Kezia handed over a heavy, green-veined key. Malachai's thick black tongue flicked out as he took it.

"Come, Lana."

Malachai and Lana descended deeper into the tunnels beneath the palace. Again, Lana wondered what she was doing there.

She was too frightened of Malachai to ask him

for an explanation.

There had been a lot of work done recently in these tunnels. Every staircase they went down and every doorway they passed through had been strengthened with fresh timber. With a miner's eye, Lana saw that the work was well-fashioned. There were parties of humans working everywhere, egged on by Order of the True minders. As she and Malachai passed down a long, rubble-strewn corridor, the floor shook. Dust fell from the ceiling.

Malachai pounded on, taking no notice.

At last they arrived before a pair of heavy stone doors, as thick as castle walls. Malachai inserted the key into a chiselled hole and twisted. With a grinding of rusty gears, the doors hinged open.

Malachai took a deep, satisfied breath.

"You have no idea how long it took to find these." He stepped forward, raising his lantern high so that it illuminated a pair of giant stone tablets that were twice his height. Ancient runes were carved into the rock. The stones had a strange weight, as if time and light slowed down when they touched them. Lana's skin prickled all over, fizzing with magic, and the flames that danced from her body seemed to form strange fleeting shapes – runes, symbols and figures. Lana heard a deep bass throb in her ears, and realised it was the pounding of her heart. Power surged through every part of her. This magic was unlike anything she had ever felt. It had no form. Or rather, it had every form. Its energy constantly changed – one moment it felt like quartz, then granite, then metal, then earth, then all of these at once.

"These Tablets," said Malachai with a strange gentleness, "these Tablets will save us all. They are the key to achieving the full power that we were born to. The power that created our Kind. The power that lies in you."

"I do not understand," said Lana.

"You will. And deep down, you already know what I speak of, Lana. You know the Netherplane! Look how your gift responds!"

Lana looked at her hands. They were wreathed with writhing shadows that spread out towards the Tablets as if desperate to embrace them.

"Can you believe that a human intruder entered this space?" said Malachai. "Yes, a rebel was sent to copy the spells from the Tablets. They defile the word of our great god. I have punished all the guards responsible. But the truth of it is that the humans seek this power too – they recognise the Tablets' importance. That is why it is so vital that you work with us, Lana – and why I am glad you chose to join our Order. Together we will do great things. For many years, the Order of the True has safeguarded Skin-Grave, but we were too afraid to delve into the dark secrets of the past – into human secrets. The humans had knowledge you would not believe. It is what makes them so dangerous. They cannot be allowed to access these secrets. We must take this knowledge from them. Many in the Order thought what I said was blasphemous, but I outwitted my enemies – that silly cat-Kind Rahziin, for one. I had my priests search every corner of this city, and when they found this key I knew we had uncovered something special. It was marked with the symbol of 'C', the symbol of the Creator, the same symbol that emblazons the sigil of the Order of the True."

Lana could feel the truth in his words. Standing near the huge stones felt like standing at the top of a tall cliff. Magic was welling up around her, twisting and shivering into her skin. She felt buffeted by a huge wind – but more than that, she was conscious of the drop. Of the vastness that lay beneath her feet. One more step and she would be falling for ever.

"We will need your help, Lana. The truth of it is that these lesser-gifted mages – like that snivelling

Kezia – are incapable of containing the power of the great spells that are written on the Tablets. Our experiments have unsettled the ground. You see how unstable the walls are; all these new cracks . . ."

"Wait," said Lana. "You want me to cast the spells that are written on the Tablets?"

"You must," said Malachai. "It is the only way we can unlock their full potential. If we channel the raw magic of the Netherplane, we can wash away the human stain with a great flood. It will be the Cleansing, when balance will finally be restored to the world."

Lana blinked, trying to take in Malachai's words. Exterminate the humans for good? Surely that wasn't possible with magic alone. And surely he couldn't expect her to cause such a terrible disaster. But how could she refuse Malachai? What would it mean for her family, for Jun?

"But what if I can't do it?"

"You will do it, Lana, when the time comes. It is meant to be. This is the prophecy spoken by the Creator, seen in a vision. Your mother's vision. Her delusions were real – she was not mad. She was visited by the Creator, heard his words. The Cleansing is coming, Lana. And I believe you are the one who will make it happen."

Lana shook her head. "My mother died. What she saw killed her."

Malachai took Lana's hands.

"Her mind saw into the Netherplane too many times. It could not handle it. But you are more powerful than her. You have a shadow-blessing. You contain shadow, pure magic, *within* you. You can channel the magic of the Netherplane, turn it to your will. There has never been a conjuror as powerful as you, not since the evil human wizard Dalthek. You will carry out your mother's prophecy. It is your destiny. You will succeed, because blood is everything. A truth that cannot be denied."

Lana felt the magic of the Tablets swarm through her, energising every particle of her body. The magic seemed to urge her on, to respond to Malachai's words.

Malachai was looking deep into her eyes, as if he was trying to hunt down the fear that roamed within her.

"You will do this, Lana," he said. "You have the power."

"Master!" A nervous acolyte shuffled towards them.

"What is it?"

"Master . . . A work party has reported intruders

in the lower levels. Human intruders. A boy and a girl."

"Thieves and spies! Why did you not tell me sooner?" Malachai spun away from Lana and cuffed the acolyte. "After them!"

19

The Last Master

As soon as Jonas fixed the manacles to Halima's wrists, she ran, pushing Jonas off. Jonas clicked his fingers. The manacles pulled Halima back, her feet dragging on the floor.

"There is no point," Jonas said. "Believe me. I can control the magic of these manacles, just as Grashkor controls mine."

Halima looked up, fury in her eyes. "I can make this difficult, you know," she said. "There's many Order of the True priests patrolling down here. They will assume you are helping me, that you are with the human rebels. Generally, they tend to be the kill first, ask questions later type. If I shout, you won't get very far before they get here."

"They don't scare me," said Jonas. He wasn't bragging. He said it with a heavy heart.

Seth materialised in front of Halima, filling the tunnels with his dark scaled flesh. "Do not speak a word, girl." He turned to Jonas. "Slayer, if guards find us we must kill them. There can be no witnesses. We don't want the Order of the True telling Grashkor to add thousands of more years to our sentence because of the murder of the priests."

Halima was brave. She did not run screaming at Seth's appearance. But horror plagued her features and she let out a hollow rasp.

"Gods! What are you, Slayer?" she muttered. "With friends like this?"

"I am not his friend," snarled Seth. "I am him. We are death."

The wyvern's voice echoed across the vast chamber.

"Death . . . Death . . . Death . . ."

The whispers came back from every corner, growing louder with every repetition. It was almost as if the giant stone statues that towered above them had come stealthily to life. Their crudely chiselled faces stared down. Their eyes were dark pits. None of them moved.

But the voices still whispered from the darkness. "*Death . . . Death . . . Death . . .*"

Jonas felt the hairs on his neck prickle. He had the feeling he was being watched from the shadows. The whispers of the dead grew louder. "There wasn't an echo before, was there?"

Seth's ears were pricked, his head held high as if he was listening intently. "The spirits sense us. Time to move."

But Jonas stayed where he was. The whispers of the dead semed to call his name now. *Jonas . . . Jonas . . . we sense you . . . we feel your hurt . . . Jonas . . . your destiny is yours . . . Jonas!*

"I don't like this place," said Seth. "We cannot dither. We are so close to freedom. Can you not taste it, brother? Freedom from Grashkor." Seth turned to hurry away.

But Jonas did not turn with him. The whispers seemed to merge at the centre of the tomb, and from that point a faint glimmer of light pierced the air, like a firefly. It grew and grew, and the whispers grew louder with it. "Jonas . . . Jonas . . . Jonas!" The whispers no longer came from inside his mind, but from the room itself. Halima could hear it too – she was staring around her, searching for the voice.

A faint, shining figure had appeared in the centre of the chamber. It looked small, tiny even, surrounded by those vast blocks of stone and the deep dark.

"Jonas," the figure said. "We have been waiting for you. Come."

"It's a trap," said Seth. "Don't do that."

Halima was staring at the shining figure, open-mouthed.

Jonas ignored the wyvern. There was something deeply familiar about the voice. He walked closer. The figure did not move or say any more but waited calmly.

It was certainly a ghost, Jonas saw as he drew near. The ghost of a tall, bearded man dressed in golden plate armour. He was faintly see-through, in the same way that Seth was, although this man merely glowed and had no ghost fire licking over his skin.

He smiled at Jonas. "You have no fear of me."

"I don't," said Jonas. "It's strange. It feels like I know you. How did you know my name?"

"A fair question." The ghost nodded. "I was told it and I have not forgotten, though I have forgotten many other things. The taste of blueberries. My mother's name. The feeling of the sun on my back. But I have not forgotten your name. You see, I have been waiting for you to arrive here for a very long time. You are connected to death. I feel your presence from the Land of What Was. Here, in the ancient place where the boundary is weakest, I have come back to you. I see that I am not the only spirit to have found you. This ghost has latched on to your life force. Be careful. He will have his own agenda. Do not let it interfere in your destiny."

"Jonas's destiny is his own!" growled Seth.

"Exactly," said the ghostly human spirit. "Not yours."

"Begone, human spirit. Begone with your lies and deceit!"

"What do you want?" said Jonas. Although he wasn't scared of the ghost, the idea that he had been expected was troubling. His mind shied away from all the enormous things that might mean. That he had a purpose. He wanted no purpose. Purpose cost too much. He didn't want people relying on him.

"I want to tell you who you are."

"Who are *you*?" said Jonas.

"I am Thom. I was a Master of the Kind a very long time ago. This chamber is the Tomb of the

Keepers. There are many of us buried here." He gestured with his hand. Before each of the great statues marching off into the darkness, small shimmering figures appeared. Some of them waved.

Until this point, Jonas had not realised quite how large the chamber really was. There must have been more than a hundred statues, and just as many ghosts.

Nor did he realise that Halima had come up behind him until she spoke. "So the legends are true! The Masters of the Kind were real." She was staring at the ghosts with a look of wild joy.

"All true. All of these ghosts were Masters once. Year after year, century after century, we fought against evil. We tried to keep the balance between humans and the old-Kind. But we failed, and now we are forgotten."

"Not by everyone," said Halima.

"This doesn't have anything to do with me," said Jonas.

"There, you are wrong." Thom shook his head. "Some have called me the Last Master. After me, the Masters began to lose their influence, their power. But our blood lived on, passed down the generations. *You* are the Last Master, Jonas. You have been chosen to bring balance, to unite the

Kind and the humans, and to fight the forces of chaos and evil."

"Him?" said Halima, shocked. "That monster?"

Jonas took a step back. "She's right," he said. "I'm no Master, or any kind of hero. I'm Slayer."

The ghost's expression hadn't changed. "Your destiny is what you make it, Jonas. The Cleansing is coming. A great change. A great rebalancing. But what that is is yet to be decided. Only the living can decide that." Thom glanced meaningfully at Seth.

"You're wrong." Jonas felt as if the floor had just dropped away beneath his feet and he was hanging there, in mid-air, about to fall into the deep.

"I am not wrong about this."

"You said Masters fought evil. That's not what I do. I've done terrible things. I've killed . . ."

Jonas couldn't finish the sentence. Thom was still staring at him with the same forgiving half-smile, as if Jonas was a child who'd trodden dirt over a washed floor but Thom wasn't going to make a fuss about it.

"Death is not just destruction, Jonas. It is as natural as breathing. We all must die, as our fates decree. But those that die are not truly gone. They have merely moved on; and some day after that, they will move on again."

"So? Why are you telling me this?" said Jonas. "I *kill* people, don't you understand? I've killed a lot of people."

"And now you have a job to do. You have a destiny, Jonas, whether you like it or not. You must choose what it is. But it is coming. The Cleansing is coming."

The ghost pulled his breastplate from his chest and held it out towards Jonas. The armour was incredibly finely worked – thousands upon thousands of tiny golden circlets decorating the shining surface.

It was beautiful.

"Take this. It is yours. It belonged to all the Masters before you. It has been buried down here for too long."

Jonas reached out before he knew what he was doing. When his fingers touched the armour, it turned real and solid, and Jonas could feel its cool, riddled surface. He was surprised how light it was.

Suddenly Jonas wanted no part of it. The burden of what the armour meant was far too much. He let go.

The breastplate clanged on the floor.

"Jonas, do not fear what you are capable of. You are a hero. You have it in your veins!"

But Jonas was walking away. He did not hear what Thom said.

When Jonas turned back, the armour and the ghost were gone. Halima was standing in the darkness alone.

"Let's get of here," he said. His voice trembled with anger. "I'm taking you to the Pinnacles now."

20

The Enchanter

A gnarled lynx-Kind priest led Malachai and Lana down twisting paths to the deep tombs. The air was stale and heavy with dust, and the shadows were black and filled with bones, but with every step, Lana felt more at home. Reassuring tonnes of earth hung over her head. It was just like the mines. Her power, too, felt stronger here. It fizzed inside her, like an itch wanting to be scratched.

At a crossroads, another acolyte was waiting, a tall ostrich-Kind, who bowed her long neck as Lana and Malachai approached.

"They ran in there, Master," she whispered, pointing. "There. Into that big chamber."

"Good." Malachai cocked his head to one side and tasted the air with his tongue. "And do you hear that? I believe it sounds as if they are walking out now."

He was right. Footsteps were approaching.

"Back behind me, Lana," said Malachai. "These human devils will be desperate."

He pulled back the sleeves of his robe and flexed his fingers like a wrestler before a fight. His fingers crackled slightly and Lana sensed a magical energy build around the enchanter.

Two small figures emerged from the darkness. Neither looked very dangerous or very happy. One of them had her wrists shackled and her head slumped in defeat. The other was a slim teenage boy with a frown and haunted eyes.

"You will go no further," said Malachai as he stepped out into their path.

The two humans stopped. The boy remained very calm and still, sizing up the tall lizard-Kind that towered over him. Lana was more impressed by him now. Most humans would certainly have been more cowed and, perhaps, terrified by Malachai.

"You are a thief," said Malachai. "You stole something precious. You must pay."

The boy said nothing.

Malachai raised his hand. Lana sensed magical energy in the room when Malachai swirled his claws. She knew Malachai was a magic-Kind, but Lana was still surprised by the strength of the magic energy that flitted over her scales like a million scurrying spiders.

"The price will be your death," he said.

Malachai pointed his claws towards the girl's hand then raised them. As he did so the girl's hands raised too. She was clearly not in control of her limbs, but she began to gasp and stare down at her hands as they approached her neck.

"You are enchanting me! Stop!"

Malachai grinned and then he brought his claws together and squeezed. The girl's hands copied the lizard-Kind as she began to throttle herself against her will, fingers gripping her own neck.

Lana froze. She didn't know what to do. She'd never seen anyone die before. The thief was just a girl. Her eyes bulged. Lana wanted to help her, but still paralysis stopped her limbs from moving. If she did stop this, would Malachai kill Jun, and Lana's family too?

Lana looked at the boy next to the thief, begging him with her thoughts to do something. The boy was calm.

He muttered a word, and the girl's arms were dragged away from her throat. The manacles around her wrists glowed faintly.

"You defy me, child?" snarled Malachai. "Do you think I don't know who you are?"

"Then you will know I have a bounty contract to deliver this thief to the Pinnacles of the Damned," said the boy.

"I commend you for tracking her down, Slayer," said Malachai. "But it was I who made your contract in the first place. I am Malachai, Arch Protector of the Order of the True. And now that you have succeeded in your task, release her."

Lana couldn't believe what happened next. A large beast – a dragon or wyvern of some Kind – suddenly appeared behind the two humans.

"The thief must go to the Pinnacles," it said. Its voice was cold as ice. "The bounty is our freedom. It is the law, and it is our right as bounty hunters to see our contract *through*."

Lana was frightened then – she had never seen anything like this. She looked at the ghostly vapours that whispered between the wyvern and the boy. They were clearly linked somehow, although she had never heard of anything so strange before. She wondered if the others could see it.

"Release her from those manacles so I can kill her," said Malachai. "If you do not, I will treat you as guilty, just like her. There is no freedom in treachery."

As the boy considered this, he turned to look at the wyvern. Some communication flashed between them, Lana was sure. "As you wish," said Seth. "Jonas, we must let the girl die. We will be free."

"Good, Slayer," Malachai said. "I am impressed with your work. Perhaps I can find a role for you myself. I always have need of trackers and assassins, even human ones – though you are not truly human, are you? You are unique, a human bound to a new-Kind. You are unnatural, Slayer, but as long as you keep to the shadows I could use you."

The boy's eyes were vacant, almost like a ghost's. "I don't know," was all he said.

Malachai's eyes glowered. "I will make it easy for you." Malachai raised his claws at the boy, and this time the boy turned and began to choke Halima.

"I can't stop it," said the boy, his whole body straining against the enchanter's magic.

"Don't try to," said the ghostly wyvern. "You are death; this girl means nothing."

"Fran! No, I can't!" shouted the boy. He tried to pull his hands away but he couldn't. The thief-girl's eyes began to go vacant as life seeped from her. Lana felt a sense of dull horror filling her. She was watching the girl die.

A screeching filled the tomb out of nowhere – or everywhere. The sound was so monstrously loud it echoed off the walls and floor, as if Lana was inside the noise itself. She ducked to the ground, her hands over her ears.

A wind like a hurricane battered her body, throwing her backwards. She was aware of Malachai skidding to the ground next to her. Rubble and dust fell everywhere.

A vast . . . *thing* appeared in the cavern. Lana could not comprehend what it was for a moment.

Dragon! she thought – even though dragons this size were not meant to exist any more.

Then the creature shook its wings, and she saw it was a vast crow – much larger than any creature she had ever seen. Ten times the size of the biggest bear-Kind she had ever seen. Its feathers were white and brilliant in the darkness. The creature filled the cavern completely and when it landed on the ground, the stone floor trembled.

It smelled like old books.

Rocks were falling from the ceiling. Dust filled the air. Lana cowered away. The ostrich-Kind priest was less lucky and was crushed by a boulder, her scream suddenly silenced with a sickening clack of rock on rock.

Malachai raised a hand, muttering a desperate spell. Before he could complete it, the crow's huge yellow talon reached out and grabbed him like a beetle. Flapping its enormous wings, the crow rose up and tossed him hard against the wall. The lynx-Kind priest fled, bounding on all fours from the chamber. Malachai began to rouse slowly on the ground, hissing in pain. The crow slammed its talons into the wall where Malachai had fallen and then gouged at some supporting pillars. Cracks snaked up the wall where Malachai lay on the ground. The walls shuddered and fell, and the ceiling collapsed with a mighty roar.

Lana crouched as the dust and rubble tumbled around her. She waited for death. She was very surprised when it didn't come.

She raised her head. A great white wing spread over her. It had protected her from the fallen rubble. Malachai was buried. The other priests were dead. The crow looked at Lana. Its eye was yellow and ancient and somehow half-amused. It was also the size of a wagon wheel.

Is that an old-Kind? wondered Lana, lost in the

depths of its eye.

Then the eye closed and the crow vanished, and Lana was left alone in the darkness. The boy, the wyvern and the thief had disappeared as well.

Lana went over to the spot where Malachai had been buried.

She reached out with her hands and the rock melted away like mist, revealing his body. It was twisted at an awkward angle, and there was a lot of blood. She leaned closer and felt his breath faintly on her cheek. He was alive. Just about. But looking at his injuries Lana wasn't sure if he would stay alive for much longer.

"What in the name of the gods just happened?" she asked. She could hear shudders echoing through the chambers around her. And clouds of dust swelled through openings in the collapsed chamber, rippling from other collapsing parts of the tunnel complex.

A boom from a nearby cave-in shuddered the ground beneath Lana's feet, and she gasped as a shockwave of immeasurable magical energy passed through the chamber. The shadow on Lana's right side exploded into a great wreathing, flaring mass of licking black flames that engulfed the entire space within the remains of the chamber. Lana knew it instinctively. She knew it the same way you sense when someone is watching you.

The Tablets of the Creator had been destroyed. They must have been crushed by the cave-in.

The fireball of shadow shrank back to a normal shape, licking gently across Lana's scales. For a brief, passing moment, Lana considered leaving Malachai down here. Without the Tablets, Malachai might not need Lana any more. And it went without saying that humans across the Four Kingdoms would be a lot safer without Malachai in charge of the Order of the True, manipulating the Emperor like a puppet. Malachai wanted to use Lana to destroy all humans. But leaving him seemed just wrong. Besides, a small, knowing part of her realised full well that without Malachai, she and her family would be in jeopardy. Malachai was her patron, her protector. And there were still the translations from the tracings that Malachai's followers had made of the tablets.

Lana twisted her hands in front of her, shaping a pocket of air into a dense cloud, using it to lift Malachai up from the ground. She didn't have long. The shockwave from the destruction of the tablets was causing more instability and she could hear more tunnels collapsing. Lana ran, controlling the blanket of air on which Malachai lay with a sweep of her hand. The magic felt easy, seamless, and

Lana was aware of the way her shadow wreathed once again as she channelled her magic, just as her shadow had done when the shockwave passed through her. Had she absorbed some of the Tablets' power? She felt the same limitless potential, like standing at the edge of a sheer drop, just as she had when she stood before the Tablets. She felt excited. She felt more sure of herself than she ever had.

For the first time, she felt truly in charge of her own destiny.

21

The Choice

Jonas had picked up Halima and ran for his life as soon as the giant bird appeared. Seth huffed in Jonas's ear as they charged through the catacombs. Cracks spread along the walls and debris dislodged from the ceilings. "Flee, Slayer. Quickly!"

"What do you think I am doing?" shouted Jonas back. "Help me with Halima."

Halima – just as terrified as they were – did not complain as they carried her away from the monstrous white crow. A great boom split the air and a shockwave of energy threw Jonas off his feet. The skull-lined tunnel began to collapse behind them in a ripple of exploding rock and bone. Jonas charged on, dodging past falling rocks until at last the thunder of falling rocks was a distant echo. Then they stopped, and breathed.

"What . . . was . . . *that*?" said Jonas, bent double. "That giant bird."

"The answer to our problem, I suppose." Seth shrugged. "Strange things in these catacombs – best not to worry, eh?"

"You saved me," said Halima, feeling her throat. There were livid red marks where Jonas's fingers had gripped it so tight. "Right after you tried to kill me."

Jonas resisted a smile. "Sorry, I didn't mean to try to kill you. The priest made me."

"I know," said Halima. "Malachai's enchantments are irresistible."

"And I only saved you to protect my bounty."

"All right then, villain, have it your way – but thanks all the same."

Once again Jonas was reminded of his cousin Fran. When they were children she would get into a grump if Jonas outfought her in a wrestle or snared a rabbit before she did. He had shouted his cousin's name when that enchanter Malachai had made him throttle the girl. Her face had just come to him then, and he was filled with the sickening dread of a nightmare as the girl lost consciousness. He tried to bury the memory – tried not to think about Fran, or what was, what would never be again.

"How do we get out of here?" said Jonas.

"Would be easier if we knew where 'here' was," Seth muttered.

Jonas jumped, adrenaline surging and the death-song flaring, as a giant shape appeared from thin air in a rustle of wings. As it dropped to the ground, the monster bird dwindled, shrinking fast. By the time its claws hit the floor, it was wearing boots and a long, dark hooded cloak. Jonas pulled his blades free of their scabbards.

This new figure was normal height for a Kind, not so much taller than a man – a crow-Kind with greyish feathers. He was looking down his long yellow beak at them, with an amused expression.

"I can help you leave this place," he said, "if you'll bear with me a moment . . ." The bird reached into his cloak and fumbled around. "Best we all leave before any of those robed buffoons see us. We can only hope Malachai is dead."

"Who are you?" said Jonas.

"I am Gael. Now, kindly get close to me. And put those nasty-looking weapons away." Jonas obliged. There was something about the way the crow-Kind talked that made it impossible to disobey him. With a flourish, Gael swirled his cloak.

There was a bright flash of light, and the next moment, Jonas felt like the ground had been pulled from under him. His whole body felt weightless and tingled with such force he thought he might be disintegrating. Suddenly everything went still and they were all standing in a forest clearing. Nausea welled in Jonas's stomach and he bent over and threw up on the grass. Next to him, Seth was coughing and wheezing. When Jonas finally looked up, he saw the walls of Skin-Grave were visible in the distance. A bird was trilling and the sun was warm on their backs. It was a pleasant day.

Gael patted Jonas on the back, half coughing, half laughing. "Don't worry, lad," he wheezed. "Teleportation can be very unpleasant – even for the terrifying Slayer himself! Still, vomiting is quite rare. Maybe too much excitement. Or too much dinner."

"Gods!" Halima sank to her knees. "I never thought I'd leave that tomb. And I definitely never thought I'd do so in the company of a death-blessed boy and a shapeshifting old-Kind."

Gael was coughing again. "Every time I teleport," he croaked. Gael's coughing fit subsided. "It's not so much shapeshifting as spatial manipulation. It's very technical, don't worry yourself. The point is it's quite hard to fit in, you know, when you're bigger than a house. This tidier shape feels more comfortable to me, really. Don't bang into walls so much."

"How do you shapeshift?" said Halima. "Sorry – spatially manipulate yourself."

Gael pointed at a funny-shaped amulet around his neck. "This charm. It's a tentacle of an old-Kind shapeshifter. Very, very powerful. Unique. Priceless."

Halima's eyes were wide. "Could it make me the size of an old-Kind, or small as a mouse? That could be useful for stealing things."

"Yes, of course, but you'd have to steal it from me first. And, well, you don't want to see me in my true form, not when I am irritated. I find thieves particularly irritating." Gael turned to Jonas. "Really, boy, this shapeshifting token is not a fraction as rare and powerful as that armour you carelessly left on the cavern floor. The Golden Breastplate of the Masters of the Kind! Not everyone gets gifted that, and from Thom himself! The legend, the hero, the most important human warrior of all."

"So you've been watching us?" said Jonas.

"Every step of the way since you entered the

tombs. You weren't difficult to follow." The crow winked at Jonas.

"I should get quieter boots," said Jonas, with a smile. Something about the crow's wry grin was infectious.

"It's not your boots, Jonas. It's you." Gael pulled a gyrating instrument from his pocket, which swirled when he moved it towards Jonas.

"*Phwoof!*" Gael clacked his beak. "Very high reading here, m'boy! Powerful death magic indeed. Strange that the descendant of the Masters should have such an unsavoury blessing as yours, poor boy, but fate works in mysterious ways. I think Thom himself used to say that, or was it his wizard Dalthek? I can never remember."

"You knew them?" said Halima breathlessly.

"Of course," said Gael. "We carried out a few tasks together, back when humans and old-Kind worked to keep the world in balance. Thom seems to think you are fated to do the same. To create peace rather than war. This could be your destiny, my boy."

"He could have many destinies, all of them great," said Seth.

"You are a curious one," Gael said to Seth. "Your magical energy feels unusual. I have come across revenants that use a living creature's life force to preserve themselves after death. But you feel more powerful, different. You feel like a destiny-Kind, a creature interested in ensuring a certain destiny is carried out. Am I right?"

"I am ghost-Kind. I am loyal to death and to Jonas. I only seek to unleash his full potential."

"Hmm, we shall see," said Gael. "Now, what say you, Jonas? Are you ready to take up the human cause, to take up the mantle of the Masters of the Kind?"

"No. No, I don't want to hear about it," said Jonas. "I'm not anyone. I don't owe anyone anything."

"Funny. Until very recently, I thought the same thing. Until a human girl changed my perspective – an assistant of mine. I used to think having friends only led to hurt – but that is better than emptiness. Sometimes your desire to stay out of a fight becomes a fight itself. Sometimes destiny has chosen you, and you must not turn from your duty. Your true duty. The duty of your people, to ensure peace and do what is right. Ha! Listen to me! I sound like a do-gooder."

For half a second, Jonas considered running away or cutting the crow in half, but both options seemed a little pointless.

"Suit yourself." Gael shrugged. Something in his expression made Jonas think he could see exactly what he was thinking. "I can't force you to do anything. Hmm." He looked down. His instrument was swirling again. "Funnily enough, you aren't the only one giving off a reading."

His magical device was clicking like mad as he ran it over Halima as well. Halima's face became furrowed in worry.

"What have we got here?" said Gael, taking two steps closer. Before Halima could stop him, Gael's quick fingers had grabbed something at her belt and pulled it away. It was a small leather bag, nothing really – except Halima struggled like mad to grab it back.

Gael danced away. "Amazing! I haven't seen a Magic Mouth for a thousand years. What have you got hidden inside, then, eh? Don't worry, I'll give it back."

He opened up the bag and peered inside.

"Hmm. Very interesting." Gael shoved his entire arm, all the way up to the shoulder, inside the tiny bag. He rummaged around and drew out a sheet of carefully folded wax paper.

"You can't take that!" said Halima. "It's . . ."

She didn't finish her sentence. Gael chuckled as

he tucked the parchment away inside his cloak of many pockets.

"I know what it is, and I know where you were going to take it. Don't worry, Halima. I will take it there far quicker than you. I predict things will turn out all right." Halima scowled. She didn't look convinced. "I'll give you your pouch back nonetheless," Gael said. "Maybe you'll find some use for what else it contains. A purpose that lies closer to hand."

Jonas was tired of the crow's riddles. "Can you transport us away from here?" he said. "I want to get to the Pinnacles."

"Still set on giving the Gaoler what he wants?"

"I am," said Jonas. "I want my freedom. I need to get to the Gaoler so he can remove my manacles. I just hope Malachai doesn't intervene."

"I don't think we will be hearing from Malachai for a while. If he isn't dead, then he won't ever be the same again. I knew the Gaoler of old. He's not a kind or generous fellow. You sure he'll keep his side of the bargain?"

"Can you get us closer or not?"

Gael squinted, considering the question.

"Best I can do right now is south Morta. That's the closest without totally draining my energy. I was actually there a few weeks ago, inspecting a magical disturbance. A few strange events have taken place in that location, in fact. I can take you there. It's easier to teleport somewhere I have been before."

Jonas just wanted to get away from this bird, and this place, and all the awkward questions. He really didn't like the uncertainty that the crow tumbled up in his mind.

"Take us there. I don't care. Quicker the job's done the better."

"As you say, Slayer," said Gael. "But just remember, no matter who you are, you always have a choice. It took me hundreds of years to remember that. Now, are you ready? Please try not to vomit this time. I won't be coming with you but the smell might make it through the remnants of the pathway."

There was a flash of light. Jonas felt himself being pulled apart then pieced back together, like sand falling into a mould. Jonas retched on to the dusty ground as he reappeared.

"Breathe," muttered Seth. "Your nausea is infecting me. Breathe!"

As Jonas took in long, calming inhalations, he recognised the feel of the air in his lungs – the freshness, the dryness. He recognised the feel of the wind, the sun above, the feathergrass around his ankles. There was the smell of wildflowers and dry soil. It could mean only thing. He was home.

He didn't realise quite how true that was until he opened his eyes and saw the carcasses of the insect-Kind all around.

It didn't rain much in Morta. The nights were cold. Bodies left out in the open tended to dry out before they rotted away.

The fields around his camp were filled with the dried-out husks of insect-Kind corpses. Their bodies still bore the signs of the terrible wounds that had killed them. Their faces were frozen in their death-agony.

For some reason, the scavengers had stayed away. Jonas spotted Rahziin's body and turned away.

"Who did this?" said Halima.

"I did," said Jonas.

He couldn't quite believe that Gael had transported him to this precise spot. Had he done it on purpose? Was this his idea of a joke? The crow seemed to know far more than he let on. Was he trying to tell Jonas something by making him remember his old friends and family, trying to manipulate Jonas into doing as the crow wanted? Into doing 'what is right'?

Jonas remembered something else. What had the crow said – that he had come to inspect a magical disturbance here? And he had said other strange events had taken place at the same location. Did he know something about what happened to Jonas's tribe?

Jonas cursed. Even when the raven wasn't here, he stirred up awkward questions.

"You know the Reader told us about you, Slayer," said Halima. "She said there was a human warrior in that terrible prison, who scared even the new-Kind. The Reader said you could be a powerful weapon against the new-Kind. We just needed to convince you to join us."

Jonas remembered the way the Reader had seemed to be speaking directly to him when she made the speech to the rebel camp in the forest. Had she known he was there? Was she also trying to manipulate him, to force him to take a side? Grashkor, Seth, Thom, Gael, the Reader, all these people trying to get him to do what they wanted . . . He was sick of it. "You're wasting your time," said Jonas. "Come on. We've got a long trek."

He started walking. Halima followed even without the manacles' pull. Their route took them through the field of corpses. Jonas instinctively avoided going inside the camp itself.

"This was your tribe, wasn't it?"

"It was."

"What happened to your people?"

Jonas was silent. He didn't want to look at his people's last camp. At the familiar tents, at the discarded pots, the broken crockery. He tried to keep his eyes on the ground, but when he did that, he just found himself staring at more bodies of Kind that he'd slaughtered.

"I don't know. I need to know. Once I'm free, I will find out."

"My village was slaughtered too, Jonas. The new-Kind did it. They killed everyone. That's what new-Kind do to humans. They probably killed your tribe too."

Jonas said nothing for a moment. Then he stared hard into Halima's urging eyes. "You know what it's like to lose everything," he rasped, his voice taut. "How can I move on, when I don't know what I'm moving on from?" When Jonas looked at Halima, he saw his cousin Fran in her again. It crushed his heart.

"I know how much it hurts," said Halima. "You know just how much they took away from both of us. But I can't *imagine* how much it would hurt if I had been accused of killing them myself. That would be worse than death."

Jonas looked away, tears in his eyes.

"I understand you, Jonas," said Halima. "I understand why you are taking me to prison. I used to be the same: full of regret, hate, the need for vengeance. I wouldn't let anyone stand in my way."

Jonas stared at her. "I'm really sorry," he said.

He began to cry. The tears had been a long time coming. He hadn't wept for years – but once the rain started falling, it didn't stop. It felt good, letting it all out – all the pain, all the hurt, all the fury. It was like poison drawn from a wound.

Halima placed a hand on his shoulder.

Jonas heard Gael's words in his head.

You always have a choice.

"I will let you go, Halima," Jonas said, and he reached down into his boot, pulling out the slim gold key. "I'm sorry. I'll find another way to be free." He inserted the key and unlocked Halima's manacles. "Please leave before I change my mind."

"JONAS!" Seth screamed into his ear. "Not again. Don't make the same mistake as you did with Rahziin. Grashkor will kill us. We are so close. Do not let this girl get into your head. We are so close. So close to freedom!"

"No, Seth. Halima, you are free. I will face the wrath of Grashkor."

"And sooner than you think," said a loud voice, like thunder and grating metal all at once. "You are so very predictable, Slayer. I've been waiting for you to come back here. Do you always drag your prisoners back to the scene of your terrible crimes? I think you've got a guilty conscience, boy!"

Jonas jumped to his feet, rubbing the tears from his eyes. His death-song surged within him, thick and choking. Something bad was here.

The Gaoler was lounging on top of a large rock, watching Jonas. He must have sneaked up without Jonas realising. The speed and stealth was remarkable considering Grashkor's size.

"You can take your conscience to your grave. This is the second prisoner you have freed. I should have killed you when you failed to turn in the cat-Kind priest. No matter. I will execute you and the thief!"

The Gaoler jumped from the rock, drawing his broadsword.

The ground shook when he landed.

Jonas tried to draw his own swords – but his wrists drew together. He tried again. They were locked in place. Unshiftable.

The manacles at his wrists glowed.

The Gaoler laughed. "You don't think I'd be stupid enough to fight fair, did you?"

22

The Showdown

The huge sword slashed across Jonas's belly. Blood gushed red on the sand.

The heavy blade bit through Jonas's neck. His head bounced across the dust.

The Gaoler grabbed Jonas's body and tore him in half. He screamed his triumph at the sky.

Jonas had never experienced a death-song like this. Blizzards of violent death swirled inside him. He screamed and died, then did it again. Over and over and over.

It felt good. Maybe this was the time that he really would die. It was, in a strange way, a relief.

"Jonas!" Someone was calling his name. "Jonas! Stir yourself! He's coming."

Jonas blinked. Halima was shaking his arm. He smiled at her. Time had slowed down to a trickle. Her mouth was moving too slowly. Her words didn't make any sense to him.

He wanted to reassure her that everything was fine. That there was nothing he could do. The manacles had seen to that. But by the time he tried to speak, he was dying again, and he forgot what he meant to say.

It was hard to concentrate when your head was flying through the air.

"JONAS!" another voice screamed in his head. "YOU HAVE TO MOVE!"

But even Seth's terrified howl did nothing. Jonas smiled as the Gaoler stomped towards him. The monster's great sword was raised high, ready to strike.

Jonas grinned. The less he did, the closer death approached.

And the better and more powerful he felt.

A blur of movement came from the sandy dunes to the left. Seth was flying low to the ground. His teeth flashed in the sun. Just before his body shifted from ghost-form to solid, his scales pulsed with an electric pink glow.

Jonas had never noticed that before.

He watched in amusement as the Gaoler pivoted to meet the wyvern. The Gaoler's feet moved well. Sidestepping twice, his feet kicked up delicate little puffs of sand. He brought his blade round so quickly that it seemed he must have been expecting Seth's ambush.

All this took so long that Jonas had time to glory in every detail.

He saw Seth's eyes widen with surprise as the sail-sized blade swept up out of nowhere.

He smelled the rank sweat puddling beneath the Gaoler's armour.

He heard Halima's shocked moan.

Seth swerved suddenly, desperate to avoid the scythe-edge swinging inexorably towards his neck.

He just about managed it. The Gaoler's blade caught only the tip of his wing. It gashed a tear across the leathery flap.

Seth screamed, rolling into an awkward, angular spinning ball of limbs and wings and spurting green blood. Jonas's arm screamed a mirroring pain. Seth tumbled towards Jonas.

Jonas couldn't move to avoid the impact.

He watched Seth skidding towards him. All he could think was that being pancaked by his soul brother would be a very funny way to die.

Halima pushed him. She threw all her weight against his body, so the two of them tumbled together.

Seth bounced over the top of them and landed in a growling heap.

"How touching," said the Gaoler. "Thank you for prolonging my enjoyment."

"Quickly – there's no time," hissed Halima.

She scrabbled for something at her belt and pulled out a glowing object of shimmering light.

"You've got to put this on," she said. "Or you're going to die."

"Hey!" The Gaoler stomped closer. "What are you up to?"

The death-song was still howling in Jonas's ears. With everything so slow, he had plenty of time to admire the craftsmanship of the golden armour that Halima had taken from her magical bag. He was amazed she'd thought to keep the ghost's unwanted present.

Kneeling on the floor, he closed his eyes. He didn't want it. Even more, he didn't want the burden he saw in Halima's pleading eyes. If he just died now, none of this would be on him any more.

"Take it, Jonas, for the Masters' sake!" screamed Halima.

Jonas could feel the earth tremble with each of the Gaoler's footsteps. He was very close now.

It would be so easy to die.

"Lift your arms!" said Halima.

Jonas complied without thinking, raising his bound wrists slowly towards the sky. Halima shoved the breastplate against his chest, and pulled his arms back in front of him. His thoughts were numb, as weightless as his body, as if the final nothingness of death was already embracing him, taking away all thought, all feeling, all resistance. "What good is this armour?" he muttered. "It is over, Halima. I am beaten." Jonas had the strange sense that the armour was moulding to his body, shrinking and tightening across his chest and abdomen.

Halima fastened the straps at his shoulders. "Fight, Jonas!" she urged him.

"What is this cursed magic?" snarled Grashkor, watching the armour with narrowed eyes. "Is that . . . no. The Golden Breastplate. Curse that ancient human magic! Curse the treacherous Masters!" The Gaoler lowered his arm in the direction of Jonas's wrists. Jonas's manacles locked against his waist, stuck there as if welded to his belt. The magic was irresistible. He couldn't raise his arms. The Gaoler swept his blade around so that it would slice through

Halima and Jonas in one blow.

Jonas raised his arm, knowing it was pointless – his manacles would stop him.

Pure, wondrous power surged through his muscles, a strength that flowed from the armour, hugging his body. He felt the manacles trying to resist that movement, but the golden armour was far too powerful. The manacles trembled and whined as their magic failed.

Jonas pushed Halima down with his knee and brought both his wrists up together like a shield. The Gaoler's giant blade crashed straight into them.

The blade stopped dead. The manacles shattered.

There was a clashing, rending screech, as if the sky itself had torn apart. In a flash of blinding light, Grashkor was thrown backwards.

Jonas did not move an inch.

The Gaoler bounced hard and grabbed at his face. Shards of manacle had stabbed into his skin.

Blood gushed through his fingers.

"MY EYES!" he screamed.

Jonas was already on his feet. He swept up the Gaoler's blade with one hand and pirouetted, feet moving like a dancer, so the giant blade whirled around his head.

He heard Halima gasp behind him. Truth be told

he was himself a little surprised by this. No human had even dreamed of lifting such a blade before. But with the armour and the death-song in harmony he felt strong enough to shift the world on its axis.

It was a glorious feeling. He felt in balance at last. The death-song gave him furious purpose; the armour cleared his mind, stopping him from going out of control with hunger for killing.

Jonas spun the black blade around his head. The edge sang as it cut through the air.

Once, twice, three times the blade whipped round. And then it came down hard, like a judgement.

Blinded, the Gaoler heard the sound of his own death approaching.

He stretched his neck to meet the blow.

23

A Gift for the Reader

Gael was coughing like a drowning thrush. This was partly due to his usual portal sickness, and partly to the choking sulphur stink in the air.

"Volcanoes!" he moaned. "Remind me again why we're coming here? The air is soot!"

"I thought it was a suitably impressive place to hold your 'secret' meeting with the human rebels," said Roshni innocently. Her face was wrapped in scarves to protect against the smoke. "Why don't you ask yourself?"

"Oh, I wanted to test our mysterious friends. I wonder who they are. Any ideas, Roshni?"

If Roshni did have an idea, there was no way of telling. She didn't reply and the expression on her muffled face was unreadable.

They trudged up the path. There were signs that others had passed this way recently. Fresh footprints marked the stones, printed neatly in the ash.

"Looks like they're punctual, at least. I'd say about twenty humans came through before us," said Gael, peering at the marks. "Some soldiers in armour. Maybe an hour ago? Let's hope they really are friendly, eh?"

He didn't sound too worried.

Again, Roshni said nothing.

But Gael was perfectly capable of keeping a conversation going all by himself. As they climbed the shoulder of the hill and passed into a steep-sided valley, he gave a short lecture, interspersed with coughs, on the significance of the hallowed ground they were walking into.

It was an awe-inspiring place. A still-smoking volcanic peak rose at one end of the valley. A wide crystal-blue lake fringed with wildflowers reflected the sky and the towering pillar of smoke that climbed needle-straight from the volcano's mouth. There was no wind, nor any trees, because they were too high for that, but the meadow grass grew thick and tall, fuelled by the soft snowfall of feathery ash.

"This is an ancient place," said Gael. "Though

it is much changed since I was last here. It was devastated then by a terrible eruption. All this is *new,* if you can believe it, grown in the last thousand years. The old volcano mouth was beneath this lake."

Gael stared at the water, flat as a mirror.

"It must be very deep. That peak you see smoking up there is merely the child of the vast monster beneath our feet. This was the volcano – stop me if you already know this – from which the phoenix-Kind Aephos was born. Back in the days of the humans, they called her volcano Stonewind."

Gael glanced at Roshni.

"Really?" she said. "That's fascinating. What happened to Aephos?"

"Well, after the Spawning, Aephos returned here. It is said she slumbers still, in the fires beneath the lake. But who believes in old legends, eh?"

Roshni pointed ahead. A slight rise in the path had revealed a group of humans waiting in a fold of the lake.

"Two dozen, just as I guessed," said Gael. "Not very smartly dressed, are they?"

As they drew closer, they saw that several of the humans were badly injured. Most were bandaged in some way. Their clothes were tattered and stained with blood and dust.

A tall woman limped towards them, raising her hand in greeting.

"Welcome, Gael," she said. "I am Alia. I thank you for calling this meeting. I lead the rebels' armies – what's left of us, anyway. The Reader assured us you would come."

"I *bet* she did," said Gael. "As she always knows exactly what I'm doing. She's a very clever girl . . ." He paused dramatically. "Isn't that right, *Roshni*?"

Roshni pulled down her mask. She was grinning through her surprise.

"Oh. Oh dear. When did you guess?"

"That you were the secret magical leader of the human rebels, who went by the rather boring name the Reader? Well, there were a few things that made me suspicious. When you left the Tower, supposedly to go to the market or sleep in the hills, you often came back smelling of Anoros cooking. You used the striding stone to teleport yourself, of course. Your shoes were often stained with mud even though it hadn't rained for months in the Hallowed Vale. You asked too many questions, and I lost count of the number of times you nudged me to help the humans. And then there was the pronounced magical interference when you use the Trickster Ring. You are a very magical being, Roshni – although you hide it well. Oh, and another clue: when I first met you, Malachai mentioned that he didn't recognise you. I think your human spies among the palace servants got wind that Malachai was intending to summon me on this quest to find out your identity, and you ensured you took the place of one of Malachai's servants. You dropped that platter of food on purpose. You intended Malachai to attack you. I suppose you guessed I would come to your aid."

"It was a mistake to think I could hide anything from you, Gael," said Roshni with a smile.

"But how did you find out about me?" Gael asked. "Why did you think I would help you?"

"We've read about you. You are mentioned in the Chronicles of Havanthya quite considerably. We have been studying those ancient stories of the great human civilisation, of the Masters and the wizards, of the kings and queens. We've been borrowing parts of the anthology from the Hallowed Vale, making copies, learning of our history and the knowledge the Kind seek to destroy. I would watch you often when I sneaked into the Tower – yes, I have my own methods of invisibility. I am a psychic, a rare type of magic-Kind. I can read people's thoughts, and I can even control those thoughts for a short time, influence what they see – or what they don't see. Malachai underestimates us human magic-Kind. He doesn't realise we have powerful witches and wizards across the realm. Many who are not members of the Council of Magic-Kind. As I watched you in the Tower, I read your heart. It was cold, but I sensed goodness in it. I knew you would come to the aid of the oppressed, of the people you once helped long ago. In the times of Havanthya when humans and old-Kind kept peace, together. That is what we seek to restore, Gael. That balance. The natural state."

"I see," said Gael. "I can't pretend I don't find you watching me a little creepy, along with the idea of you reading my thoughts, or indeed controlling them."

"Don't worry, Gael. My influence is only temporary – I only used my magic so you did not notice me in the Tower. I would never try to manipulate your thoughts – such spells can cause permanent harm. Besides, you would only have changed your mind as soon as my spell wore off. I had to convince you to come to our side. I had to make you believe, in your heart, that to do so was just and right."

"Well, you've succeeded brilliantly!" said Gael. "I

am quite persuaded that the humans are right: that maniac Malachai *must* be stopped. It is unfortunate that word has got to me that he is alive. I saw what he was doing down there in Skin-Grave. He wants to unleash a plague of pure destruction on the world. He's evil, plain and simple. If he goes ahead with his plan, he will destroy not just you humans, but our world, and quite possibly all the *other* worlds as well. The Netherplane magic contained in those Tablets is much too dangerous to meddle with."

At the end of this long speech, Gael coughed, rummaged around in his cloak and drew out a neat packet of folded paper. The papers were covered in marks traced in wax crayon.

"I thought we might need these. Tracings of the Tablets taken by Halima. They record all the runes, all the spells, all the power needed to unlock the horrors of the Netherplane – or to stop Malachai from doing so. Now we are on the same team. Me and the humans, united once more, just like old times!"

Roshni's eyes were wide. "Did you get this from Halima?"

"Oh! I kept some secrets from you, Roshni. How does that feel, I wonder?"

Roshni shook her head wryly.

"Oh no! Is Halima dead?" said Alia. "What became of her? Why didn't you save her too?"

"I thought it best to leave her where she was. She still had important work to finish. Buttons to press, that sort of thing."

"Was she safe?"

"No," said Gael. "Not even a little bit. But she is an admirably capable girl. And I have full faith in Jonas."

Roshni looked at him. "I understand your plan. You put faith in Slayer. His presence at one of our rebel camps led to many of my people dying. He has darkness in his heart. Rage, and fear. I hope you know what you're doing." She was examining the papers. Her eyes were bright as she read the ancient runes.

"There is one spell in particular I was after," said Roshni. "Which is why I wanted to meet in this place. I know of Aephos well, Gael. And I know how to translate the Tablets. We have been studying for years, decades, learning the language of the Old Ways, of the ancient human runes. I was hoping I could use a resurrection spell . . ."

"Ah!" said Gael. "I see. Be careful, Roshni. These spells are dangerous. They use Netherplane magic. You do not know the forces you are dealing with."

"We have no choice," said Roshni. "We must fight fire with fire."

"Literally!" said Gael.

"Indeed. For the resurrection rite all that is needed is a remnant of the being wished to be brought back," said Roshni.

She drew out the Talon of Aephos from where it hung around her neck. "And you gave this to me two months ago!"

"Ah, I do like to get my pieces into position early," said Gael.

Gael watched as Roshni stood on the banks of the lake. A small pile of rosemary and dried willow moss burned in a copper pot.

She called out the words that she had memorised. Her voice rolled across the lake. Gael had made sure that everyone else was standing well back, but to those watching, it seemed as if each word took life and fluttered away across the water like a butterfly.

Roshni held the Talon above her head.

As she continued to speak, the water in the lake began to boil. First great clouds of steam rose up and then geysers spouted vast plumes of water into the air.

The earth trembled. The smoke pouring from the volcano turned black. Fire began to spark from its mouth and then jets of hot lava burst forth.

"Are you sure this is a good idea?" said Alia.

"Too late now," said Gael. "The spell must be finished. Or the raw magic channelled from the Netherplane will be let loose. It must be channelled into fire magic. It must be directed into the volcano."

The ground was shaking now. The lava was rising in the lake.

"COME, FLAME BIRD! COME, AEPHOS!" Roshni spoke the spell into existence. Her voice shrieked above the howling earth. "I CALL YOU BY YOUR NAME!"

The Talon was glowing brighter than the flame.

The volcano boomed and shuddered.

From the clouds of boiling smoke and shrieking steam a monstrous shape emerged.

A flaming bird, wreathed in fire. Its wings burned brighter than the sun. It shrieked its fury at the sky.

"Behold one of the greatest old-Kind!" breathed Gael. "Behold the Flame Bird herself!"